12⁵⁰

A DESERT OF PURE FEELING

A DESERT

OF PURE FEELING

Judith Freeman

PANTHEON BOOKS NEW YORK

Library of Congress Cataloging-in-Publication Data

Freeman, Judith, 1946–
    A desert of pure feeling / Judith Freeman.
      p.   cm.
    ISBN 0-679-43290-6
    1. Women—Nevada—Las Vegas—Fiction.   2. Women
authors—Psychology—Fiction.   3. Friendship—Nevada—
Las Vegas—Fiction.
    I. Title.
PS3556.R3915D47   1996
813'.54—dc20   95–26155
                                            CIP

Book design by M. Kristen Bearse

Manufactured in the United States of America

First Edition

9 8 7 6 5 4 3 2 1

PRINTED AND BOUND BY:
THE COUNTRY PRESS INC.
MIDDLEBOROUGH, MA

For
Jerry Freeman
1948–1994
and
Daniel Gundlach

Malevich, of course, back around 1915 pared everything down to those empty white squares on their white ground. Everybody looked at those and moaned, "Oh no, everything we love is gone." And instead he replied, "Ah, but we have found *a desert of pure feeling!*"

—ROBERT IRWIN

A DESERT OF PURE FEELING

ONE

From the window of my room I can see a small portion of a pool. The water is slightly agitated, stirred perhaps by the electronically powered waterfall I can't see from here but which clicks on and off throughout the day. Or perhaps it's only the wind rippling the water, although this seems unlikely, for now that I look again, I see how the palm trees are hardly moving.

Water is everywhere here where you don't think it should be. It fills ponds and pools, forms moats around fake castles, erupts from sprinklers and fountains and runs off oversaturated lawns. I asked a taxi driver yesterday on the drive from the airport, "Where does all this water come from?" I imagined he would say Lake Mead, the Colorado River, Hoover Dam. Instead, the cabbie jabbed his finger downward. "Aquifers," he said. "It all comes from underground," and somehow, as he said this, I could see all that water lying in dark pools deep beneath the earth. I envisioned it being sucked to the surface and erupting in a fine blue spray blowing out over the sand and sage and bunchgrass, landing like a mistaken blessing on the tawny and desiccated earth.

I've taken a room in a motel called the Tally Ho Inn. The only thing at all attractive about the place is the little kidney-shaped pool and two palms growing nearby. Otherwise, this is Motel Nowhere, a generic and slightly rundown structure in the heart of the heart of the Mojave.

On one side of the Tally Ho is an empty lot dotted with dry tumbleweeds and bits of broken glass. I walked out there this morning. Little fans of dust rose around my feet. The milky cocoons of sun-baked condoms lay split and torn among the clay-baked cracks. Yellowed sheets of newsprint were embedded in the earth amid the weeds. In the distance, tall monoliths appeared grotesque and wavery in the blazing sun, like something seen through thick glass—liquid shapes shimmering in the heat: a pyramid, King Arthur's castle, Treasure Island, a Mayan palace, giant Easter Island heads—the whole plastic panoply of cargo-cult history reinvented in the desert.

An Indian family own this motel, a middle-aged couple with a teen-aged daughter and an elderly grandmother who's ancient, as bent and thin as a gnarled stick, and wears the most exquisitely beautiful saris; she peeps at me from the window when she thinks I am not looking.

Why have I come back here?

One answer is I've come back to the place where it all began— here in Las Vegas, only a few short months ago, months that now seem attenuated in length, as if the events that occurred during that time consumed a much greater part of my life than they did.

I had been invited to attend a conference, along with several other writers, the theme of which was "Is the Novel Really Dead?"

It seemed like a pleasant excuse for a free trip to Las Vegas—a prospect I admit many people wouldn't find so inviting.

But I've always had a fondness for Vegas.

My family used to stop here during our long vacation drives through the West. Even then, when the town was only one motel deep, it seemed like the world's greatest carnival, a meta-theme park arising amidst a surreal expanse of windblown nothingness.

To a child it was a luridly beautiful place.

But there's another reason I like Las Vegas, an even deeper connection, one that goes back much further. Las Vegas was first settled by my ancestors. I like to think of what they started, and what it has become.

The conference turned out to be well attended. Several writers whom I held in high esteem were present. There were speeches in the morning, then we broke for lunch, and later reconvened for an afternoon of more talks and panel discussions.

When finally called upon to speak during one of these discussions, I began by saying I didn't see how the novel could be dead when so many people still wrote novels, and so many others still read them. I said I felt that many people continued to turn to literature looking for a means of illumination.

Not so, one of my colleagues argued. Novels had become mere entertainments, their power usurped by more modern forms of expression--by movies, television, computers--and, he insisted, even by terrorism. One could argue that terrorism had become the most powerful form of modern expression. How could a mere novelist expect to compete with a terrorist for the attention of the world?

I knew something about terrorism. My son had been killed eight years earlier while living in a country in Central America, and whoever had taken him--whoever had been responsible for his death--must surely be called a terrorist. I quietly withdrew from the conversation, and no one even seemed to notice, because there were others most eager to take up the question.

The day ended with a discussion of the fiction of the future, which, it was argued, would no longer be printed on paper but would appear on computer screens. This egalitarian system would do away with publishing houses and booksellers and even authors as we know them, and instead enable anyone not only to read a book but to write one and distribute it. This prospect seemed to please many people, but I found it a rather troublesome idea. I was thinking of the beauty of the object, the way a book felt in one's hands, and I thought I should never like to see that come to an end.

As I prepared to return to my hotel late that afternoon, one of the other writers caught my eye and approached me suddenly. I had met him on a few occasions, once at a reading where we shared the podium. Another time we had dined together at the house of mutual friends. Although originally from the West, he now lived in New York City. He was a formidable writer, and a rather elegant man, now graying with age. I'd always admired him. And I was flattered that he sought me out at the end of the day.

"Ah," he said, clasping my hand, "we've had an interesting time today, haven't we?"

I agreed, and told him I had especially liked his comments, which dealt with the way our stories shape us as a culture, and the continuing importance of novels in helping to shape those stories, and with them, our future.

"When I learned you were going to be here, I was surprised," he said. "I didn't think you came out of hiding anymore. How are things up in Montana?"

"Idaho," I said, gently correcting him.

"Idaho, of course. How are things in Idaho?"

"All right," I replied.

"Don't you miss the city?"

"Occasionally. But I get over it rather quickly."

"Listen," he said to me, "the reason I want to speak to you is, I've got a proposal you might be interested in."

He then went on to explain how he had agreed to be a guest writer aboard a luxury ocean liner on a five-day voyage across the Atlantic. But something had come up, and he was going to have to bow out. He'd agreed to find a replacement, and now he wondered if I might not be interested in filling in for him. I'd only have to give one reading during the time at sea. Everything would be paid for by the company that owned the ship--all my expenses, plus a return air ticket from any city in Europe.

He had caught me off guard, and I stood silent for a moment, looking at him, considering what he had just said.

"You'd have to leave in a few weeks," he said. "That's the only rub. It's pretty short notice. But think about it. It would really let me off the hook."

"Where does the ship sail from?" I asked. "And where does it land?"

"New York to Southampton," he said. "They give you a free return on the Concorde if you choose to come back from London or Paris. It's a nice opportunity for a little vacation. A free trip on an ocean liner."

"I'd have to think about it."

"Don't think too long," he said. "I've promised to find a replacement soon." He gave me a number where I could reach him the next morning with my answer.

TWO

That afternoon I returned to my motel room and for a long time lay on the couch, thinking about a trip across the ocean, something I had never done before. The more I thought about it, the more attractive it became.

For a number of years I had been living on a ranch in a valley that was so remote and so beautiful I often thought of it as a paradise. I had moved there shortly after my son was killed. I suppose it was grief and despair that drove me to retreat from the world, to search out such a distant place and settle into a solitary life. Grief and despair—and a fear I had never felt before, a sense of what a dangerous place the world really is.

There were times when I felt there could be no safer, no quieter place on earth, no better spot for me to be. Mountains rose all around me, and a wide and beautiful river ran next to my land. In the mornings clouds often ringed the mountains so that they seemed to dissolve into some heavenly realm. Bald eagles roosted in tall cottonwoods near the river. Geese often woke me at dawn, honking as they sailed low upstream, and in the evening deer came down into my hayfields, circling my cabin in a silent procession. A human being was the most insignificant figure in such a landscape, and it was an equation to my liking.

Yet as much as I loved this place, I had begun to feel unsettled. The summers weren't so bad. But a fierce loneliness often overtook me in the winter months when darkness descended early and the evening hours grew long. Cold seeped into the cabin from every crevice and window, and to move from the fire was to enter a bone-chilling realm, made colder by the absolute darkness outside and the idea of the long hours that stretched before dawn.

My cabin stood alone in a wide valley with no other houses, except for my neighbors, Manuel and Hortensia Archibeque, the couple who took care of my fields and lived in a trailer set back among willows near the river. We moved about like shadows that occasionally lengthened and intersected, only to quickly disengage and return to separate shapes.

Sometimes when I stepped outside at night, I felt my aloneness intensely. Gazing up at a sky glittering with wildly pulsing stars, I felt so small and disoriented it seemed I might be drawn upward into another universe and simply disappear. At these times I often felt my failure at love most intensely, for I was alone now and I had been this way for a very long time.

Yet I had taken myself to this place after my son's disappearance precisely because I wanted to be alone. My aloneness, however, had become a bad habit, one I found increasingly difficult to break. "How do you like it out there in the country?" my friends in cities used to ask. And I would reply, "It's beautiful but boring."

Initially, I said this not so much because it was true—in fact, every day delivered new and remarkable discoveries in this natural setting—but because I didn't want anyone to join me in my little wilderness. I thought if I made life sound mundane enough, I would be left alone.

But the truth was, life *had* become mundane, and I had been left alone, perhaps more than I wished.

I had begun to dread another long winter. Sometimes, in January and February the temperature didn't rise above zero for days. The world became a bitter and solitary place, and the hours of sleep were gradually extended until I began to feel like an animal caught in woolly hibernation.

As I lay there on the couch, entertaining the idea of an ocean voyage, I began considering different possibilities. For some time I had had a desire to visit Cornwall, where my mother's ancestors had come from. If I were to take the boat to Europe, I realized I wouldn't have to return to the ranch immediately. Manuel and Hortensia could look after things for a while. I might spend some time in Cornwall, and then go on to Ireland and Scotland, other places I'd always wanted to visit. The whole idea of such a trip began to excite me.

There in my hotel room in Las Vegas, with the air conditioner humming in the background and the sun fading outside, casting a peach-colored light on the walls, I began imagining distant places, conjuring up visions—a small hotel in a charming village, a green countryside, the sea breaking on a white beach—and I could also see myself sitting at a little table, writing, looking out over the water, or at rooftops spreading out before me.

Yes, I could definitely see myself this way. In a hotel. Near the sea. Writing . . .

For some time I had been trying to work on a new book, but with little success. I wanted to tell a sweeping story, to spin a fantastic tale about the people who lived on this continent and those who had come to claim it. It was to be a monumental work—a gigantic epic, with sea journeys and battle scenes, descriptions of a fabled New World and its inhabitants, a tale of Spaniards and Portuguese, conquistadors and Maya, the lust for gold and power—the story of an old barbarism loosed in a new world.

I intended to call this work *The Book of the Damned*.

I had managed to write a number of chapters, but then I found that I could only think in small and rather personal terms. The harder I tried to focus on my grand themes, of discovery and conquest, the more personal were the events, the smaller the ideas, that overtook my imagination.

I became frustrated and put *The Book of the Damned* aside. Instead, I began writing a series of short stories. Some were set in cities, with the homeless and immigrants for characters. Others were about my childhood and my early marriage at the age of seventeen—and of course many dealt with the death of my son, my only child.

I seemed compelled to embrace the little tale of personal suffering. I began to think that for some reason I was fated, as an American, to plumb the sorrowful shallows of the *individual*. Yet I wished to write a *global* story, one of historical significance. But no matter how hard I strived, I could not break the pattern, and *The Book of the Damned* remained unfinished. My imaginary opus, my tale of the New World, remained untold.

There was something else to consider as well. I thought about what had been said during the conference that day, how the novel was in trouble, how it had lost considerable power in this electronic age. Much as I didn't wish to admit it, there was some truth to this.

The written word lay like a yellowed fallen angel, a dying figure in the dust, its brittle wings fluttering in the cadaverous light cast by television and computer screens. Somewhere, somehow, as someone said that afternoon, novels had become mere entertainments. But I had never felt this way. And I thought, why not take this voyage? The chance to read my own words might give me the opportunity to breathe life back into my own troubled prose.

And so in the morning I packed my bags, and when I'd finished I picked up the phone and called my colleague and said I would take him up on his offer.

What I could not have known was how this decision would lead me back along the path of my own life, how it would open old wounds and lay them bare and create new ones I hadn't expected. What I did not know was how it would bring me once again face-to-face with Dr. Carlos Cabrera.

THREE

What can I say about Dr. Cabrera? Dr. Carlos Ricardo Fernandez Cabrera?

The first time I saw him, he was standing in the corridor of a large hospital with his back against a wall, his face illuminated by the glare of fluorescent lights. In one of the rooms nearby, my son Justin lay in a little crib encased by plastic sheeting. The steady hiss of oxygen filled the tent around him with a fine mist. The sound of babies crying in faint and intermittent mews filtered out into the hallway of the chidren's ward. On this day a baby was wailing—not merely crying—and the noise shattered the stillness and set my nerves on edge.

Dr. Cabrera was standing just beyond the nurse's station, waiting for me. He wore the uniform of his profession, a long white coat with a silver stethoscope hanging from around his neck. He was tall and rather thin and had aristocratic features—an aquiline nose and high cheekbones and a clear, straight brow.

Several other things about him struck me immediately.

He was younger than I imagined he would be.

He was very handsome.

And he did not look Guatemalan.

I was surprised, for I had been told the surgeon I was to meet was originally from Guatemala. Yet he had fair hair and very blue eyes and pale skin.

"Ah," he said when I stood before him. "You must be Mrs. Patterson?"

I nodded, and said that I was.

"Your husband is not here?" he said. His voice had a lovely singsong accent which I later came to understand was the result of the five languages he spoke, all fluently, though the predominant influence was Spanish.

I explained that my husband couldn't make it.

"Listen," he said. "I wanted to talk to you before we operate on your son tomorrow."

"Yes," I said.

"You know the situation is very bad," he said. "Very critical."

"Yes, I know that," I said.

"We've been able to stabilize him somewhat, but you realize he is still in poor shape. His liver is depressed, indicating the seriousness of his condition. His lungs are not in the best state. Yet we have no choice but to operate. To wait any longer would be a mistake. You understand this?"

"Yes," I said, "I do."

"I'm not one to give percentages on these things, but in this case, I would say we have less than a fifty-fifty chance of success."

"Fifty-fifty," I repeated.

"You realize I wish I could be more positive. More *upbeat*, as you say in this country." He smiled, and I realized he was making a little joke with the word *upbeat*, which sounded so utterly wrong coming from him. When I didn't respond, he went on.

He took a pen and a pad of paper from his pocket and made me a little diagram of the heart, indicating, as many doctors before him had done, the exact nature of my son's congenital deformity.

My son had a transposition of the great arteries of the heart. The pulmonary artery and the aorta were switched—their positions transposed—a fatal condition had it not been for the fact that a tiny hole between the lower chambers of my son's heart allowed a little oxygenated blood to reach his body. It was this hole, this tender defect, that kept him alive.

Dr. Cabrera's drawing of Justin's malformed heart was so delicate, like a little work of abstract art. He then quickly made another sketch, of what Justin's heart would look like after surgery, providing all went well. He said he would be using a piece of pericardium—the sac surrounding the heart—in order to reconstruct the heart from the inside, creating an S-shaped baffle to better divert the flow of blood. It all looked so simple, so promising, no more complicated than realizing a pattern of some sort. Cut here. Stitch there. Reassemble the parts. He used a fountain pen to make these drawings. The deep blue of the indigo ink looked beautiful on the paper.

"So you understand?" he said at last.

"I think so," I replied.

"I've talked with the surgeon who did the first operation on your son. He agrees with me that we shouldn't delay attempting this procedure, even though conditions are far from optimal."

He looked at me intently for a moment. Then he said: "Forgive me, but I'm curious. You seem so young. I mean, so young to have a two-year-old child."

I didn't know what to say to this, but he saved me from having to respond by quickly going on.

"You're from Utah, is that correct?"

"Yes," I said. I could imagine what he was thinking. That I was from such a backward place, where girls had babies while still teenagers. I thought he was going to say something about this, but he took the conversation in an entirely different direction.

"I believe the skiing is very good out there, isn't it?"

I said that it was.

"I myself am not so good at skiing, you understand. But I enjoy it, bad as I am. You, of course, are probably an expert."

"I'm pretty good," I said, and then immediately regretted it. In fact, I was an excellent skier. It was one of the few things I did truly well. But it embarrassed me, for some reason, to say so.

"Ah," he said, "just as I thought. An expert."

"Not, not an expert."

I found it odd to be discussing skiing. He must have sensed this, too, because he quickly folded up the little drawings and put them into his pocket and said, "Well, then. Unless you have any further questions, I will see you tomorrow, after surgery."

"Just one thing," I said. "Would you mind if I kept the drawings?"

"The drawings . . . ?"

"The little drawings you made of my son's heart."

"Of course," he said. He handed them to me with a sort of bemused smile on his face. "They're a little crude. You must forgive me. I'm not exactly Michelangelo." He laughed, and then he touched my arm lightly.

"Listen, try not to worry, eh? We'll do our best tomorrow. That's all we can do."

Only later did I realize how often he would begin his sentences this way, with this word *listen*. It was as if he wished to capture you completely with this word, and then hold you suspended, caught up in the delicate web of his sentences, like a fly caught up in silvery threads.

For a long while after he'd left, I sat near Justin's bed as he slept. His pale blue lids were closed over his eyes. His hair was coated with wet light. He looked so frail, so beatific in his stillness, as if not of this world. In a crib nearby, a pale boy with bruises on his legs, who was suffering from leukemia, rocked back and forth and whimpered. Every once in a while, I looked down at the little drawings again, studying the diagram of the walnut-shaped heart. It seemed to me the formula for my future was encoded there, in those intricate lines.

FOUR

The hospital where Dr. Cabrera was to operate on my son over-looked a wide river, the Mississippi, whose muddy waters flowed serenely past banks lined with willows.

Not far from the hospital, a mere two or three miles, stood a small liberal arts college, a maze of old, ivy-covered buildings and narrow walkways that crossed green commons—a lovely little college called Macalester—small and intimate, with a reputation for drawing bright students from privileged backgrounds.

This was the place where my husband Walter and I moved a few weeks after arriving in St. Paul. We lived on campus, in a ground-floor apartment of a coeducational dormitory where Walter had gotten a job as a counselor.

We had decided to move to Minnesota at the advice of the surgeon in Utah. Take your son to Minnesota, the doctor had said. There's a brilliant young heart surgeon there, Dr. Carlos Cabrera, one of the best in the field. He's your best hope.

We had left Utah in haste, taking all our belongings with us, driving day and night through the Midwest with our frail little boy, who grew sicker, it seemed, with each passing mile. We had driven across country with all our belongings because we intended to stay in Minnesota. Walter, who was several years older than I, had just gotten his undergraduate degree in social work. Within weeks of arriving in the city, he not only found the counseling job at the dormitory, but was accepted into graduate school at the University of Minnesota. I spent my days locked in a state of suspended being, sitting beside our son in one hospital room after another.

We lived with four hundred students who were stacked up on five floors above us. Although Walter was officially their counselor, we were both regarded as dorm parents who were expected to be there for the students in any crisis.

At the age of nineteen, having grown up in a little town in the rural West and never having left home before, I became a dorm mother in a building where most of the students were older than I was.

They were not only older, but far, far worldlier.

The morning Justin was taken to surgery Walter left me alone at the hospital for a while in order to turn in a paper that could not be late, he said. I was sitting in the little waiting room on the children's ward. When he'd gone, I sat there quietly for a long time, thinking of Justin and how at that moment he lay on an operating table, his chest opened, his tiny heart exposed. The TV on the wall was tuned to a game show and the gaiety of the participants, their laughter and false banter with the show's host suddenly grated on my nerves. Two children, both with Down's syndrome, were throwing blocks at each other in one corner of the room, and a stray block flew my way and hit me hard in the back of the head. Something snapped in me. I wanted to yell at the kids, and yet when I turned to face them, and saw their broad, flat faces and rather sweet, uncomprehending looks, my anger suddenly dissolved. I felt myself close to tears.

I got up and began walking rapidly down hallways until I found myself standing outside the hospital in the bright and startling sunlight of a winter's day.

It was clear and cold and I headed toward the river, walking at a brisk pace. I began thinking of how my life was set on a course and I was powerless to alter it. Happiness and sadness no longer figured in. There was only the drifting on the current of events, the waiting, the suspension of what I imagined to be my real life, a life that seemed to exist as if waiting for me to claim it, running parallel and unseen next to the life I had somehow become caught up in.

Something had broken in me, I knew that, and it seemed like that thing was the capacity for intimacy.

Something had begun shutting down in me at the moment of Justin's birth, when he was taken from me, blue and struggling for breath, before I could even touch him. For a long while I had felt myself growing increasingly cold inside, as if protecting myself from a loss that seemed imminent. It had been a long time since I'd wanted Walter. I endured sex with him by thinking, It'll be over soon, just as I endured Justin's illness by thinking the worst would never happen. He wouldn't ever die. But at that moment, standing on the banks of the Mississippi, the phrase *fifty-fifty* kept rolling through my mind, and I no longer felt sure of anything.

What I could not endure was the thought that this numbness in me would last forever. And yet what, I wondered, would release me from it?

I began thinking of my childhood, leapfrogging back over the years to the time when life seemed to have such a simple and immutable order.

I had a vision of my mother standing in the kitchen frying venison in a heavy cast-iron pan with the sweet and gamy odor of the meat filling the room, while beyond the window that overlooked the lake a red sun was setting and casting its bloody light over the water, and one of the boarders who rented a room from us coming up the stairs in his heavy work boots, his feet sounding on each step, walking into the kitchen and shuffling to a place at the table and my mother turning and saying to him, "I have to inform you that I cannot continue to do your laundry unless you change your underwear more frequently; I must insist on cleanliness in this house," and the boarder, whose name was Eldon, looking down at his hands with their nicked and blackened nails and replying, "Yes, ma'am," and then my mother saying, "One more thing, about those boots you're wearing, the heels leave black marks on my floor and I must ask you not to wear them in this house," and the boarder sniffling, and he always sniffled as he spoke from some region of his poor clogged sinuses, saying again, "Yes, ma'am," and then the family being called to dinner and the plates of meat and potatoes being set down at the table and every seat filling up until last of all my father came in smelling of the leaves he'd been burning along the ditch bank, that warm smoky odor of ash and the outdoors clinging to his clothes and filling the room, and how our lives went on then, past the black marks and the dirty underwear and the moment of tension, past the money that was never enough and the work that was never finished, to a meal eaten by each child so secure in his sense of belonging to that room and those smells and that time, that something like happiness descended on us all.

I remembered other things, orchards stretching to the foothills, the trees gnarled and black against red cliffs, baskets of peaches and pears in the August light, and the keening calls of seagulls wheeling over newly ploughed fields.

And then I began thinking of the thing I had shoved out of my mind for days because I couldn't bear to contemplate it. I had told myself I would think of it later, after Justin's surgery was over, but I could no longer ignore it, and I was forced to admit the thing I hadn't wanted to believe, the thing I hadn't yet told anyone—not even Walter, who surely had a right to know—and that was the fact I was pregnant again.

There was no doubt that a new life was growing inside me, a life so unwanted, so feared, that I had tried to deny its existence for weeks. I didn't believe any child born to me would ever be whole, would ever be free of imperfection. I was afraid I would never be capable of bringing anything but damaged goods into this world. Yet I knew I would have this child. Just as I knew in my heart that I didn't want it. In my world, in the world in which I was raised, there was no other choice but to accept this as fate.

For a long time I sat there by the river, rearranging the dis-aligned elements of my life, until at last I came into the possession of something like peace.

When I returned to the children's ward, Walter was waiting for me.

"Where have you been?" he said. "I was worried about you when I came back and you weren't here."

"I just went for a little walk."

"I don't think it was very responsible of you to leave the hospital," he said. "Do you?"

He held out his hand to me, and reluctantly I took it. At that moment my fragile peace departed.

Many hours later Dr. Cabrera entered the waiting room and stood before us. I had been dozing and opened my eyes to find him gazing down at me. He still wore his surgical clothes, a green gown and a small green cap that fit closely over his hair.

"Listen," he said, "we had a very difficult time in there during surgery. Very difficult. But Justin came through. He's still in very critical condition. The next twenty-four hours are most crucial. You understand that we aren't—how do you say—out of the woods yet."

I nodded but didn't speak.

Walter asked Dr. Carbrera a few questions about the surgery, and Dr. Cabrera answered each one carefully, at some length. I listened and I did not listen to the conversation. Mostly, I was thinking, He made it, he's alive.

"Can we see him?" Walter asked.

"You can see him for a moment," Dr. Cabrera said. He hesitated, and then he spoke directly to me. "You mustn't be shocked by how he looks. I want to warn you that you should be prepared."

"Okay," I said.

Dr. Cabrera led the way to the intensive care ward to see him then.

I stood looking down at my son, the smallest, frailest child imaginable, so pale his skin appeared translucent. An incision stretched from his neck to his stomach, intersecting the incision from a previous surgery, which ran from the center of his back to his chest, creating a little half moon beneath his arm. His body was clamped, sutured, bruised, and painted with antiseptic. So many tubes entered and exited his tiny being he appeared to be a fleshy little conduit for the numerous machines surrounding him. He lay semiconscious, drugged, his eyes partly open in a vacant stare. I knew he was there and yet not there before me, that his life hung in the balance, and that what he occupied was an ethereal realm where life and nonlife met like the amorphous edges of two distant clouds.

Later that night I awoke with a searing, clutching sensation in my abdomen. My thighs felt moist and sticky. It was dark in the bedroom except for a bluish beam of light which shone through the window and came from the streetlamp outside. I heard Walter breathing beside me, the tick of the clock, the traffic outside, and the soft snoring of the dog on the floor.

Quietly, I got up and made my way to the bathroom, doubled over with pain. I turned on the light. There, against the whiteness of my nightgown, I saw the stains of red. I saw how the blood had seeped from between my legs and covered my gown.

I sat down on the cold rim of the porcelain tub and began to weep. Amid the spasms of pain that rolled through me, there arose a feeling of such profound relief it felt like deliverance.

By morning it was over. The life I hadn't wanted had left my body of its own accord. I couldn't help feeling that the soul of one being had been exchanged for another. And I gave thanks for this small good thing.

FIVE

I take one look outside my window in the Tally Ho at the sunlight glaring on the asphalt and close the drapes, then switch on the lamp sitting on the table in the corner, where my books and papers are stacked, thinking I will write again this morning.

Funny how I was able to finally begin yesterday to set this story down. I think I was right to come back here.

But as I look over the pages I wrote last night, I find myself thinking of Carlos. There is so much sadness associated with these thoughts that I begin to weep—an act so unpremeditated it catches me by surprise. The sudden burst of tears subsides almost as quickly as it erupts but nonetheless leaves me feeling exhausted.

A few moments later I become aware of voices coming from the room next door.

I hear a man say "I'm getting the fuck out of here," and a woman begins yelling. There is the sound of something crashing against the wall and more angry, though not entirely decipherable, words being exchanged.

Then the voices grow louder. The man begins shouting. The woman screams back at him. I have no trouble now hearing what they say to each other.

"What did I expect from a whore?"

"I did just what you told me to. It's not my fault things didn't work out."

"Bullshit! You had your instructions and you still blew it. You fucking blew the whole job! You were supposed to play the machine opposite us, wait until we'd finished, and then walk over and pull the handle on the other one the minute we moved away. And what did you do? You stood there shoving quarters into the wrong damned machine and didn't make your move. So what happens? We set up a win, and somebody else walks over and fucking collects. How stupid can you be?"

"I didn't see you move. My back was turned—"

"Don't give me that shit. You're too stupid for this business, that's the problem. You haven't got the brains. Sid isn't going to give you another chance and neither am I."

"I won't mess up next time—"

"There isn't going to be a next time, honey. I'm leaving. And you're out of the deal. Period."

"What about the money? You owe me! I could go to the cops, you know. Don't screw with me."

"Tell that to Sid and he'll break your face. He might break your face anyway, just to teach you a lesson."

"You really scare me."

"You're so stupid you don't get it, do you? You think you're playing with a bunch of Sunday School teachers? Don't make threats, honey. Just cut your losses and beat it."

After a while I hear a door slam and it grows quiet next door, and in the eerie silence I take up my pen (yes, pen, my beautiful Montblanc pen—no computer here), and after a few moments, I begin again. . . .

From the moment I arrived at the dock where I was to board the ship called the *Oceanus*, I felt the strong sense of excitement. I'd never traveled on an ocean liner before. The *Oceanus* rose before me like a great tiered behemoth, a white whale of a ship with great black smokestacks. I joined the line of passengers standing at the bottom of the gangplank, waiting to board the ship. The day was gray and overcast. There was a slight drizzle, and the passengers were impatient and pressed forward against each other, anxious to present their tickets and be allowed up the gangplank.

A faint smell of wet wool and dampened fur permeated the crowd. As I stood in line, I looked over the faces surrounding me. It was an older group of rather affluent-looking people. I could hear accents and foreign languages being spoken around me. Men were dressed in thick coats and mufflers and a few women wore full-length furs. As I presented my ticket, a tall, bearded man stepped forward and introduced himself as Gil Rawlins. He informed me he was the social director on board ship and he'd been waiting for me to arrive in order to show me to my cabin.

"We're delighted to have you on board," he said, shaking my hand. "I just finished reading one of your books. We're always honored to have an author join us for the crossing."

I thanked him and told him I was looking forward to my time at sea.

"Follow me," he said, "I'll show you to your cabin." He led me up the gangplank and into a large circular room on the main level of the ship where a few passengers had gathered.

They were standing near a brass railing, looking down at a man wearing a tuxedo, who sat in the middle of a little recessed pit playing a tinkly sort of music on a grand piano. On the wall was a picture of Queen Juliana of the Netherlands, clasping her purse with one hand while breaking a bottle of champagne over the bow of a ship with the other.

"Is this a Danish ship?" I asked.

"It's owned by an international consortium," Gil Rawlins

replied, "but it was reoutfitted in Denmark three years ago, and sails under the Danish flag."

I followed Gil Rawlins past the piano player and up a stairway. We made our way to an upper deck, following narrow hallways, ascending several more staircases, and then walked down another long corridor, which was lined with pretty little watercolors of ships and seascapes.

"As I'm sure you know," he said at one point, turning to face me, "there are not many ships of this caliber still at sea. Luxury ocean liners are a thing of the past. But we like to think there are still a number of discriminating individuals left in this world who prefer this method of travel."

I had to smile when he said this. So often the word *discriminating* simply meant "monied," when in fact taste and money quite often formed an uneasy alliance, one either terribly predictable, or downright garish. Yet everything about the *Oceanus* was in fact rather subdued and tasteful, as if every effort had been made to create an ambience of luxury.

"The dress for each evening is formal," he went on to say. "I'm sure you're aware of this. Tuxedos for men, evening gowns for woman. As for meals, there are two dining rooms—the Queen's Room for our Luxury Class passengers, and the Poseidon for First Class. You have been assigned a table in the Poseidon."

"I see."

When we arrived at the last cabin, at the very end of a long corridor, he unlocked the door and stood aside for me to enter.

I found myself inside a pleasant space, small, but comfortably furnished. There was a narrow bed, a built-in dresser and vanity, and a tiny adjoining bathroom. The walls were lined with wood paneling, the bed covered in pale green chintz. One small, round porthole let in a cheerful light and offered a view of the Hudson River and some old buildings on the far shore.

On the dresser, a bottle of champagne was cooling in a metal bucket, and a vase of red roses stood next to it.

"The flowers are compliments of the captain," Gil Rawlins said.

"How nice."

"I hope you'll be comfortable in these quarters."

"I'm sure I will. I was hoping to have a window. It would be terrible not to have a view at sea."

"Porthole," he said, correcting me.

He motioned toward the TV set, which had been mounted on a wall opposite the bed.

"Also, you have the ship's channel," he said. "Any time you can turn on your TV set and get a view from the bridge of the ship! And I must say, it's absolutely the best view."

He reached up and turned on the TV, and a strange black and white image flickered to life. It took a moment to realize it was a fuzzy panorama of the skyline of New York.

"I think you'll enjoy the crossing," he said. "The *Oceanus* is no ordinary ship, nor are her passengers ordinary travelers. We hope you will mingle freely. Our passengers enjoy getting to know our guest lecturers and authors. Anything you need, please ask for it. I'm always available and at your service."

"I think I'll be quite comfortable," I said.

"There's a bon voyage party just starting on the upper deck. I hope you'll join us as we leave the harbor."

"Thank you."

After he'd gone, I laid back on the bed and stared up at the TV. A few seagulls occasionally animated what otherwise appeared to be a frozen scene. Then a barge passed. I watched the ripples it left in its wake, and then I closed my eyes for a few moments, turning my face toward the light falling through the porthole. A very deep sense of happiness suffused me. I cannot say why, except I think it was the sort of happiness one feels at the beginning of a journey.

After a while I made my way to the upper deck and looked down at the crowd of people standing on the dock below. The *Oceanus* was about to depart. There were several loud blasts from the ship's horn that seemed to hang on the air and continue to echo through the woolly grayness of the afternoon. Streamers made of brightly colored crepe paper had been thrown up over the railings, so that the ship seemed attached to the dock by a latticework of festive little ribbons. People were waving from the dock and calling goodbye to relatives and friends, who stood at the ship's railings, waving and calling back.

Later, as the *Oceanus* began to slip away from the dock, I stood alone, looking out at the city of New York. Waiters wearing white gloves and coats with gold buttons appeared and began handing out champagne. It had stopped raining. The sky was gray, leaden with a bank of low clouds. The massive ship, escorted by tugboats, began slipping between the banks of the Hudson. People stood at the railings, on three different levels, gazing out over the city. All around me, and below me and above me, were couples and families, clasping each other's hands and staring out over the wheeling seagulls and the skyscrapers and the tugboats guiding us down the main channel of the river. There was a very festive feeling, a great air of anticipation thrumming through the crowd. As I stood there, my coat collar turned up against the brisk air, I looked out at the city, washed from the rain, and it seemed at the moment that it wasn't the ship that was moving at all, but rather the city that was pulling away from us, being siphoned into the distance.

And then, as if crossing an imperceptible line of some sort, I found myself looking out at a watery world, with no trace of land in sight. There was the sea, all around me, wrinkled, glinting in the broken light, not blue, but gray and silver, crawling toward a flat horizon. And the world in which I had lived all my life became a new world, one I had never seen before.

SIX

Soon after my father died, he began to occupy a different realm inside me, although it didn't occur to me immediately that this was happening, or how it could happen, how a person can be dead and gone, and yet begin to assume a new and even more prominent role as a ghostly presence.

Not long after the funeral he began appearing, in the thoughts that sometimes seemed to waft beyond me and beckon him to me until I could see him very cleary like an actor whose face was projected on a screen before me. This began to happen more and more frequently, until I could feel him taking up more space in my consciousness than he had when he was alive.

He visited me at odd moments, appearing suddenly, his face hovering before me, staring down at me, a man who certainly bore a resemblance to my old living father but who in many important ways was quite different. For one thing, his ghostly self was kinder. He always looked down upon me with a gentleness I hadn't known before. Sometimes he was smiling, his lips drawn back over his teeth, as if filled with a great joy. Often I felt he was inviting me to join him in that ineffable realm of happiness. As if he were saying, Don't be so troubled by your worldly cares.

Most often in his real life—I mean the life I knew him to have on earth—he was not a happy man. But I remember one time when he appeared so unfettered, so truly, carelessly happy in a way I had never seen him before, that the memory of that moment remains indelible.

It happened in the days before I left home, so many years ago, when my father used to call me up on the phone almost every morning. My son Justin was only a few months old, and struggling for his life. Those calls from my father—I knew he was simply checking in with me, letting me know he cared.

One day, in the middle of one of our brief conversations, he said to me, "Why don't you meet me for lunch today?" My father never invited me for lunch, so the suggestion came as a surprise.

"I'm going to the hospital to see Justin today," I said.

"You can go up there later. Have lunch with me first."

"All right," I said. "Where do you want to meet?"

"Zito's," he said. "Meet me at noon."

Zito's was a steakhouse out on Highway 89, a place I'd seen only from the outside. I was surprised my father wanted to meet there. Zito's had a reputation as the sort of spot where serious drinkers went and got loaded in the middle of the day. But it wasn't far from the Air Force base where he worked, and I thought maybe that's why he'd picked it, because it was close to his work.

When I arrived, he was waiting for me, sitting at a table in a dimly lighted corner. I was startled to see he wasn't alone. A middle-aged woman wearing a bright dress sat next to him, a woman I had never seen before.

As I approached the table, he stood up and introduced me to her. "This is Louella," he said, "Louella Wadman." She worked with him out on the base, he added. She was his secretary.

Louella looked up at me and said, "I keep him in line," and they both laughed.

I sat down at the table opposite Louella, and almost immediately a thought came to me, a thought so strange I wanted to refuse
it but I couldn't. I knew at that instant that Louella and my father
were lovers. Given everything I knew about my father, it was a
completely preposterous idea, yet I was sure it was true.

"Your father's always talking about you," Louella said, smiling
across the table at me. "He's so proud of you. Of course, he's proud
of his whole family. All his kids. But especially you. And you're just
as pretty as he said you were."

My father glanced knowingly at me and I found myself looking
away from him, suddenly uncomfortable. At the next table a
woman was sitting alone, drinking a martini and looking off into
the distance. She was smoking, and I noticed how the hand that
held the cigarette shook slightly. Her face appeared indescribably
worn and sad, and when she turned and caught me staring at her, I
turned away quickly.

"What are we going to have?" Louella said brightly, picking up
her menu and studying it. Her eyebrows had been shaved off and
she'd drawn in new ones with a dark pencil, thin and imperfect
lines arching above her eyelids, which were coated with blue
shadow. I noticed she wore a great deal of jewelry—big rings,
gaudy earrings, and a heavy necklace made of large glass beads.

She was an entirely different sort of woman than my mother
was. She was thin and dark-complexioned, and as my father would
say, she was all dolled up. My mother was plump and rather plain
and often appeared tired from the drudgery of her life, a life devoted to her ten children and the boarders she took in in order to
make ends meet.

"Order anything you'd like," my father said with uncharacter-
istic generosity. He had trained his children to always think of cost,
especially when ordering in restaurants. But today he said, "Go
ahead. Have whatever you want. It's my treat."

"Oh, Ray," Louella said, "you're always treating. I think you
should let me pay for a change."

"Absolutely not," he said.

She reached over and patted his arm.

"What am I going to do with you, Ray?" she said. "What are we going to do with him?" she asked me.

I cleared my throat and stared down at the menu. I could feel a flush rising to my face, a hotness that started at my ears and was rapidly burning its way across my cheeks.

"I believe he's one of the most generous men I've ever known," Louella said. "Too generous, I'm afraid."

"What's it going to be, gal?" my father said to me. "Steak? Shrimp? How about the steak-and-shrimp combo?"

"Just a hamburger," I mumbled.

"Well, I'm going to have the pork chop sandwich," Louella said. "I shouldn't, but I'm going to anyway."

"Why shouldn't you?" my father asked. "You couldn't put on weight if you tried. She eats like a horse," my father said, turning to me. "And she never gains a pound." I thought of my mother, whose heaviness was a source of great sorrow to her.

"I don't gain weight because I only eat in the middle of the day. I never eat much for supper," Louella said. "Who wants to cook when you live alone? That's no fun, is it?" she said to me.

"I guess not," I said. I had no idea what it would feel like to live alone, or what I would cook for myself if I did.

The waitress appeared and took our order. After she left, my father said: "I told Louella you were a good kid. It's not often I tell you that, so I want you to know what I really think and what I tell other people about you."

I stared down at my hands. I wondered what I was doing there, why I'd agreed to meet him. I wondered what he thought he was doing, asking me to come here and have lunch with Louella Wadman. Did he expect me to approve of her? Was he looking for a confidant? A coconspirator? Or was he simply proud of her, and wanted to show her off to someone he felt he could trust?

"When I was your age," Louella said, leaning slightly toward me so I caught the full force of her perfume, "I didn't have half the responsibility you do, honey. I was just a flighty thing, and here you are, already so grown up and having to deal with so much. I sure hope everything comes out okay with your little boy. Ray told me all about his heart problems. I just say little prayers for him."

"What I don't understand," my father said, "is how we can believe in a God who would cause an innocent child to suffer so much. You have to ask yourself why He would do such a thing."

Louella shook her head. "Your father's always asking these kinds of questions. He always wants to know the answers to big questions that don't have answers."

"Like what?" my father said.

"Like why God makes little children suffer! You can ask that, Ray," she said, as if scolding him. "There are things you've just got to take on faith. You know that."

My father laughed. "She doesn't let me get away with anything."

The waitress brought our food. I noticed the woman at the next table had ordered another drink. The smoke from her cigarette drifted in my direction, making me feel a little nauseated. I didn't feel like eating, but I ate anyway.

My father and Louella began discussing something at work, a shipment that had come in damaged that morning. My father worked in the purchasing department at Hill Air Force Base. Sometimes when he called me up on the phone, I could hear planes taking off and landing in the background. His office was in a quonset hut near the runways. He was always complaining how he didn't like his job, but he never made any effort to look for anything else.

"I'm sure it wasn't shipped that way," Louella said. "That box must have sat out in the rain somewhere."

I ate my hamburger in silence, listening to my father and Louella talk about people they knew at work, things that had happened that week at the office, nothing that really interested me. Yet I was glad they were doing all the talking and I didn't have to say anything.

At one point my father said, "Why so quiet?" and I shrugged

and said, "I'm just thinking about Justin, you know, wondering how he is today."

In fact, I wasn't thinking of Justin at all. I was thinking about my father and how at that moment he seemed a complete stranger to me.

"You know," he said, as if reading my thoughts, "we all like to think we know a lot about the people closest to us. But I think it's impossible to ever really know another human being. Take parents. They think they know their children. But they don't. Any more than children know their parents. Have you ever thought what it would mean if we could really see inside each other?"

"There you go again, Ray," Louella said, shaking her finger at him. "Wanting to know such big things. Do you know what he told me the other night?"

I shook my head.

"He said to me, 'Louella, I think when we go to sleep and dream, we actually leave our bodies and travel to those places we dream about.' Now that may be very possible, as I told your father. But nobody knows that's true, and nobody will ever know, will they? Still, your father's got to wonder about these things."

When lunch was over, we walked outside and stood beside my father's car.

"This has been a very special treat for me," Louella said, taking my hand in hers. "Just to meet you, to have the chance to talk to one of Ray's kids. You're just as pretty as he said you were. I know I already told you that, but that's the kind of thing a gal can't hear too often. So young, and so very pretty."

"Thanks," I mumbled.

"I believe you could have been an actress if you'd wanted to. That's how pretty you are."

My father leaned down and kissed my cheek. Then he laughed. He laughed at nothing that I could understand. He seemed to be laughing simply because he felt so good.

"I'll call you tomorrow." He started to get in the car and then he stopped and looked back at me and our eyes met.

I stared at him, as if really seeing him for the first time. He was balding and his face appeared bloated and white, and there were dark circles under his eyes. He wore a rumpled suit and a tie that looked ridiculous, a big wide thing that was bright yellow and had maroon circles printed all over it. I noticed how his glasses sat crooked on his nose and caused his face to appear lopsided. He seemed too plump and too old and too bald and too ridiculously ordinary to be anyone's lover. And yet I had a quick flash, a picture of him embracing Louella, of her thin body pressed against his, conforming itself to the bulge of his ample stomach. He smiled at me one last time. I returned his smile, feeling a sudden wave of love for him flow over me, and began backing away from him, waving.

I watched the two of them get into my father's old Plymouth and begin to drive away. It was the dead of winter and it had begun to snow sometime while we were inside having lunch. The parking lot was now slick. There was a little incline leading up to the highway, and the wheels of my father's car began spinning on the ice. He had trouble getting traction. He kept having to back up and take another run at the hill, until finally he managed to get up enough speed and crested the hill, driving away in a plume of exhaust, with Louella waving at me exuberantly from the window.

I didn't go to the hospital until much later that day. After I left Zito's, I drove out toward the lake. I wanted to be alone for a while.

There was a little back road I knew. It followed the river through the canyon, down past the town of Uintah, and came out at the marshes at the edge of the lake. I parked under a cottonwood tree and sat for a long while in the car, just staring out over the water.

I wondered how my father could justify his infidelity. I wondered what my mother would think if she knew. I tried to imagine what sort of intimacy my father and mother had managed to have in life, beyond bringing ten children into the world. I wondered if everybody at sometime or other in his life got bored with what he had and wanted something else. I even wondered what Louella looked like when she washed her face at night and her eyebrows disappeared. Had my father ever seen her this way?

Odd thoughts continued to come to me.

What, I wondered, would I cook for myself if I lived all alone like Louella? Would I even bother to cook, or would I eat fast food and takeout? And how would I fill up the empty hours in an evening with no one to talk to? What did people who lived alone do?

Would I ever find myself alone, I wondered? It seemed possible I would. I could suddenly picture it, though I didn't like to think of it, or the events that would lead up to it.

I thought about the word *adultery*. It had the strangest sound to me. And some new connotation seemed to attach itself to the word. *Adultery.* Something *all* adults did, or wished they did, or feared they might do, as if it were the inevitable—the normal state of being adult—the natural condition of adultness, this act of voluntary, and perhaps inexorable, infidelity.

The snow had stopped. I got out of the car and walked toward the lake. My boots broke through the thin layer of snow and the crust of salt covering the marsh. A viscous mud sucked at my feet with each step, and I had to curl my toes and walk carefully to keep my rubber boots from being pulled off.

It seemed there were so many incongruous elements in the world, I wondered how anyone made any sense of anything. I thought of what a religious man my father was. I remembered his hands heavy on my head anointing me with oil and giving me a blessing when I was sick, how he had whispered prayers over me. I thought of his deep voice in church. I saw him leading the congregation in the singing, holding the thin white baton, waving it in the air like a magician with his wand, and all the while a bright and beatific light shining on his face.

I thought of us as a family, the way each evening, before supper, we had assembled in my parents' bedroom, kneeling down around their bed, the same bed where each of us had been conceived. Ten children, my father and mother, all kneeling at that bed, that common altar covered with a chenille spread—folding our hands atop that surface of tight little knots—how we prayed there, giving thanks for all that we had, each taking turns, praying for our health, praying for the goodness locked in our hearts to be released, praying for a sick cat to be made well and a lost bike to be found (these were the prayers of the youngest), asking for so little really, so very, very little compared to all we offered up to God, which was our own souls, our very beings.

And then I thought of the woman I had just met, Louella Wadman, and the way she had said my father's name, Ray, and some deep realization worked itself up through my body. I believed then that my father was right and we never can know another person, not really, not even if we live with him our whole lives. He was a stranger to me. And in some sense I was a stranger to myself. I felt in time I would become someone other than who I was, but I did not know who that person would be, only that she would be different, this other me I sensed coiled deep inside.

It had grown colder, and my feet were now wet, my boots heavy with mud. Big shapeless flakes were falling out of the sky. A wind came off the lake and rattled through the branches of the cottonwoods. I could see the thin layer of river water and, where it met the salt water, how the two had not mixed. The river water had frozen into a hard and beautiful sheet over the salt water, which never froze, not even in the coldest weather.

Far out over the lake this layer of frozen river ice extended in a wide path while the lake water, driven by the wind, rose into white-capped swells around it. The river ice was so firm and beautiful, it was as if a part of the world had stopped and grown still amid the surrounding chaos.

It was at that moment I saw the coyote. He was crossing the ice, moving in my direction. He did not see me standing there, half hidden by a cottonwood tree. He held something in his mouth, and as he came closer, I saw that he was dragging a lamb. He appeared to be trotting on the surface of the water, so clear and smooth was the path of ice that extended like a tongue from the mouth of the river. The lamb was dead, I could see that from the way it hung limp, like a soiled rag clenched in the coyote's teeth. Blood covered the lamb and spilled onto the ice, leaving a little trail. I realized the coyote had crossed over to the island on the little narrow path of ice lying over the lake and taken the lamb from a flock that wintered there. Now, in the yellow light of the afternoon, he was bringing the dead lamb back to the shore.

Much later this day would come to haunt me. The memory of my father sitting at the table at Zito's, laughing so freely. Louella beside him, with her penciled brows, saying, "oh, Ray, what shall we do with you?" The limp body of the lamb spilling its blood on the ice, and the way the word *adultery* came to have some new meaning for me.

Much later I would come to understand that nothing is ever as simple as it seems, and no one is ever so innocent as they might wish.

I would often think back on this day, recalling certain things. I would replay that lunch with my father and Louella and wonder, Was I right about them, or was I wrong? In time, I realized I'd never know. I never saw Louella again, and my father never mentioned her after that day.

SEVEN

I'm sitting in my room at the Tally Ho this evening, working at the little table in the corner, when suddenly there's a knock on the door. I open it to find a woman standing there. I've never seen her before. Yet there's something familiar about her voice when she begins to speak.

"Hi," she says, "I know this is weird, but I need help. Can I just come in for a minute?" She looks over her shoulder, and then without waiting for an answer, brushes past me and enters my room.

"Close the door, okay?" she says. "Hurry. I don't want anybody to see me."

For reasons I don't quite understand, I do as she says, and then I turn and look at her.

She's young, and she looks extremely upset. Frightened would perhaps be a more appropriate word. She's wearing a red miniskirt and white high heels, and her leather jacket is open, revealing a skimpy black top. A wild fountain of dark hair half hides her face, and earrings the size of lollipops swing from her ears.

"I just need to stay here for a minute, okay? Then I'll go."

"What's the matter?"

"I'm not going to rip you off or anything, if that's what you—"

"But what's going on?"

She sighs and looks at me pleadingly. "Just let me hang out here for a minute. Could you do that? Please?"

"Okay. But . . . who are you?"

"I'm staying in the room next door."

"Oh." It begins to make sense. That's where I've heard this voice. Through the wall.

She is standing there, teetering unsteadily on her little spiked heels, as if waiting for instructions as to what to do next.

"Why don't you sit down?"

She crosses to the bed and sits down awkwardly on the edge. I wonder, What's happening here?

"I've seen you a few times, you know, coming out of your room and getting in your car and stuff. I wouldn't have come here except you know it was like I just had to do something fast and I saw your door and that was it."

"What's your name?"

"Joycelle," she says. She tries to smile as she says her name, but the smile ends up looking strained.

I introduce myself, and then wait—for what, I don't know. We're both sitting there, waiting for the inspiration of a conversation opener, when I hear a noise outside in the parking lot. There's the sound of a car pulling up, a door slamming, and men's voices.

The men outside begin arguing. I can make out only a few words, among them the names "Joycelle" and "Sid," and the words "Fuck her," which are repeated an astonishing number of times. Then a man yells, loud and clear, "Get rid of her before she fucks up again." There's the sound of a car door slamming, and then the car drives away and it's quiet again.

When I look over, I notice Joycelle has begun weeping, and I get her a box of Kleenex and then sit down again across from her.

"Why don't you tell me what's wrong?" I say to her gently.

This brings on a wave of fresh anguish, and she buries her face in her hands and shakes her head.

After a while her sobbing subsides. She stands up as if she's getting ready to leave. Instead, she crosses to the mirror on the wall next to the TV and looks at herself, bringing her face right up next to the glass. Her mascara has run, leaving black streaks on her cheeks, and she wipes away the smudges, then fluffs her hair. While I watch, she carefully applies lipstick in a thick layer and blots her lips with the same tissue she's used to wipe her cheeks. All this is done with deliberateness and a complete self-absorption, as if I were no longer in the room with her. When she's finished, she stands back slightly and smiles faintly at herself.

"Are you in trouble?"

She turns and looks at me and begins laughing. "That's what you think?"

"Just a guess."

"Yeah, well . . ."

"I'm just wondering what's going on."

"Listen," she snaps, "there's a lot you don't want to know about that goes on around here."

"Like what?"

"Like slime-bag crooks threatening people."

"Is someone threatening you?"

She shoots me a hard look. "I didn't pop in to tell you my life story."

"Is this just a social call then, Las Vegas–style?"

"You're real funny," she says.

"You don't actually seem amused."

She folds her arms across her chest, looks down at her shoes, and points one toe.

"Listen, I don't care, really," I tell her, and I feel a tiredness come over me. "But I think you should know this. I'm good at keeping secrets. You asked me to let you in, and I did. You can't expect me to just let you walk out and not wonder about what's going on."

Her face softens, as if my little speech has moved her. She appears even younger to me then.

"The reason I can't tell you anything is not cause I don't want to but because they'll smash our face in if they think you know anything. It's not *good* for you to know anything."

"Okay," I say, "I can understand that. But I'd still like to know who you are."

"What do you mean?"

"I just want to know something about you, that's all."

"I told you I didn't come here to talk about myself."

"You're not going to let . . . ?" I say, and then something stops me from going further. Why should I get involved? I decide to give it up.

"Okay, if you don't want to tell me anything, fine. Stay here a while if you need to."

I pick up the book lying next to me and begin to read. In fact, it's impossible to concentrate. I'm just staring at the page while thinking about her, very aware of her standing across the room, still staring at me, leaning against the built-in vanity. We go on like this for some time. She doesn't stir, and neither do I. Finally, out of the corner of my eye I see her pick up her purse and start for the door. I don't look up, not even when she opens the door and cautiously peers outside.

"Hey," she says, just to get my attention.

Then I do look at her, and see how much more composed she is now, how all the fear is gone, replaced by a toughness: she's bolstered by an attitude of confrontation, a false bravura leaking from her like a bad odor.

"You want to know about me? I been on my own since I was thirteen and my parents died and I ran away from a shithole of a foster home. There isn't anything I haven't done when I needed to do it to survive. There you go, my life story. How'd you like it?"

"Not much," I say. "But it doesn't sound like you do either."

"You know, just because you sit there with your face in a book, you shouldn't go feeling you're smarter than everybody else," she says. And then she walks out and shuts the door.

She leaves me feeling confused and a bit unsettled. I just don't know what to make of it. Who is she? What if somebody ends up injuring her? I don't feel good about any of it, what I'd said to her, the fact I'd let her walk out when clearly there's some sort of threat to her. For a long while I sit there, immobile.

To exorcise the worry from my mind, I turn back to my work, to the little pile of paper that has begun to accumulate on the table.

EIGHT

The first day at sea the water was calm, and the ship rode the swells smoothly. Darkness seemed to fall early. The November night closed in abruptly around the *Oceanus*. One moment I was lying on my bed in the fading light, looking at an old movie on TV, and the next time I glanced out the porthole, I found a dark world with only a seam of the faintest vermilion running through the world.

That first evening I ate dinner alone, sitting at a small table in the dining room. Waiters hovered about me during the meal, bringing course after course, removing one plate after another, unctuously inquiring after my needs, until I felt I could hardly take a bite of food without the waiter materializing at my elbow to ask if I needed anything. But what really disconcerted me was the fact that I seemed to be the only person in the entire room who was dining alone.

I looked around me, wondering if it might not be possible to join another table. The dining room was arranged with tables for two and groups of four set around the periphery, with a few larger tables placed in the center. I recognized a few people from earlier in the day, having seen them gathered on the deck for the bon voyage party—the well-dressed couple I'd heard speaking French, the woman who wore a turban and her husband with the shaved head, the elderly couple who both appeared unnaturally youthful, as if each had had a face lift.

A number of tables had empty seats, but one in particular caught my eye, a table of three people—two men and a woman. The woman was blond, rather thin and attractive, and the men on either side of her were carefully dressed and athletic-looking. They were young—that is to say, under forty—younger than most of the passengers aboard the *Oceanus*. What really got my attention, however, was the way they seemed to be enjoying themselves. They were laughing and engaged in an animated conversation.

I thought I might approach them later and introduce myself, but when I had finished my meal, something kept me from doing so, an old reluctance that reflected, in equal measure I suppose, both my desire for company and my fear of intruding. Instead, I chose to simply leave the dining room, but by a route that would take me near their table, and as I passed by, I heard the woman say something to one of her companions—a little comment so extraordinary it stuck in my mind: "You have the most exquisite imagination, Devie, and what is imagination except the muscle of the soul?"

I was still thinking about this later as I sat in the lounge, nursing a drink and looking out the window at the blackness of the night, aware of the slight lifting and lurching motion of the ship and the chatter of the passengers who came and went around me. I had never heard such a lovely definition of imagination, and I couldn't help wondering about the person who could make this sort of remark.

I felt a pleasant anonymity that evening, sitting in the lounge, but I also felt myself in the presence of my old nemesis—a loneliness so complete it soon engulfed me. I did what I often do to cure myself of this feeling: I opened my bag and took out a book and began to read. But after a while, my attention began to wander, and I got up and made my way down a long corridor, which suddenly opened onto a very festive scene.

I found myself in the ballroom. A little orchestra was playing. Couples were dancing beneath the faceted lights, which created a little strobe effect, causing their movements to seem slightly jerky, as in an old film. Other people stood in groups, clasping drinks, or sat on the leather banquettes at the edge of the room. I spotted Gil Rawlins, talking with several people whose backs were turned to me. He caught me looking at him and waved for me to join his group.

I had not realized until I approached him that his companions were the blonde and the two men I had observed in the dining room.

"Let me introduce you," he said. "Lucy Patterson, this is Constance Milward, and her brothers, Archibald and Devon."

"Constance, Archibald, and Devon," Constance Milward said, pointing first to herself, and then in turn gently poking the chests of the two men who stood beside her.

"How are you?" she said abruptly. She extended a hand with extremely long fingers, on one of which was an enormous diamond ring. "And *who* are you?"

Her brothers laughed. One of them said, "Don't be bad, Constance."

"Lucy is a writer," Gil Rawlins said. "She's our guest author on this crossing."

"Really? Does that mean you'll be giving a reading or something?" Constance asked.

"On Thursday night," Gil said before I could respond.

"I had no idea this was to be such a *literary* voyage, such an *educational* experience. And we thought we were going to be bored stiff, didn't we, duckies?" Her brothers seemed to cringe a little. One cast his eyes disapprovingly at his sister, the other looked toward me and smiled.

"Don't mind my sister," he said. "We're trying to wean her from a disastrous love affair. She really doesn't want to be here. She'd rather be home, consorting with a misogynist."

"It isn't that Gilbert is misogynistic, darling, as I've told you before. He's *misanthropic*. He makes absolutely no distinction in terms of the depth of his loathing for almost everything and everyone." She turned toward me and added, "In that respect he's terribly egalitarian."

I realized that she was a little drunk—from the slight slur to her words, the way her upper body seemed to weave ever so slightly, making a minute rotation occasionally, starting from the axis of her waist and traveling up her torso in a widening circle. She was an exceptionally tall woman—almost six feet, I guessed, and these occasional weavings of her upper body seemed to cause her to sway gently like a tall tree in a wind.

"Is everything all right?" Gil Rawlins asked me. "Your cabin fine? Your table in the dining room?"

"He means, are you having *fun* yet?" Constance said. "That's his job, you see, as social director, to see that the level of fun doesn't drop too far."

"Actually, there is something I'd like to ask you," I said to Gil, ignoring her remark. "I seemed to have been assigned a table to myself. It's not very pleasant to eat alone and I was wondering—"

"But you can join us!" Constance said. "Can't she, Devon? Archibald?"

"Of course," Devon said.

"Yes, there are only the three of us at our table," Archibald added. "You must come and take your meals with us."

"I'm not always such a bore," Constance said, leaning slightly toward me. "Don't let me scare you off."

"Actually, I'd like to join you," I said. "That would be very nice."

"Oh good, it's settled then," Gil Rawlins said.

"We really ought to go now," Devon said suddenly. I noticed he'd taken hold of his sister's elbow in an attempt to steady her. She had begun to list badly in his direction.

"I'll see you tomorrow at breakfast then."

"Yes, see you then."

When they had gone, I stayed and spoke to Gil for a while longer until someone drew him away, and then, suddenly feeling rather tired, I left the ballroom and made my way to my cabin, where I fell asleep almost immediately.

In the night I was awakened by the rolling motion of the *Oceanus*. My body was pressed against the mattress as the ship dropped into watery troughs, then grew lighter, rising weightlessly and almost imperceptibly, as a wave bore us toward its crest. On and on it went all night, this feeling of my body sinking and rising, growing alternately heavier and lighter in a rhythm like breathing.

In the morning the sky was clear, but the water was still rough. I lay in my bed, looking out at the sight of a sea flecked with white-caps.

I got up and took a shower and then set about trying to make the small cabin feel more cozy. I stacked my books on the little dresser next to the bed. I arranged my clothes in drawers. My note-books and pen were laid out next to my books, and I draped a scarf over a lamp in order to soften the light. All the while I was doing this I could feel the movement of the ship as it ploughed the deep waters. The *Oceanus* seemed lost amid such a watery vastness, no more than a tiny speck on an immense and heaving sea. When I had finished arranging everything in my cabin, I dressed in a warm sweater and slacks and, taking my coat with me, I made my way to the dining room.

Archibald and Devon were already seated at their table, but Constance was nowhere to be seen. When I asked about her, I was informed by Devon that his sister *never* ate breakfast, and in fact, rarely rose before noon.

"She's a nocturnal creature," Archibald said.

"It suits her somewhat dark nature," Devon added.

"Besides, she's sulking."

"Over what?" I asked.

"She's disappointed in our accommodations. She thinks we should have booked Luxury Class."

"Never mind that the difference in price was *exorbitant*," Devon said, rolling his eyes.

"Intensely expensive," his brother added.

"Still, she feels cheated. She wants to eat in the Queen's Room instead of here. But it's too late to change. So what can we do?"

"Yes. What can we do?"

"Put up with her moods, that's all."

"Not an easy assignment," Archibald sighed.

Over breakfast I learned that the Milward brothers lived in Santa Barbara, California, and that their greatest passion in life was polo. Their father had been a very wealthy banker. He'd died recently and left them a lot of money (all this came out with a forthrightness, I thought, that was admirable), and both Devon and Archibald had quit their jobs as investment bankers and gone into business together breeding polo ponies.

I was pleased to find we had something in common—namely, a love of horses—and as we ate, we talked about polo and which breeds were most suitable to the sport, and then we talked about California, and about earthquakes and whether or not Santa Barbara might one day end up in the sea. They were charming men, so similar they could have been mistaken for fraternal twins.

In fact, Archibald was forty-one, the older by a mere ten months. Neither he nor Devon had ever married, and by their own accounts, had no wish to ever do so.

"Our parents divorced when we were young," Archibald explained. "They each remarried, my father several times but never with much success. My mother had equally fatal taste in spouses. They each ended up rather sad and lonely, rattling around in large houses with a few cranky servants to take care of them. It's not the sort of family history that sends you running to the altar, I suppose."

"But it might have had the opposite effect on you," I said. "You might have resolved to better your parents, to find the right partner and to make a marriage last."

"Had we been the marrying kind," said Archibald stiffly.

"Which we're not," added Devon, raising one eyebrow and peering at me.

"Besides," said Archibald, "now I'd be suspicious someone might only want me for my money. And wouldn't that be dreadful?"

"Quite the worst," said Devon. "The absolute worst."

They were like Frick and Frack, I thought—eccentric, but somehow perfectly matched in their oddity. Even the way they dressed suggested their similarity—matching polo shirts and cashmere sweaters and khaki slacks. Yet I found them easy to be with, and considered it a stroke of good fortune to find myself sharing their table.

When the breakfast ended, we all left the dining room together and said our goodbyes standing in the hallway, promising to see each other again at lunch.

It was midmorning, I was ready for a walk, and I decided to go out and explore the decks.

Initially, I found it very confusing to try to make my way around the ship, to discover the stairways that led from level to level, and to find the doors that offered access to the decks outside. I found myself in the casino, then took another wrong turn and ended up in a small and darkened bar where a few midmorning drinkers had gathered and were playing cards in the light cast by a solitary porthole.

In a way I didn't mind bumping around the ship. It was a way of discovering its contours, of beginning to sense the configuration of what seemed to be a great floating labyrinth. By accident I ended up in the Queen's Room, the Luxury Class dining room, which had strange murals of nymphs and neoclassical scenes painted on the wall. Somehow I kept turning up in the same cul-de-sac where I had seen the man in the tuxedo playing the piano when I first came aboard. I could not remember how I had gotten out to the upper deck for the farewell party the day before, and I began to feel frustrated at my inability to do something as simple as find the right door. Finally, by asking directions, I discovered a passageway on the upper level that ended at a heavy metal door, and, opening it, I stepped out into the sea-fresh air.

It was a beautiful morning. I could see the horizon, in every direction the same crisp definite line where sea met sky. The sky was a robin's-egg blue with small clusters of soft clouds here and there. A pale light rose from the horizon, like a fluorescent glow. The water was rough, a heavy rolling swell that seemed to bear the ship forward in a lifting motion.

The wind was brisk out on the deck. I pulled a beret from my pocket and wrapped up in my coat against the chill. As I began walking, the air stung my cheeks in a fine salt spray. I passed other passengers who were also taking the morning air out on the decks. I overheard bits of conversations in French and German. There seemed to be many Europeans on board. I noticed how pleasantly people treated one another, and how happy they appeared to be. I passed an old man, who removed his hat when he said good morning to me. There was a polite, Old World ambience that I liked out there on the deck. I especially felt this among the older passengers, many of whom were dressed rather elegantly in clothes befitting a sea voyage. One man stood at the railing in a pea coat and white scarf, smoking a pipe. The sweet smell of his pipe tobacco wafted out to me. As I passed by, he turned and said, "Lovely day, isn't it?" and I replied, "Lovely," thinking what a nice picture he made, in his blue coat and white scarf, with the sea behind him.

I had just made a complete circle of the entire deck, and settled myself with a book on a chaise lounge facing the sea, when I happened to look up to see two men walking toward me.

What struck me immediately was the rather intimate atmosphere that seemed to exist between the two men, the way they leaned slightly toward each other in conversation, and how each gestured as he spoke, using his hands as Europeans often do to emphasize some point or another. As they drew closer, I could hear them speaking in Spanish to one another.

One of the men was young and very good-looking, with dark

hair and olive skin.

The other was older—beautifully dressed in a long camel's hair coat and pale scarf. He had the most astonishingly white hair—thick, beautiful hair, but absolutely white—so white it appeared unnatural—as white as snow. His head was slightly bowed, and when he lifted his face and turned to speak to his companion, I saw how his thick eyebrows were also white. His skin, too, was unnaturally pale, so that it occurred to me he might be an albino.

As the two men drew closer, I glanced up from my book to steal a look. The man with the white hair looked briefly in my direction.

At that instant I recognized him, although for a moment it seemed so thoroughly impossible that it was really him striding toward me and not some ghostly white-haired impersonator that I doubted my eyes. But when he had almost reached the place where I sat, there was no longer any question in my mind.

It was Dr. Carlos Cabrera walking toward me.

As he reached the place where I sat, he turned to glance at me. I looked directly into his eyes and I saw him experience the same abrupt shock of recognition.

I stood up slowly, blocking his path, and smiled at him.

"Carlos," I said.

He stopped dead still. His brows furrowed, then he raised a hand to his temple.

"My God," he said, "I don't believe it. Lucy?"

"Yes."

We both were so caught by surprise it did not occur to us how foolish and awkward we must appear, standing frozen before each other, not moving at all, as if all time and events had been suspended. The complete transformation in his appearance—the white hair and eyebrows and his extraordinarily pale skin—caused me to stare in bold astonishment.

Carlos recovered first and said, "My God, I can't believe it," and then he leaned down and very quickly kissed me, first on one cheek, and then the other. Then he turned to his companion.

"Dr. Ramirez, this is Lucy Patterson."

I shook Dr. Ramirez's hand.

"You know each other, then?" Dr. Ramirez said.

"Yes, from very long ago."

"How strange to meet again on a ship!"

"Very strange," I said.

"Out here in the middle of the ocean," Dr. Ramirez added.

Something faint and almost imperceptible passed between Carlos and myself as we continued to look at each other.

"Are you traveling alone?" he asked.

"Yes. And you?"

"Dr. Ramirez and I are headed for a medical conference in London. But what are you doing here?"

"I'm giving a reading aboard ship."

"That's why your name is familiar to me!" Dr. Ramirez exclaimed. "Of course, Lucy Patterson, the writer. *The Invention of Light*!"

"Yes."

"Wonderful," Dr. Ramirez said. "I enjoyed that book very much. We mustn't miss her reading, Carlos. When is it?"

"Thursday night."

"Of course we won't miss it," Carlos said, and I thought he looked momentarily confused. It occurred to me he might not even know I had become a writer, that I'd published any books.

It was at that moment I looked up and saw in the distance two women walking toward us. It didn't take but a moment to realize that one of the women was Isabella Cabrera, Carlos's wife. I recognized her only from a picture I had once seen. I had never met her before, and I had no wish to do so now. I looked at my watch quickly.

"I'm afraid I have to go," I said. "I'm supposed to meet someone at noon."

"Could we get together later?" Carlos said. "For a drink, perhaps?"

I nodded, and again my eyes drifted in the direction of the women. I saw that Carlos, too, was aware of his wife approaching, and again something unspoken passed between us—a little feeling of urgency, a sense of mild alarm I knew only too well from the past. There was something beseeching in his look as he said, "Would you meet me in the First Class bar at five o'clock?"

"Yes," I said, "I'll meet you then."

As I turned into the wind, I felt its full force against me. The sky had grown overcast, and the sea was no longer cobalt but had turned charcoal and darkened under the leaden sky. I hurried along the deck, head down, until I reached the heavy metal door that led inside the ship, and hastily stepped inside.

NINE

My mood is low this morning. Another sleepless night at the Tally Ho, with more arguing next door.

I dreamed of Justin last night. It was the old recurring dream, the one where he is still a baby and I have misplaced him or lost him through some act of negligence on my part. In last night's dream, I finally do locate him, but he has withered and shrunk into the frailest little thing. How many years have I been dreaming this dream, or some version of it? Fifteen? Twenty? Since long before he disappeared. And as always, it leaves me with a haunted and hollow feeling.

As always, I am left with an old feeling of guilt.

In those months following Justin's surgery, I lived in a curious state. He remained in the hospital, recovering from a staph infection that had invaded his chest and which required that his incision be opened and left open until the infection cleared up.

I felt relieved that he was alive, although the first time—after the reopening of his incision—that his bandages had been removed in my presence and I had gazed into the open cavity of his chest to see muscle and tissue quivering to the beat of his tiny reconstructed heart, I felt much of the joy leave me. How was it possible to be alive with such a gaping hole at the center of your being?

I went to the hospital to see him every day. But he remained isolated in a germ-free room, and my visits were limited to two fifteen-minute periods daily, during which times I often found him sedated and sleeping. After years of caring for him—all the days and months when he had been the center of my life and consumed all my available energy and time—I now found I had hours and hours in each day to myself.

Slowly, I began exploring the new world in which I found myself. The city of St. Paul was unlike anyplace I had ever known. The dormitory on campus where we lived was at the corner of two intersecting boulevards, one a busy main thoroughfare and the other a beautiful quiet street lined with trees and divided by a wide meridian of grass. The houses on this street were large and very old, with gated gardens and beautiful trees, and often I took this route to the river, walking beneath the lovely old trees and wondering about the lives that went on inside such elegant houses.

It was 1968, and so much was in a state of flux. Each morning students lined up on the street outside our apartment and marched back and forth carrying signs denouncing the Vietnam War. At night they came and sat in our living room and discussed events in the world—the invasion of Prague, the rise of ecumenism, the possibilities of free love, and the civil rights movement—in short, their belief that the world was on the threshold of some great and liberating revolution.

All of my life up to that point had been lived in the shadow of a religion so devouring in its messianisms it had robbed me of most of the available imaginative space. Now, as I sat listening night after night to the conversations of the students, a deep and curious liberation began to occur within me.

Some mornings I would leave the apartment and begin walking toward the river, taking the scenic route to the hospital, down the quiet avenue with the large houses to the pathway that followed the Mississippi. Winter came on and brought with it a bitterness, a cold beyond anything I had known, and still I often bundled up and walked at least a part of the way to the hospital. Sometimes I caught a bus if the cold became too much to bear.

Even the act of riding a bus was a new experience. It gave me an opportunity to study people, to observe their differences. They seemed quite unlike the people I had left behind in Utah. They dressed differently, and spoke differently, often exhibiting a studied indifference to each other, at other times demonstrating a certain openness, a sort of instant, if fleeting, camaraderie. Often I tried to strike up a conversation with a fellow passenger, but usually with little success. But occasionally I had a very pleasant, if brief, exchange with a total stranger and this in its own way felt adventuresome. All this was new, and sometimes perplexing to me. Old rules often didn't seem to apply. The social codes had changed along with the landscape when I left home. And the mixture of races I encountered during my bus rides and walks around the city was also something quite different. I felt as if I had joined a much more cosmopolitan world, one that seemed utterly fascinating in its diversity.

Justin came home in December, in time for Christmas. His incision was still open to allow the infection to drain, and it was my task each day to remove the bandages covering his small body and clean his wound—that's what they called it, his *wound*—as if he were some little soldier, the survivor of a war injury that had left him with a hole in his chest.

He was an uncomplaining child, rather silent, with large, sad eyes that seemed to bear constant witness to his suffering. His sternum, which had been split down the middle for surgery and later closed with wires, had been unwired to allow the infection to drain. The edges of his split sternum formed the rubied, raw lips of his open wound. Every day, using a large glass syringe—which I first boiled to kill any germs—I rinsed his chest out with a sterile saline solution, patted him dry, and bandaged him again. After a while, it was nothing for me to do this.

I saw him slowly begin to develop a little strength, and some of the sadness lifted from him as he began to move about and play, loping down the hallways of the dormitory on his thin and unsteady legs.

The students were happy to have a child in their midst, especially one so obviously fragile, so in need of their attention, and often they came to take him away for a few hours, making snowmen with him on the commons, taking him for hot chocolate in the student union, tossing balls with him in the long hallways. I felt a weight lifted from me. The singular responsibility for his care was now divided among others. For the first time since his birth, I had free time on my hands. The question was, what should I do with so much time?

In mid-January, when the next semester started, I enrolled in a class. As the wife of a faculty member, I could take classes for free, and I began with a literature class. With a feeling of trepidation, the strange commingling of eagerness and fear, I took my place among students vastly more sophisticated and well read than myself.

In the house where I grew up, there had been few books, and those that were there were all of a religious nature—books with titles like *A Marvelous Work and a Wonder* or *Answers to Gospel Questions*. I had grown up largely without reading, except those books that were forced upon me in school, which somehow had never interested me very much.

Now everything changed.

I became a reader. I discovered Hardy and Joyce, Lawrence and Woolf, Cather and James. I devoured their works, one after another. It seemed to me that encoded in these books were the keys to understanding the secrets of life. Why humans suffered, and failed, and tried again—in short, why struggling itself was a necessary and immutable condition of existence. In class I was often silent, preferring to listen to the opinions of my fellow students and the professor, a pock-faced, chain-smoking man with a dry wit and affable nature named Dr. Blakemore.

One day, at the end of a discussion of *Tess of the D'Urbervilles*, Dr. Blakemore called on me to answer a question. The question was this: Of the two men in Tess's life, who was the more injurious to her, Angel or Alec?

I knew the story well, and it was a difficult question to answer.

One man—the sensuous, wealthy, pseudoaristocratic Alec— had seduced young Tess, leaving her pregnant, unmarried, and shamed (though it must be said he did not know of her condition until long after Tess's baby had died).

The other—Angel—son of a minister, had married her without knowing of her past, and when it was discovered, had abandoned her.

So who *was* the more injurious?

I found I couldn't answer Dr. Blakemore's question right away. I didn't know how to answer it. How were these things to be judged? And what experience, what knowledge, did I possibly have to enable me to make such a judgment? I knew only this much from my reading of the book—that one man had exerted a darker force on the heroine, luring her into the depths of passion, and the other had offered a more predictable picture of goodness and yet in the end had abandoned her. But somehow I felt it was Alec, the tempter, the sensuous, worldly man, who had contributed more to Tess's downfall. And so I said so. Alec was the more injurious, I said.

There was no right or wrong answer, but my opinion sparked a conversation in which both sides of the question were debated. What leads a woman into treacherous territory may also lead her into a sense of the fullness of life, lift her above the ordinary, release a sense of passion in her. But was the price of such knowledge destruction?

It was ironic, in a way, that this discussion took place at the time that it did.

That very same afternoon I came home to find a woman in my

apartment, sitting in the living room with Walter. I'd never seen her before. She wasn't one of the students from the dormitory. Walter introduced her to me as a "friend" from the university. They had the same advisor, and they had decided to study together that afternoon.

Her name, ironically, was Alexis.

The moment I met her, I perceived a current between her and Walter, the charged sizzle of sexual feeling, the surface of lust coated with a sugary kind of playacting.

I was still thinking about Tess and Angel and Alec, and really, I couldn't blame Walter. Who wouldn't want to be desired, to feel a sensuous longing stir inside them?

I couldn't blame him. But I could despise him.

When she had finally packed up her books and left, the silence she left behind was enormous, a huge sucking feeling of emptiness filling the room.

"Who is she, Walter?"

He looked up at me, and I noticed the swift and feigned placidity in that look. "We're not sleeping together, if that's what you mean."

"Not yet?"

It occurred to me right then what the worst lie was. The deepest injury. For me, for Walter. For Tess. Being faithful to a dead self, to a present rotten with lies, was even worse than being unfaithful to the old order of spent vows.

"I didn't set out to get involved with her," Walter said. "And I haven't, not really."

It's strange how little changed between us after that day. The civilities grew a little more strained. A dryness of heart settled in. The worst part was that the exhilaration I'd begun to feel with Justin's improvement and my new class became more muted. I saw how swiftly the bad follows the good in this life. Just as the good follows the bad.

Because the good did come to me again. Swiftly, and quite unexpectedly.

It was February, and I'd taken Justin to the hospital for a checkup. I was sitting alone in a waiting room on the ground floor. Sunlight was falling through the windows onto a patterned carpet creating a luridly bright block of whiteness.

I had this habit, left over from childhood, of trying to line things up in the world—disparate elements—the toe of my shoe, say, with a crack in the sidewalk, or the edge of a doorjamb in the distance with the straight line of a chair in the foreground. I was busily engaged with trying to fuse the hard edge of the block of sunlight with a stripe in the carpet—closing one eye and tilting my head—indulging my little compulsion, when I heard a voice, someone saying my name. I looked up to see Dr. Cabrera staring down at me.

"Are you all right?" he said.

"Oh sure."

"I thought you might have something in your eye . . ."

"No, I was just . . . uh . . . looking at something."

"I see. Listen, everything appears to be excellent as far as Justin's recovery. The wound is clean. It'll still be a while yet before it closes completely. These things take time, you know."

"It doesn't seem to bother him much. He's become more active. He really gets around now."

"That's good," he said. "It must make it much easier for you to see him becoming active. But . . . forgive me, if I may say so, you look so sad today. Are you all right?"

I shrugged. It bothered me to think that I wore my feelings so openly on my face. Because I did feel sad, though, I didn't think it was anything I wanted to discuss.

"Well," he said, changing his tone of voice, "in any case you shouldn't be worried about Justin. He's doing very well."

I nodded. For a few moments neither one of us said anything. Then he said, "May I?" and sat down beside me.

As he took a seat beside me, his white jacket fell open. Looking at him, I noticed his initials were monogrammed on the pocket of his shirt—CRC, embroidered in a blue script. It seemed clever to me, and exotic: I had never known anyone to wear their initials on their clothes.

"Listen," he said, "have you tried skiing since you've been here?"

I said that I'd wanted to but there hadn't been an opportunity. Besides, I didn't know where to go.

"You know there's a little ski area not far from here, only two hours away. Magic Mountain, they call it—Thomas Mann would perhaps find some humor in that, no?" I smiled at him, wondering who Thomas Mann was.

"Two of my residents went skiing there last weekend and said it was quite good. I've been thinking I might venture out myself. Perhaps you'd like to join me?"

"But why?" I asked, startled by his invitation.

The moment I said these words I realized they sounded quite wrong. Yet I was curious as to why someone like Dr. Cabrera would wish to spend the day with me—the mother of one of his patients.

"I could use some lessons from an expert like yourself."

I started to protest that I wasn't an expert, but he cut me off.

"I know you say you're not an expert, but I suspect otherwise. I'm sure this place isn't up to your standards. It's undoubtedly somewhat . . . rinky-dink, huh?"

I began to laugh then, at the way he'd said 'rinky-dink,' like the foreigner he was trying out some absurd Americanism. And he laughed too, happy, I think, that he'd finally broken my reserve.

Later, when I told Walter I was going skiing with Dr. Cabrera, he regarded me with a look of strange incomprehension, as if to say, How did you arrange such an invitation?

And in truth, I remained somewhat uncertain myself about why he had asked me to go skiing. It was all a little confusing.

The following Thursday I was waiting for him, standing on the corner, my skis leaning against my shoulder, when he drove up in a little green sports car with his skis fastened to the top.

We set off under gray skies. A light snow was falling, and soon we had left the city and were driving through the flat countryside of whitened fields and farms.

The land and the sky seemed welded together, seamlessly united. We were surrounded by a benign immensity of unstained light, the sky and earth blending into an unbroken luminosity. Dr. Cabrera instantly put me at ease with his conversation. He showed a great interest in me, in my life—a life that seemed so ordinary to the one who had lived it that the mere fact of his curiosity prompted me to begin to think of myself in a slightly different way.

In particular, he seemed fascinated by the fact I had been raised in the religion I had. This seemed an exotic detail to him.

He said he had a particular interest in this subject because he was from Guatemala, and didn't the Mormons claim that their *Book of Mormon* was partly a history of warring tribes who once lived in what is now Guatemala?

I said that was true.

"It's an amazing concept," he said. "I've read some of these writings. Extraordinary how they try to explain certain events without any attempt to examine historical facts."

I said I agreed with him.

"What most people outside the church don't understand," I said, "is that the Book of Mormon is really a history of the Americas from about 300 B.C. to roughly 400 A.D."

"Right!" he exclaimed. "There is some notion about some people arriving on this continent in little boats, no?"

"Yes. A tribe of Israelites were supposed to have crossed the Pacific in small boats, landed in Central America, and engaged in a series of wars with the dark-skinned natives, fighting their way up the continent to the last great battle in what is now upstate New York."

"From Guatemala to New York!" he said, chuckling. "Quite a trip in those days. Not as difficult as from Palestine to Guatemala, however."

"Moroni, the last record-keeper, buried the history of his people, etched on golden plates, at the end of the battle that destroyed his tribe of Israelites. These were the plates that were supposedly dug up by Joseph Smith in 1820, at the direction of an angel, and upon which he founded a new American religion."

"Extraordinary," he said again. "This guy Joseph Smith . . . I mean, one would have to say he was big on imagination, no?"

"I suppose he was."

What I did not tell him was how once, when I was about fifteen, I had worked for one of the leaders of the church, cleaning house for him and his wife, and how this man had one day taken me into his library and unlocked a safe and showed me a helmet and breastplate made of pure gold. He said they were artifacts he had obtained from an archeological dig in Central America and had once been worn by a dark-skinned Indian chief. This he said was proof of the truth of the Sacred Book, for this very breastplate and helmet had been accurately described by the prophet long before they'd been discovered. I had no idea where these things really came from, whether to believe him or not, but the beauty of the objects was dazzling to me.

"They're everywhere down there now, the Mormon missionaries," Dr. Cabrera said. "You know that, of course? They even give out free toothbrushes to the Indians."

I laughed at the thought of missionaries preaching salvation and promoting dental hygiene.

"Are you still a Mormon?" he asked.

I said no, I was not, that I had stopped believing in my religion years ago. He wanted to know how that had happened, how it was I had lost my faith, and I began telling him a story.

I was quite young, barely a teenager, I said. My father at that time was the bishop of the local church, an unpaid job, but a consuming one. Every night, when he had finished working at his regular job at the Air Force base, he would come home, change his clothes, eat a quick dinner, then go out to attend to the business of the church, returning long after I'd gone to bed. He was the head of a congregation of five hundred people, all of whom depended on him for guidance and counseling. He was very good at this. He gave himself up entirely to these people, to this job of being shepherd to his flock.

Each day after school and on the weekends, I would saddle my horse and ride into the foothills above our house. On the trails that crested ridges, I escaped from my ordinary life and created for myself an infinite realm of limitless beauty. I was an explorer in those woods. I was fearless. I was free. I escaped the oppression of the terrible roles I could see even then were assigned to females. I felt temporarily genderless, as strong and swift and well seated on my horse as any boy. Every day of the week, even Sundays when I was supposed to stay at home and read the funny papers after church like everyone else, I instead headed for the foothills on my horse.

One day my father came to me and said, "I'm sorry to have to do this to you, but I'm afraid you can't ride your horse on Sundays anymore." He said this because apparently he'd received complaints from members of the congregation. How could they expect their children to observe the Sabbath, the day of rest, to refrain from all activity, when they could see me, the bishop's daughter, riding into the hills every Sunday? "If it were up to me," my father added, "I'd say go ahead and do it. But it's not up to me. We have to set an example for others, whether we want to or not."

"That's when it all began to change for me," I said, turning to glance at Dr. Cabrera. "When my father said, 'If it were up to me, I'd say go ahead.' At that moment I realized he didn't really believe in it, and I thought, Why should I believe if he doesn't? I'm not sure I ever really believed. I was just a child who went along with things because I didn't have a choice. But I realized, at that moment with my father, that I did have a choice. And I began to reject it, right there and then. From that point on, I turned against it. I gave up riding on Sundays. I still went to church because I was forced to, but I never really believed in any of it again."

He looked at me and his eyes became slightly hooded—I later realized he had this habit of closing his eyes slightly when he was thinking deeply about something.

"Very smart," he said after a long pause. "Very perceptive of you."

"I don't know that it's all that perceptive, or even that it's so clear as I've made it sound."

"It all sounds rather sane to me."

"But religion isn't about sanity, is it? It's about faith. You either have faith or you don't, and if you don't, there's not much you can do about it."

"What a curious person you are," he said, looking over at me with a little smile.

"Do you mean *curious* as in *strange*, or *curious* as in *inquisitive?*"

"I mean *curious* as in *novel.*"

"It's not so terribly novel to believe in nothing—"

"Nothing? Is it really so bad as that?"

"What should I believe in?" I felt a certain defiance at that moment, a wish to challenge him.

"You might have faith in the individual, in free will," he said. "The Manichean concepts, the Nietzschean man. I myself am a dialectical materialist."

"Right," I said. I didn't even bother asking what a dialectical materialist was, for I began to feel myself getting in over my head. These were all things, after all, which I knew nothing about.

A little while later we came to Magic Mountain, which I was surprised to discover was not so much a hill as a hole in the ground.

The ski runs actually descended from high ground into a gorge some seven-or-eight hundred feet deep. In the bottom of the gorge there was a little frozen river lined with willows and a warming hut that served soup and hot chocolate to the red-faced skiers who came in for a break.

We put on our skis and chose a run and pushed off. The snow was hard and fast, and although the run was short and not terribly challenging, I felt exhilarated, stimulated by the feeling of speed, the sensation of flight, the beautiful buoyancy that results from perfectly carved turns. My legs were solid beneath me. I felt the power

and the strength in me, and I felt something else, an old joy returning. It was as if I had never been off skis, as if this were my natural
métier, my chosen method of travel across the surface of the earth. I
was good at this. I had forgotten just how good. By the time I had
reached the bottom of the run and pulled up in front of the little
warming hut, it was as if I had been reunited with an earlier self, a
more capable and unstoppable and carefree self, a self that resembled the child who had exhalted in her freedom from the back of a
horse.

I looked up the hill and watched as Dr. Cabrera descended the
lower part of the hill. He looked very graceful, very elegant as he
carved long wide turns, using the rather old-fashioned European
technique called Arlberg. He skied very precisely, standing erect on
his skis, and looked quite formidable in his jacket made of some
sort of fur and a cap trimmed with the same material. It was difficult to recognize him as the same man I had seen at the hospital, the
surgeon in starched clothes. He appeared younger, more vibrant.
As he skied toward me, he held his poles slightly out to the side, his
arms flung open, as if embracing the empty space before him.

When he pulled up beside me, he regarded me with a bemused
look and said, "Just as I thought. An expert. You're going to kill me
if I try to keep up."

"I thought you said you weren't a very good skier."

"But I'm not! As you can see for yourself."

"Well, you're not bad."

"Is that a compliment?" he said, laughing, and turned and
headed for the lift again.

We skied run after run, sometimes following one another,
sometimes skiing far apart, but always aware of each other, always
coming together at the bottom of the hill for the chairlift ride back
up.

As the day wore on, I felt there arose between us an unspoken
sense of how completely pleasurable we each found this experience.
It was very cold, and yet it hardly seemed to matter. We stopped
only once for a quick bowl of soup, and then we were back on the

slopes again. Dr. Cabrera began to ski faster and faster, taking his cue from me, and he seemed to exalt in such speed. By the end of the day a certain intimacy had sprung up between us, born of sheer collective joy in the doing of a thing together that we each so obviously loved.

It had been a long time since I had experienced such happiness. There was something so pure about that day. On the way home we stopped at a little German restaurant along the road and ate supper together. I think we each wished to extend the day, to see it not end quickly.

As we ate, I asked about his life. He said he would give me an abbreviated account.

"I was born in Italy," he began, "in a little town called Positano, overlooking the sea. My mother was only sixteen at the time of my birth, and my father not much older."

"So you were not born in Guatemala?"

"No. I spent my youth in Europe. My grandfather was the Guatemalan ambassador—first to Italy, and then France—and my family had lived in Europe for sometime before I was born—in Italy, and then later Switzerland and France, and finally Germany. Actually, my most pleasant memories are of the years we spent in Paris, where my grandparents lived in a suite of rooms in the Ritz Hotel."

"They *lived* in the hotel?"

"Yes. It was a rather extraordinary existence. I remember as a child going to the spring fashion shows with my mother and grandmother, eating in the most fashionable restaurants, being taken to museums at a very young age." He paused for a moment and then asked, "Have you ever been to Europe?"

"No. I've never been anywhere," I said. "This is as far from home as I've ever been."

"Then there's much ahead of you. A whole world awaits your discovery."

"I'd like to think so. But tell me more."

The Cabreras were a political family, he explained—a distant relative had once ruled as president, and many of his uncles had held high government posts in Guatemala.

"So you never really spent much time in Guatamala as a child?

"I made frequent visits as I was growing up, but I did not return there to live until I enrolled in medical school in Guatemala City. There was a dark period in my youth, and I finally realized I wished to leave Europe and all it reminded me of, and that's why I chose to return to Guatemala."

"What do you mean, 'dark period'?" I asked.

He seemed reluctant to explain, but finally the story came out.

In 1939 when war broke out in Europe, he had been staying with his mother and widowed grandmother on an estate in Germany, and they had somehow become trapped there. He didn't elaborate, but said only that his grandmother had refused to leave, and so he and his mother stayed with her, and later it had been impossible to get out. He had spent the entire war in Germany. With his Aryan looks and aristocratic background, he had quickly been absorbed into the Hitler Youth organization. His athletic prowess was so great, he was quickly singled out and rewarded with leadership roles and went on to excel in sports, to become the ideal Aryan youth.

"You are looking at the 1942 Ping-Pong champion of the Hitler Youth," he said dryly, and then he fell silent.

I didn't know what to say. I felt his discomfort intensely, and I also felt that he didn't often reveal this information, and therefore I couldn't help feeling flattered that he had chosen to take me into his confidence. But the effect was that in telling me about himself he had not decreased the sense of mystery surrounding him but had compounded it.

"You must find all this rather strange, no?" he said, breaking the silence.

I wished to put him at ease, and so I said, "No more strange, perhaps, than my being raised as a I was."

"Forgive me, but I must disagree. As constricting, as difficult as your upbringing must have been, I don't think it can compare with the complexity of my own experience—particularly the experience of war."

I think at that moment we both felt the extreme oddity of our present circumstance, the unlikelihood of the two of us sitting there in a German restaurant in a little town in the Midwest, discussing our radically different lives.

"At any rate," he said, "the past is a country we shouldn't visit too often."

"A country of ghosts."

"Well put."

"The present is a lot more interesting. But nothing fascinates us like the future and it doesn't even exist, though we are always thinking of it, aren't we? Always wondering what it's going to be like."

He gave me a rather penetrating look, and then said, "That's quite true."

The waitress appeared and he ordered a bottle of wine. The waitress hesitated, looking at me.

"I'm afraid I'll have to see her I.D.," she said.

This embarrassed me, but it was even more upsetting to Dr. Cabrera, who said to the waitress, "Surely you must be joking."

"No, sir," she replied. "You have to be twenty-one to be served liquor in this state."

"She is twenty-one, I assure you of that," Dr. Cabrera said coldly. "Please bring us the wine without any more nonsense."

The waitress, confronted with his implacability, went off to get the wine.

"America," he said with thinly veiled contempt. "I suppose they think they're protecting your morals. In Europe children are raised on wine, and somehow they don't crumble into degeneracy."

"You know I'm not twenty-one."

"You're not?" He smiled. "Then I *am* contributing to the deliquency of a minor! You are also guilty, however, of consorting with a very old man."

"How old?" I asked.

"Thirty-nine, I'm afraid to say, and in a rather decrepit state as you could see for yourself today on the slopes."

"You're really a very good skier," I assured him.

"Such lines," he said laughing, "and from one so young. Already I can see the moral degeneracy setting in."

"Can I ask you something?"

"Of course," he said.

"Why did you ask me to come skiing with you?"

"I assume you do realize that you're a very attractive woman?"

"I—I don't know," I stammered.

"Well, I find you so," he said. "Perhaps part of your charm is that you don't seem to realize these things. But I see I have made you uncomfortable."

I shrugged. "Perhaps a little."

"The real answer to your question is, I thought it would be pleasant to spend a day in your company, and I haven't been disappointed."

I looked away from him, not wishing him to see the effect his words had on me.

A little band had begun playing. There was a dance floor near our table where a few couples had begun dancing.

Suddenly, he stood up and, extending his hand, said to me, "Perhaps we should dance a little before we leave, no?"

"In our ski clothes?"

"Believe me, in this *joint* no one will notice."

"But I'm not a very good dancer."

"Ah, then perhaps it's my turn to lead you."

He was an extraordinary dancer. He moved with exquisite grace. Much later I would learn that in his youth he had won prizes in dance competitions, mastering the tango and the merengue and the mambo. But that night I was only aware of his extreme confidence as he held me lightly in his arms and moved me across the floor.

At one point, he stopped and stepped back from me and said, "With dancing, it all comes from the hips, you know. The upper body stays very quiet. Everything from here . . ." and he began moving his hips fluidly, stepping rhythmically in place, demonstrating what he meant.

"And your hand," he added, "if you will place it like this, very lightly, on my shoulder, keeping your arm against mine, you'll be able to feel what I'm going to do next, to anticipate my movements."

As he gathered me up again in his arms and we began dancing, I could feel what he meant. I could feel that and much more.

It was late when we finally drove back into the city and he pulled up at the curb in front of the dormitory.

"I hope your husband won't be worried," he said.

"Will your wife?" The words came out before I could stop myself. There was really no question in my mind that he was married, although he had not once mentioned it directly.

There was a rather long pause, and then he said, "No, she will not be worried."

"Well . . . thanks for the nice day." I gathered up my skis and poles. We were standing under a streetlamp. Little snowflakes were drifting down through the circle of light like chips of silvery mica. They clung to his coat and glittered briefly before melting and disappearing into the dark fur.

"It was fun, no?"

"No. I mean, yes," I said, laughing.

He looked unusually handsome to me at that moment, his face flushed from the day outdoors. He seemed almost too perfect with his bold good looks, not of this world or any other world I had ever known, a stranger from a strange land, a distant traveler who didn't belong on this street corner in this ordinary city in America, and I felt a sudden wariness of him, as of the unknown, so mysterious and uncomprehensible did he seem at that moment. He dispelled that fear, however, with a look that was guileless, profound, confidant, trustful, and somehow very intimate.

"Can we do this again?" he said.

I nodded.

"Next Thursday? It's my day off."

"Yes. Next Thursday."

I watched him drive away, following the pinpoints of the red taillights until they disappeared into the whiteness of the storm, and then I turned, and with a feeling of euphoria inside me, stepped out of the light and into the darkness.

TEN

The knock on the door came from some distant realm, an ambiguous sound that drifted to me as if from the fuzzy region of dreams.

"Oh God," Joycelle said when I opened the door and she saw me standing in my robe. "You aren't even awake yet."

"What time is it?"

"Almost ten."

"I'm afraid I had a little too much to drink last night." I stepped aside for her to enter.

"I can come back."

"It's all right, come in."

She came inside and I closed the door against the blinding sunlight. She was wearing spiked heels. The shoes looked too large for her feet. Her ankles wobbled when she walked, and yet she managed to stride briskly into the room. She seemed filled with energy, her mood distinctly brighter than it had been the first time I'd seen her.

"I know what it's like to be hungover," she said. "God, that terrible furry feeling in your mouth."

I saw that we were not without common ground, Joycelle and I.

"Hey," she said, "I just wanted to apologize for being so—well—what can I say . . . so *bitchy* to you the other night. I get upset and I just take it out on the nearest person, you know."

"A common condition. That's why I live alone. I can limit my sphere of damage."

"Living alone isn't a solution, believe me, I know, 'cause then you just take it out on yourself."

"I'm afraid that's quite true."

"I thought you might want to get some breakfast and then we could go over to the Mirage and see the white tigers."

"The white tigers?"

"You haven't seen them? Oh God, you've *got* to! You're not going to believe how beautiful they are. I'll even buy you breakfast—steak and eggs and a Bloody Mary, that's what you need for a hangover."

My stomach took a bad turn.

"That's very nice of you, but I planned on working this morning," I said.

"Yeah, well, it's okay. I didn't really think you'd want to go." She turned toward the door, and her disappointment was palpable; her whole frame curled beneath its weight.

"Some other time," she mumbled.

It moved me to reconsider. There was something fresh and eager in her manner this morning, something so unguarded, a quality of youthfulness and energy, and I couldn't deny I felt an absence of these things in my own life.

"Maybe some breakfast wouldn't be a bad idea after all," I said. "Give me a few minutes to get myself together."

Her face broke into a grin. "I'll wait for you outside."

The day was hot, a dry wind blowing from the south. Out on the Strip the tourists were already trudging along the dusty sidewalks, shading their eyes from the sun, as if searching for something on a distant horizon. We were in Joycelle's car, a battered old Chevy convertible that backfired with alarming volume and regularity.

"We'll get some breakfast at Treasure Island," she said, "and then we can take the skywalk over to the Mirage. If you want after that we could go over to the Luxor and ride the barge around the lobby, maybe even play some bingo. You like bingo?"

"I rarely test my luck."

"What I love about this town is how every single minute of the day there's something to do. The city that never sleeps."

"Considering how little sleep I've been getting lately, it seems the atmosphere is infectious."

We pulled into a parking lot next to the Mirage and were just getting out of the car when Joycelle suddenly was overcome with a fit of coughing. She sat back in her seat and held on to the steering wheel while her whole body shook, racked with spasms she seemed powerless to control.

"Shit," she said in a thin, weak voice when she'd finally managed to calm herself. By then I was standing next to her, near the driver's door, looking down at her. There were goose bumps on her arms. Her hands were trembling.

"Are you all right?"

"I got this cough," she said, dragging herself wearily out of the car. Her eyes had watered badly and she leaned against the car for a moment, wiping the tears away with the back of her hand. "I don't know what it is. It started a few weeks ago. Sometimes I wake up in the night all broke out in the sweats. I guess I just got a bug of some kind."

"Perhaps you should see a doctor."

She shot me a meaningful look. "Doctors are for people with insurance, hon. The rest of us just wait for things to pass." Her voice was laden with cynicism. There was something about her that seemed terribly sad to me at that moment.

"Well, let's go get some breakfast," I said, "then you can show me those tigers."

"Righto," she said, tossing her wild mane of dark hair out of her face. As we started across the parking lot, I felt her loop her arm through mine as if she needed a steadying presence. It felt so thin, so weightless, as if a small bird were caught next to my ribs, fluttering against my blouse.

At breakfast she picked at her food, shoving it around her plate with the tip of her knife, and then she began playing with the sugar packets, all the while keeping up a steady stream of talk. She talked about what she would do if she had money (buy a BMW, take a cruise to Acapulco, get her own tanning machine). She mentioned how much she didn't like her job, although when I asked where she worked, she said, "You don't want to know." She went on about why she thought women made crummy friends, how the only real friends she'd ever had in life were men, and they weren't very reliable either.

"Women only like you if you're dumber and uglier than they are."

"I find that a particularly dismal view," I said.

"I'm not saying I couldn't be friends with you, don't misunderstand me. It's different with older women. They aren't so threatened."

"I would think it might be just the opposite," I said. "Older women might find someone like you—someone so young and attractive—very threatening."

"Only if they had some big fat bald husband who wanted to screw me," she said with a sneer.

I found it difficult to warm to her. One moment she seemed open and cheerful. The next she showed a sort of vulgar, banal contempt for almost everything around her. I didn't see any point in engaging with her remarks, so I continued to eat in silence.

"You married?" she asked suddenly.

"No," I said.

"Were you ever?"

"Once. A very long time ago."

"Do you have any kids?"

"No," I said quietly.

She took a cigarette out of her purse and lit up. She let the cigarette dangle from her lips while she rummaged around in her purse looking for something. The smoke curled up into her eyes and she squinted against it, contorting her face into a grimace.

"Ah hell, forget it," she said, tossing the purse onto the seat. "I was going to show you a picture, but I must have left it back in the room."

"A picture of whom?"

"Forget it. It's not important."

"I don't think it's such a great idea for you to be smoking with that cough, do you?"

She grinned at me, cocky, defiant. Then she leaned across the table and pointed a finger at me with the hand that held the cigarette.

"You," she said, "would make someone a very nice mother." Then she dissolved into shrill and foolish laughter.

After breakfast we crossed the skywalk connecting Treasure Island and the Mirage. It was a long glass tunnel, several stories above the ground. It afforded a sweeping view of Las Vegas and the mountains in the distance.

In the middle of the walkway she stopped and pointed toward the horizon. "That's Sunrise Mountain out there," she said, indicating a single cone-shaped mountain that appeared washed out in the hazy purple light.

"This guy once took me out there, you know, he said he wanted to show me something—" She suddenly changed her mind about whatever she was going to tell me and said, "Never mind, I'm sure you don't want to hear *that* story. I don't know what I'm thinking of." She looked away from me and sort of rolled her eyes up at the ceiling.

For some reason I wanted to hear what she had to say. Or maybe I was just tired of her broaching subjects then backing away from them.

"Maybe I do want to hear it," I said.

"Naw, you don't want to hear it."

"Look, Joycelle. Just tell me. You keep starting something and not finishing it."

"Okay, okay." She sighed, blowing air out through her nose in a little snort.

"I went out there with this guy one day, he said he wanted to show me something out at Sunrise Mountain, and I figured, you know that it was going to be something pretty, some nice spot with a view. But we get out there and he just drives off the highway into the desert on this little dirt road and there's nothing there, just sand, some broken glass, and some old tires and stuff. He stops the car and says we have to get out and walk, it's just a little bit further. So we start walking. It isn't easy because I've got on these high heels. I start complaining, I don't want to go any further, I don't believe there's anything out there anyway. And then suddenly there's this bad smell. And a lot of birds. I get a real bad feeling even before he leads me up to the edge of this big pit. It drops about fifteen feet straight down. And you know what's in the pit?" She hesitated, as if I was supposed to guess, but I simply said no, I didn't know what was in the pit.

"Dead animals," she said. "Lots of them. Bloated old cows and horses. Dead sheep. Even dogs and cats. All maggoty and rotting. It was a dead-animal pit. I couldn't believe he'd brought me out there to see this. I got so mad I turned around and shoved him. I meant to just push him away from me. I didn't mean to shove him in, but that's what happened. He lost his balance and fell right into the pit." She put her hand in front of her face and began laughing.

"He landed on this big fat old bloated cow and it kind of gave way under him. He just sunk into it and started wallowing around in all that rottenness, screaming at me. I just turned and ran, I tell you, I did *not* want to be there when he got out. When I got to the highway, I hitched a ride back to town."

"Quite a story," I said, trying to hide my revulsion.

"Not the best story to hear right after breakfast, is it?" She laughed. "I just couldn't help thinking of it looking at that mountain."

"What about the man? What did he say when you saw him the next time?"

She gave me a look that suggested I was stupid. "He wasn't anybody I *knew*. He was a *john*," she said. "Don't you get it? He took me out there because he was a sicko. He probably thought it'd be real fun to have sex out there. There are guys like that, you know. Guys sicker than you can imagine. So I figure he just got what he deserved."

We arrived at the Mirage just as the fake volcano in front of the casino was erupting, an on-the-hour occurrence. Hundreds of people had gathered to observe the spectacle. The volcano itself looked like a gargantuan cone made of papier-mâché, a great molded and wrinkled mountain, concave at the top, and surrounded by sick-looking palm trees. The fronds were tattered and brown, as if the constant eruption of the fake volcano had been too much for them to bear. Smoke began belching out from the top of the volcano, and then flames and sparks erupted, shooting straight into the air. The volcano roared and rumbled, and the crowd roared with it and began clapping. The whole thing lasted less than a minute. Then the flames and the sparks and smoke subsided and the crowd began to disperse, seeking shelter from the sun, so real, so brutal in its merciless heat compared to the fake fire of the volcano, and all that was left was a strange smell lingering on the air, the odor of a steam iron left on too long, the smell of a spent firecracker sizzling toward extinction.

"That was lucky," Joycelle said, "getting here just in time to see the volcano erupt."

"But you must have seen it before?"

"Oh, lots of times. But I never get tired of it. I mean, how often do you get to see a volcano go off?"

"You act like we've just witnessed a real event!"

She turned and faced me, and I could see she was upset by my reaction. "So you didn't like it? You think it's ridiculous, huh?"

"Well, I—"

"Blow it off, then," she said, and turned and began striding rapidly away from me.

I followed her through the lobby, past the shark pool—a giant aquarium behind the check-in counter where sluggish-looking sharks cruised waters studded with Day-Glo coral, their prehistoric ferocity reduced to a glint in a malevolent eye—over a little bridge, through a simulated rain forest reeking of mildew, and down a carpeted aisle between gaming tables, until at last we came to the Royal Tiger Habitat.

And there they were—the white tigers. There were four of them, all white, and marked with the faintest black stripes.

They were visible behind slanted glass, confined in a large enclosure open to the sky, surrounded by high walls sculpted to resemble rock. In the middle of the enclosure, a blue-tiled pool was surrounded by white plaster palms. The decor was faux-Indian— white plaster elephants standing guard beneath a white Moghul archway near the white raised dais where the white tigers slept. It was all so white it dazzled the eye.

Some people were pressed against a brass railing in front of the glass, standing two and three deep, looking at the tigers. Others stood back in order to watch a narrated story of the tigers unfold on one of the six video monitors mounted above the railing, as if the tigers themselves were not nearly so interesting to them as the video of the tigers.

"Aren't they beautiful?" Joycelle murmured.

"Indeed they are."

The three females reclined on a raised platform. As we watched, the large, magnificent-looking male climbed down from the platform and began striding nervously up and down before the glass, his great black testicles bouncing against his legs as he peered out at the spectators looking in at him. He crossed to the fake palm and rose up on his hind legs, scratching at the plaster as if trying to sharpen his claws.

A shaft of sunlight fell across the face of the male as he turned his head toward me. His blue eyes held a look that was completely unfathomable to me. His head was larger than I could have imagined. There was a slackness to his body, his stomach slung low, and when he strode off lazily, making a circle around the pool and passing beneath the Moghul archway, only to circle the pool again, I couldn't help wondering how many thousands of times he had trod exactly the same path around his cage. I felt sorry for him, locked away in his phony paradise. I felt what I always felt when I saw caged animals—a deep sadness, and a sense of complicity and shame.

"Joycelle," I said, glancing at my wristwatch, "I'm afraid I've got to get some work done. Do you mind taking me back to the motel?"

"You don't want to go to the Luxor and ride the barge?"

"I'll take a rain check on that."

In the car, driving back to the motel, I hardly listened to Joycelle, who seemed to be talking mostly to fill up the awkward silence. My thoughts were disjointed, fractured into images of the fake volcano, the white tigers, the single eye of a shark, and I couldn't help thinking of the ridiculous spectacle of humans so entertained, so *thrilled*, by such sights. Of course, everything was phony in Las Vegas. One didn't come to this place to experience the splendors of the natural world. And yet it was that very world that was being replicated, reproduced in cardboard and pyrotechnics and confined behind glass, and I couldn't help thinking that this was the future, that we were all being inexorably herded toward life as a diorama.

"Are you listening to me?" Joycelle said suddenly.

"I'm sorry. I'm afraid I wasn't."

"Because there's something I want to say and I want you to hear it."

"Go ahead."

"That story I told you about the dead-animal pit. Well, I don't want you to think I do that anymore, you know what I mean. I mean, I did that for a while, but only 'cause I was broke. I'm not doing that now."

"I'm glad to hear that," I said.

"I got this job now, you know. It's not great, but it's a regular paycheck."

"What is it?"

"I'm working at this club called the Penthouse. It's kind of a strip joint. Not kind of, it *is* a strip joint. But I get to dance, which is what I really want to do. I'm trying to get a job with a revue at one of the casinos, and when I do, you can bet it'll be the last they see of me at the Penthouse."

We pulled into the parking lot of the motel, and I thanked her for breakfast and started to get out of the car.

"Wait a minute," she said. "I want to ask you something." I turned to look at her, and was surprised to see how cold her eyes were, how hard they stared at me.

"You didn't enjoy any of that, did you?"

"Any of what?"

"Anything we did this morning?"

"Well, that's not entirely true."

" '*That's not entirely true,* ' " she said, mimicking my voice rather rudely. "Well, I think it is true and you can't cop to it. What I want to know is, why can't you just let yourself have a good time?"

"Maybe I'm just preoccupied at the moment."

"Or maybe you just think you're better than everybody else. Maybe I'm just beneath you, like the tigers and the volcano and everything else. Maybe it's all fake to you and you're the only real thing in the world. Maybe I'm just some dumb person who isn't worth the time of day to you."

"I'm sorry if I've said anything to make you feel that way."

"Then why don't you say something to make me *not* feel that way?"

"I have apologized."

"What's wrong with you, anyway? Something is, I know that much. I may look stupid to you, but I'm not so dumb when it comes to people. Believe me, in my business I wouldn't be around if I was. You act like the world's coming to an end and you're the only one who knows it."

I sighed, and looked out the window, toward the pool, where Mr. Patel was working, methodically skimming the surface of the water with a net attached to a long pole. I could hear him whistling and I recognized the tune: "Somewhere over the rainbow." The water sparkled in the sun and cast liquid, glittering patches of light upon his brown face. How could I explain things to her? What could I possibly say to make her understand? Obviously, she was right. I *had* behaved badly. When clearly she had only wished to be friendly, to show me around.

"In a way, the world *has* come to an end—my world, or at least a certain part of it," I said slowly. A butterfly drifted lazily by and lit on the windshield, where it continued to flex its stippled wings.

I continued in a low and monotone voice, keeping my eyes fixed on the butterfly, on the delicate spots of purple flecking its white wings.

"I've recently lost someone—a man I loved very much. If I have been rude to you this morning, I'm sorry. Perhaps you'll forgive me. It has nothing to do with you."

I turned to face her and our eyes met. I was struck by the honesty of her expression, the frankness and openness. And the kindness that was now so evident in her eyes. A callow wisdom seemed to radiate from her in that instant and suffuse the space between us.

"Will you forgive me?"

"Yeah, I'll forgive you. But only if you'll try to loosen up a little, huh?"

"Thanks," I said. "I'll try."

"All right, then."

Joycelle has gone now, and I am here alone in my room. The air conditioner hums in the background, creating a comforting white noise. The only disturbance is a leaky faucet that drips with annoying regularity into the bathroom sink.

ELEVEN

The meeting with Carlos out on the deck of the ship had been so abrupt, so unexpected, it left me unsettled. How was I to manage over the next few days? It wasn't only Carlos I was thinking about, but also Isabella, whose very name filled me with an old sense of dread.

As I made my way toward my cabin, following the confusing maze of corridors, I bumped into Gil Rawlins.

"Ah," he said. "Just the person I was looking for. I wondered if everything had worked out all right with the change in our dining arrangements?"

"Yes, fine, thank you."

"Oh good. Splendid. I hated to think of you dining alone. I'm sorry we didn't think of that before you did."

"The Milwards were very kind to ask me to join them."

"There is one other thing I did want to mention to you, since you are traveling alone. We do have gentlemen hosts aboard ship, for ladies like you who are traveling solo."

" 'Gentlemen hosts'?"

"Yes. Charming fellows who are available for companionship. Bridge, shuffleboard, dancing, whatever takes your fancy—our gentlemen hosts are there at your service. You might like to join them and the other single ladies tonight, at five o'clock in the lounge, for cocktails and a little dancing?"

I began laughing, I don't know why, except this struck me as rather funny.

"Thank you," I said, "but I've made other plans. However, I'll keep the gentleman hosts in mind if I find I need some company."

"You do that," Gil Rawlins said merrily. "I feel it's my personal duty to see to it you enjoy the crossing."

The *crossing.* I thought about this word all the way back to my cabin. Crossing, as in traversing the sea, or for that matter, the river Styx. Or the act of opposing or thwarting. Interbreeding, or hybridizing. Or a point of intersection, such as the spot on the deck where my life and Carlos Cabrera's had just come together once again.

I stopped in the dining room only long enough to ask the maître d' to pass a message along to the Milwards saying I would not be joining them for lunch.

Once inside my cabin, I lay on my bed, rocking gently to the motion of the sea, thinking back over the years to those early days with Carlos.

We had moved swiftly, inexorably toward each other after that first day of skiing.

He had awakened emotions in me I didn't even realize I possessed, enflamed a curiosity as well as a passion that I seemed powerless to deny. He had seduced me by his sheer magnetism, an attraction that was based in equal part on excitement of mind and of body.

And yet I must ask myself, Who really seduced whom? Wasn't I full of an equal yearning? When he asked me to go skiing with him again, I went, and then I went again, and again, and then somehow we no longer needed the excuse of a day on the slopes in order to justify seeing one another.

I began slipping out in the evenings to meet him for a drink or dinner. Our conversations became more intimate, and we wore our feelings more openly, saw each other more frequently, and fell deeper and deeper into that state of utter longing, of complete fascination with one another. I only know that with the first kiss, not stolen but given—given while he held me against him as we stood in a darkened parking lot behind a restaurant, with the distant sound of voices drifting out of a door leading to a kitchen—that there was no turning back, but only a greater sense of being swept up by our desire, and a deepening urgency to our feelings.

I remembered the first night we ever made love, how nervous we were. We had chosen a motel at random, a place called the Paul Bunyan Inn. An enormous plaster figure of a bearded man, towering over a blue ox, dominated the parking lot.

We did not realize that night that a robbery had just taken place there and, upon entering the office, found policemen were still milling about, taking fingerprints and talking with the clerk who nevertheless made it clear to us we could still rent a room. It didn't seem we could leave without attracting suspicion, so we tried to act normal, stilling our guilty hearts, and checked into a room. Then, and only then, when we had closed the door behind us, did we dissolve into laughter at the absurdity of the situation.

I remember sitting on the bed, nervously undoing a scarf around my neck, and Carlos standing over me, fingering the silk scarf and saying, "You have very nice taste in clothes, you realize that?" and how at that moment I felt the double edge of his compliment.

"Do you mean, how did I acquire such taste, coming from my background?" I asked, looking up at him.

"No, I did not mean that at all," he answered quietly.

"Do you think I shouldn't know anything about clothes?"

"I was paying you a compliment, darling."

"I don't care, really, how you were raised. Taste isn't a genetic factor. It's not inherited, you know. It can be acquired. However—from whomever—in some manner, you seem to have done so."

"But you think it's surprising, don't you, that I have—"

"Stop this nonsense," he said. "Please."

"Is it nonsense?"

"Absolute nonsense."

"It isn't about wealth," I argued, unable to stop myself. It was as if I felt compelled to come to my own defense even though I knew he wasn't attacking me. I believe I was airing my own discomfort about the differences in our backgrounds, trying to enlarge my own sense of worth.

I straightened my back slightly and added, "I may be from a different background, but I know how to comport myself."

"Of course you know how to *comport* yourself," he said gently. "Do you think I could fall in love with someone with poor *comportment*?" He smiled, and I knew he was teasing me a little, and then he leaned down and kissed me tenderly, and said, "Oh, Lucy, darling Lucy."

We made love in the dark. I was struck by the slenderness and tautness of his body, and his extreme grace, his almost agonized ecstasy at the moment of orgasm. And I remember afterward turning on a light and seeing all the blood, and feeling no shame that it was mine. I had not mentioned this to him, that I was menstruating, and later when he'd washed off in the shower and come back to bed, he'd said very casually, "you're bleeding, you know," and I said, "yes, I know." This seemed to amuse him, that I felt no shame, no embarrassment, that it hadn't stopped me from coming to the motel with him. "It's nice," he said to me very gently, "I don't mind." He showed none of the disgust I would later feel with other men who recoiled from the thought of making love during this time. I was so young, so inexperienced in spite of marriage, that I didn't yet know about these things, did not even consider it, did not know what one should do or shouldn't do in such situations. I only knew that I wanted him, and that he wanted me, and lying in his arms afterward I was suffused with a feeling of love for him.

I remember he told me a story that night as we lay in bed, a story about something that had happened to him earlier, when he was still a medical student in Guatemala City.

He had been on his way to the hospital one morning, crossing through a poor district of the city, when he came upon a man who was literally lying in the gutter in terrible distress, having great difficulty breathing. The man managed to tell him that he suffered from acute asthma, and Carlos helped him to the hospital, where he checked him into a bed and began treating him.

The man stayed in the hospital less than a week, but each day Carlos checked on him, personally overseeing his treatment. As the man improved, he got to know him a little. Carlos found him to be a very compelling, very interesting character—intelligent, perceptive in his remarks, though to judge by his clothes and the condition in which he'd found him in the street, one would not necessarily have expected this.

One morning when Carlos arrived at the hospital, he found the man was gone. He simply wasn't there in his bed when he went to check on him. Carlos forgot all about him, until one day two years later, in 1959, when he was already living in the United States, he happened to pick up a *Time* magazine. There on the cover, which proclaimed the overthrow of Batista in Cuba, were the pictures of the two men responsible for leading the revolution. One was Fidel Castro; the other he instantly recognized as the asthmatic he had picked up in the streets of Guatemala City.

It was Che Guevara.

Who could have guessed that my son, that little boy whose heart had been opened and stitched and repaired by the same hands that traveled over my flesh in the darkness, would later give up his life, the life we had all struggled to maintain, there in that distant place? In poor, bloody Guatemala?

I thought I had laid my grief to rest, but it was a shallow slumber, and as I lay there in my little cabin, it awoke in me, fresh and full of new terror. I saw the face of my son, so clear and open, so youthful and full of innocence, and it was more than I could bear.

I shoved these memories aside, forced them to recede back into the dark recesses from which they had emerged, and then I fell asleep, as if memory had exhausted me and driven me toward the only remaining refuge, of dreams and deep slumber.

Much later I awoke with a start. It was a quarter to five, and I remembered I had agreed to meet Carlos in the bar. I dressed hastily, giving little thought to my appearance, thinking only of what we might have to say to each other after all these years and worrying, worrying that this meeting was destined to open old wounds, or create new ones.

I thought of all the years that had passed since we had last seen each other. What was I to say to him now? And what if by some chance Isabella should be with him? How could we all pretend that the past—a past laden with guilt and longing and pain—didn't exist?

He was sitting at a table near a window when I entered the bar. He stood up as I approached and watched me cross the room, a little smile on his face. He was alone.

"I thought perhaps you weren't coming," he said, and took my hand. He turned my palm upward and bent and kissed it, a gesture so reminiscent of the old days that at that moment it seemed no time at all had passed, and it caused my heart to beat faster. But when he raised his head and looked at me, I saw an old man, still elegant, still very attractive, but aged almost beyond recognition.

As if reading my thoughts, he said, "I look like a creep, I know, this white hair . . . a freak, no?"

I smiled and sat down. "You look . . . older, that's all."

He broke into laughter. "That's very good . . . that little pause! I like that." His laughter continued, all out of proportion, I thought, to my comment, which I hadn't intended to be humorous.

"You are being slightly dishonest, if I may say so. But that's all right. You, on the other hand, look wonderful. You haven't changed. How is it possible?"

"Carlos," I said. "I've aged, too. You can drop your Latin charm with me."

"Ah! You sound so tough. But you always were a little tough, no? I think you had to be. But perhaps you can drop this toughness with me. After all, we are . . . old friends. I think we could say that at least."

I was going to challenge him and say, Is that what we are? but I saw he was vulnerable in a way I hadn't expected. He gave me a look so laden with sadness I felt some part of myself succumb to old emotions, and the thoughts I had conjured up on my way to meet him fell away from me, so that I returned his look with all the softness I felt toward him at that moment and said, "Yes, I think we could say we are at least that."

He blinked rapidly and looked down at his hands, folded on the table, and when he looked up again, it was to catch the eye of the bartender, who came and took our order.

When he'd departed, I felt an intense awkwardness settle between us, as if we could think of nothing to say. The light was slowly fading outside, and I turned my attention to the sea, and the sky clotted with clouds, a dying sun laying down a curdled light.

"Lucy," he said softly. "Have you managed to forgive me, after all these years?"

I didn't answer his question, because it didn't seem I knew the answer. I continued looking out to sea. The band began playing, and out of the corner of my eye I saw an elderly couple get up from their table, hands clasped, and make their way to the dance floor.

I turned my face toward him. "Did you simply forget me, Carlos? Did you just erase me from your memory?"

"Really," he said, sounding slightly exasperated with me. "I think you do me and yourself a great disservice by imagining that I didn't suffer deeply, that I somehow just forgot you. You do a great disservice to us, to what we felt for each other at that time, to the genuineness of our emotions."

I was listening to him, but I was also thinking of the night Is-

abella had discovered our affair, when she had come across a receipt
from a motel in the pocket of his jacket, and how later he had described the scene to me, the tearful confrontation in the bedroom,
the hastily packed bag, the taxi called late at night, and how he had
followed her out onto the lawn and stood at the curb, pleading with
her to come to her senses, to not take the midnight train to Chicago.
He had been unable to prevent her from leaving that night, just as I
had been unable to stop her from returning a few days later and re-
suming her position as his wife, albeit a colder, angrier, more distant wife, but nonetheless one who would not relinquish her role so
readily, or so easily.

I had not known how to stake my claim, or that I even had a
claim to stake when it came to Carlos. I was barely twenty. So
young. And so inexperienced. I felt the slight unworthiness of
youth, or should I say the blindness that comes with so little expo-
sure to life? The feeling that I had no right to make claims on him,
on this man who lived so securely, so richly, within the walls of his
stately house, with his wife, who came from one of the five wealthi-
est families in Guatemala. Only once did I see the inside of that
house, one night when Isabella was away, and I still recall the
sumptuousness of the furnishings, the paintings by Orozco and
Siqueiros on the walls, the richness of the polished wood and the
fabrics covering the furniture, the sound of Mozart drifting from
the stereo. Outside, in a perfectly manicured garden, a little gazebo
stood like a tiny time capsule of happiness. Above all, I recall the
feeling of *comfort* in his surroundings. How could I possibly lay
claim to that life, or rather make a counterclaim? When it so rightfully belonged to others—a wife, three small children? When it appeared so perfect the way it was, undisturbed?

I also remember what he reported Isabella to have said that
night, as they stood at the curb arguing, waiting for the taxi, when
she pressed him for the identity of his lover, when she demanded to
know who I was, and he told her how he had met me, that I was
the mother of one of his patients. "Are you crazy?" she screamed.
"Are you out of your mind, getting involved with someone whose

child you've saved?" Until that moment it hadn't seemed so complicated, but afterward, I saw that it was, that my debt to him was
not perhaps completely inseparable from my love.

"Please, Lucy," Carlos said, taking my hand. "Talk to me. I
can't sit here and endure this silence. You owe me, I think, at least
the courtesy of your thoughts."

I sighed, and turned away from the view of the sea to face him
once again.

"I remember you once said that the past is not a country we
should visit too often. Maybe it would be better for us both if we
moved on to the present. You might tell me, for instance, about
your life now. Are you still at the Children's Hospital?"

"Yes. Even in my decrepit state I still manage a rather heavy
schedule of surgeries."

"And your children?"

"Eduardo is divorced. His life is—how do you say?—at loose
ends. Carlita has decided to be a bohemian. She lives in Paris and
works as an artist's model. If you can believe it, Juana has become
the academic. A feminist scholar, who if I may say so, lays a little
too much blame on her father for the unhappiness she claims to
have suffered in life. She has chosen to reject the male sex in favor
of liaisons with other women. It's not that I judge her for this, but I
find a certain element of hostility toward men rather upsetting."

"Of course you would," I said.

He laughed uncomfortably. "And what do you mean by that?
Am I such an unevolved creature in your eyes, such a chauvinist?"

"Not at all. I meant simply that I think most men find it dis-
comfiting, the thought that any woman, let alone their daughter,
could do without a man, that some women might find it a prefer-
able state."

"My friend," he said, a hint of condescension entering his voice,
a tone I remembered only too well from the past, "I'm not con-
demning the positive aspects of such a choice, the understandable
inclination of some women to choose relationships with their own
sex. That isn't what dismays me. It's the more negative aspect, the

hostility toward the opposite sex, that I find disturbing."

"Are we to love our oppressors then? Is that it?"

"I see I have no sympathy from you. But I'm surprised at your choice of words. Oppressors! Am I to assume you include all males in this category?"

"Not I. But perhaps Juana. And I wouldn't judge her too harshly for this."

"You must understand I can't easily accept the nom de guerre. It's not terribly pleasant to be labeled the oppressor."

"Perhaps you shouldn't take it so personally."

"But how am I to take it! She's my daughter, after all, and she's pointed the finger at me, laid the blame at my feet! And why are you smiling?"

"Forgive me. I'm thinking of something that Lawrence once said."

"Lawrence?"

"D. H. Lawrence. He once said of men and women that in the closest kiss, the dearest touch, there is the smallest gulf which is nonetheless complete because it is so narrow, so *nearly* nonexistent. Don't you see? It perhaps has nothing to do with you and your daughter. It's that wretched little gulf, all the more troubling for its narrowness—the alluring proximity of intimacy between men and women and yet the unattainability of true understanding."

"Perhaps," he said, unconvinced. "Though I myself prefer to think of it in different terms."

"What sort of terms?"

"No doubt I date myself, but there is perhaps a Freudian expla-nation for my difficulties with Juana. An unresolved Oedipus com-plex."

"I believe you have it wrong. Isn't it an Electra complex when a daughter has an unhealthy attachment to a father?"

"Oedipus—Electra—in any case, you get my meaning."

"You men have always loved Freud," I said. "He offers such neat solutions for the male of the species. You know what Nabokov said about Freud?"

"Refresh my memory."

"He called him the Viennese quack traveling in a third-class carriage of thought through the police state of sexual myth."

"Really?" he said in a rather bored monotone.

"Yes. He said it was a great mistake on the part of dictators to ignore psychoanalysis—a whole generation might be so easily corrupted that way."

"I see the years haven't diminished your propensity for generalization! Or tempered your argumentative nature."

"Quite the contrary. I've become absolutely entrenched in dogma of the most dangerous sort."

We both laughed, and the atmosphere, which had become rather intense, suddenly lightened. I realized we had very naturally slipped back into the pattern of the past where for hours we had discussed a subject, debated one another, defended what were often opposing ideas. And it was just such exchanges that had first kindled in me a love for the world of ideas.

Simply being near him again revived so many memories. Certain things I had forgotten came back to me all at once, the way he said "My friend" at the beginning of a speech, his habit of gesturing as he spoke, the way his hands moved in the air as if he were shaping a picture to go with his words. The natural elegance of his bearing—his dry wit.

"Oh, Lucy, it's so good to see you again. Why did we ever let go of each other?" he said abruptly.

I could have pointed out the fact that we didn't let go of each other. It was he who let go of me. But I had no wish to go over that ground again, and so I said simply: "We were realists, I suppose. In the hard, cold light of day, we saw the writing on the wall."

"Perhaps. One couldn't deny the enormous differences that existed between us."

"I doubt we could have ever been happy together," I said, and yet the moment I spoke those words, I felt their dishonesty.

"I would not claim any great happiness has existed for myself, in any case. And you? It can't have been easy for you. You must have suffered greatly. In particular, over Justin's death."

"Let's not talk about Justin. Not now. Perhaps another time, but not just now."

"As you wish."

Even though I had asked for the subject to be dropped, I seemed compelled to violate my own request. There was something that bothered me, and bothered me deeply. After Justin's disappearance, I had written to Carlos, a long letter explaining what had happened and telling him of my intention to make a trip to Guatemala in order to try and better understand what had happened to my son. I had asked for his help. I'd hoped he would be able to use his influence there to connect me to people in high places who might answer my questions. But I'd never received an answer from him, and I had gone to Guatemala feeling bitter about many things, not the least of which was his silence. It had been my first attempt to communicate with him in many years. Now I felt compelled to ask him why he had not answered my letter.

"But I did!" he protested. "I wrote to you immediately. In fact, I tried to call you, but I was unable to find a telephone number for you. Do you mean you never received my letter?"

I shook my head. "No, I didn't. I suppose it's not so important now."

"But of course it's important! How could you think I would not respond? Am I such an unfeeling bastard in your eyes? Did you imagine I could be so insensitive as to not respond?"

"I suppose these things happen. A letter can go astray."

"I was extremely disturbed when I received your letter and the news about Justin," he said. "Extremely disturbed. That such a thing could have happened, and in Guatemala of all places. I longed to speak to you, to somehow locate you. But you have not made that easy over the years. When I never heard from you again, I assumed you had no wish to communicate with me further."

"I longed to talk to you after Justin's disappearance."

"But why didn't you call?"

"I don't know. I can't explain it. I kept expecting a letter from you, and when it didn't come, I just gave up."

"You mustn't blame me. I think part of the resposibility lies with you."

I sighed. "It's pointless to lay blame. Let's leave the past for the time being, shall we?"

"As you wish," he said again, this time rather solemnly. "But you should know that I have never stopped thinking of you. During all these years."

I fell quiet, and in that silence I became aware of the room, how it had gradually filled up during the course of our conversation. Without my being aware of it, a festive atmosphere had developed around us. The dance floor at one end of the room was crowded. Almost every seat in the bar was occupied by men in tuxedos and women in evening gowns. The drinks were flowing, the laughter and voices mingling with the sound of the band. Outside the window the sun was setting, reddening the western sky. The sea moved in one direction, the ship in the other, giving an impression of stasis, as if we were caught between opposing forces, in a void without momentum. As I gazed out over the water, a sentence came to me unbidden: *Our lives are still sacred in their intimate sympathies.* Whose words were those? Perhaps Joyce, I thought. "The Dead."

I began to feel I couldn't remain there much longer, sitting at that table with him, without being in danger of losing my composure. I didn't want to lay myself bare before him, to reveal the extent to which he was still capable of unsettling me.

"Tell me," Carlos said, breaking into my thoughts, "what about your life now? Where are you living?"

"I live on a ranch, in a rather remote part of Idaho."

"Idaho? But why Idaho? My God, that's in the middle of nowhere, isn't it?"

"Nowhere suits me at this point in my life."

I glanced at my watch, thinking he might interrupt this gesture as an indication that the time had come to part. Surely Isabella was waiting for him somewhere.

But he seemed not to notice I was anxious to leave the bar. He leaned back in his chair and said: "You know, for a long time I didn't realize that you'd become a writer, although you will remember how very early on I encouraged you in that direction. Then one day I came upon your first book by chance, in a bookstore in New York."

"The short stories?"

"Yes, the stories."

"I'm afraid they now seem like the efforts of someone still very unsure of her voice."

"On the contrary. I recognized the voice immediately. You know, I always believed you would prove yourself in some way."

"Did you?" A faint current of cynicism tainted my voice as I said this.

"Of course I did. I think I had more faith in you than you had in yourself."

"Perhaps that's true. But then you had lived so much more, seen so much more than I did. Perhaps you were capable of seeing everything more clearly than I was. You were so much more sophisticated and worldly, weren't you? I can't help thinking you still are, that it would be impossible for me to ever catch up to you."

"I can't agree. You seem to have grown into a very self-possessed woman."

"Self-obsessed might be more accurate."

"But isn't that a writer's condition?"

"I suppose—yes."

"In any case, the differences which separated us earlier in our lives have been rather reduced at this point, I would think. You appear to have acquired a considerable level of worldliness and sophistication. Not to mention recognition."

"Sometimes I think I'm moving backwards in time now. Trying to reclaim a lost world, a simpler existence. I suppose that's why I live the way I do. Though I have to admit it's rather impossible to ever reclaim anything, isn't it?"

"Lucy . . ." he began, and then hesitated, as if he were on the verge of saying something difficult, something that required that he stop to think the thing through in order to express it precisely.

I didn't want to know what that thing was. I couldn't bear the thought of him attempting to explain or justify his past actions.

"Carlos, I'm afraid I must leave you now. I'm meeting some people for dinner."

"Could we meet again?"

"I would think it will be difficult not to run into each other over the next few days."

"I mean alone. Obviously."

"We'll see each other, I'm sure."

He grew solemn. "You don't sound particularly—"

"Particularly what?"

"I mean if . . . it it's not what you wish . . . if you'd rather not see me . . ."

"There are complications for me . . ."

"Ummm, I see. I thought perhaps we might take advantage of this time together, but I see I'm alone in these feelings. I have no wish to revive anything. I only hoped for the pleasure of your company for a few days. Consider it the sentimental wish of an old man."

"Old man! Such hyperbole."

I realized that in spite of his aged appearance, he couldn't be more than sixty-five. Hardly on death's doorstep. Yet I couldn't help feeling that he was, in fact, somehow very vulnerable. His age did seem to lie on him like a sentence he had somehow condemned himself to. But I had no wish to be drawn back into that vortex of feeling from which I never fully extracted myself. In particular, I couldn't stand the thought of arranging to meet behind Isabella's back. Perhaps that was the greatest difference between the woman I had been and the woman I was now. I was no longer willing to engage in a humiliating deception. Not for him. Not for anyone ever again.

"Then you can't agree to my request?" he said.

"I don't know what would be gained . . ."

I stood up.

" 'Gained'?" he said, a look of confusion coming over his face. "But it's not a matter of gaining anything! If you imagine—"

"I don't imagine anything," I said. "When it comes to you, I stopped imagining things a long time ago."

He rose stiffly. "Of course. I think perhaps you've quite outgrown me. I see you have changed more than I thought possible, haven't you?"

I felt a humiliating intent behind his words, and I stood very still, quietly staring at him for a moment.

"Yes, I have changed."

My next move was so unpremeditated I had no idea that I would do what I did until I actually found myself doing it.

I took hold of his face in both of my hands and brought my lips to his. I kissed him with force, acting as the aggressor, leaving him no possibility of refusing me. I did this as much out of anger as desire. I could as easily have slapped him, but I chose a different form of assault. There was a dryness, a hardness to my kiss. I wanted it to be punishment and reward, for it to contain a brutal and unloving passion. And when I drew away from him, I didn't even bother to meet his eyes to discover his reaction. I simply turned and very swiftly made my way across the crowded room.

When I had almost reached the door, I caught sight of Dr. Ramirez out of the corner of my eye. He was sitting at the bar, alone, and I realized he had been watching us. What he was now thinking I couldn't know. Nor did I much care. Turning my back on him, I strode out of the bar and made my way to the dining room, where the Milwards were already seated at the table.

They were dressed in evening clothes, and made a very elegant, a very smart-looking, trio.

"Hello, hello," I said, greeting them happily, as if they were long-lost friends.

"Sit down, ducky," Constance said. "Don't you look smashing in that black dress." She took hold of my hand and squeezed it. "We've been waiting for you."

"Yes," said Archibald, "and we've got a plan. Tell her about it,

Constance."

"We've just ordered the most expensive bottle of wine on the menu," Constance explained. "Our plan is to start at the top of the wine list and work our way down, meal by meal, bottle by bottle, until this dismal voyage is over. Since we are consigned to this second-class existence—it's the least we can do! And of course, we need your help."

And so I sat down, and soon I was thinking only about the Milwards, about how entertaining they were and the way they could make me laugh, and my spirits rose considerably. Buoyed by the wonderful wine and the pleasant company in which I found myself, I forced myself to forget about Carlos. And after a while it took no effort to do this. No effort at all.

TWELVE

I often wonder what it would have been like to have had a son when I was thirty, or thirty-five, instead of bringing a child into the world when I was only seventeen. Would I have known any more about mothering? Or is parenting like bingo? A matter of luck?

Justine never held anything against me—not the divorce, which occurred when he was five and took him from his father. Nor the decisions I made afterward. He didn't even fault me for my later self-involvement, for the way in which I put myself first, *always* first, in a splendid display of egoism.

In any case, he did get back at me later. I'm sure he didn't intend it. I'm sure it wasn't simply a matter of punishing me, though it seemed that way at the time.

It was one thing for Justin to decide to reject me when he was fourteen and left my house in order to go live with his father. That I could understand. A boy needs a man in his life at that age. I had to let him go (let's tell the truth: I was *ready* to let him go). But how could he have so fervently embraced, just a short while later, the religion I had so scrupulously kept from contaminating him? How could he have so willingly joined the church whose influence I had spent my whole adult life purging from my being?

The easy answer is, it was his father's doing. He joined a religious household—a stepmother, a half brother, and a father who had gone back to the church not long after we divorced—and they had influenced him.

But he was nobody's pawn, I know that. He was a strong boy, with a strong mind. He made his choice. I'm afraid he actually *believed*. He had a *testimony*, as he put it, of *the truthfulness of the gospel*, which he believed was being restored on earth, in *these latter days*. He *wanted* to be baptized, to go down into the waters beneath his father's hands, and emerge a newborn and cleansed being.

When he turned twenty and decided to accept a mission call to Guatemala, I had pleaded with him not to go. Believe in it all if you must, I said. But a mission? Do you really think it correct to *proselytize*? Must you try to convert those poor Guatemalans?

I did everything to dissuade him from going on a mission. But to no avail.

He had driven down to Los Angeles, where I was living then, in order to give me the news, although he didn't mention the matter of the mission right away. It had been months since I'd seen him, and as always, there was a little tension between us at first. I believe I made some comment about his needing a haircut when he first arrived, a comment he didn't like.

"Why do you always have to find fault with me?" he said. "There's always something you have to criticize, isn't there?"

"I only meant I could give you a haircut," I said. "Like I used to do when you were little. Come, let me cut your hair. I promise you'll like it when I'm finished."

He had acquiesced, and we'd gone out into the garden of the house where I was then living, in Santa Monica Canyon, a few blocks from the beach. I remember that day very clearly, the feel of the sea on the air, the bright colors of the hibiscus and ginger and oleander forming a fragrant backdrop, the whiteness of his slender torso as he removed his shirt, the feeling of his hair thick in my hands, and how it fell, as I snipped away at it, in weightless little golden clumps onto the emerald grass.

I wanted to touch him again, as I had touched him so often in the past, and I remember how we had laughed and joked with one another that afternoon while I cut his hair, and then later walked to the beach and took a swim together in the ocean, diving beneath the waves and surfacing while pelicans cruised by just above our heads.

Later, over dinner, we had argued over something silly. It began with his saying how happy he was to be an American. He was very happy to live in this country, he said, when he considered what life was like in other places in the world. With my character-istic bluntness, I had replied that perhaps he should feel a little shame, too, that he was able exist in a privileged world at the ex-pense of others—we *did* consume far more than our share of the earth's resources after all—and that simple feeling *happy* maybe didn't quite cover it. He had been offended by my remark and had grown silent.

Later, I found him sitting in my study, staring out the window into the blackness of the night. He looked so fragile, so confused and hurt, that I had gone to him and laid my hand on his newly shorn head and told him I was sorry. I said I didn't mean for him to take what I said *personally*, it was simply a *political* observation.

"It's all right," he said.

I wanted to repair the damage I'd done. At that moment I very much wanted him to love me, and for him to know that I loved him. I wanted all the misunderstanding of our lives to disappear, all the hurt and struggle and longings to fade away. I wanted to be for-given for all my shortcomings—for my bluntness and insensitivity, for the way I had uprooted him time and again in his youth. For the loneliness he had suffered being an only child of a single mother. I stroked his hair and said, "I wasn't the best mother, was I? But I wasn't the worst, either."

He had looked up at me and said, "You were a good mother."

"Do you really think so?"

"Yes, I do."

"What did I manage to give you? That's what I'd like to know."

"You showed me that it's possible to do anything in life. I saw you do it. I think that's what you gave me, more than anything else. You wanted to be a writer, and you became one. I guess that means I can do anything, too."

I had been touched by his words. For a brief moment I felt that I had perhaps not failed completely, that in spite of my insensitivity and self-absorption I had managed to give something valuable to my son.

"Nothing was ever more important to me than you were—are—Justin."

"I know that," he said. "I guess I've always known that."

It was our last moment of intimacy, of real. And I cannot help thinking now how he had used the past tense when he said "You were a good mother," as if foreshadowing the end, and how I said "Nothing was ever more important to me than you were" before I thought to correct myself.

He waited until the next morning to tell me about his mission call. And once again we were at odds.

I remember the day I decided to leave his father. It was April, and the ice was breaking up on the Mississippi River. A winter's worth of snow had been sullied by exhaust and soot, and everywhere a grime blackened the mounds of hardened granules that lay in thickened ridges everywhere in the city. By then, Walter and I were both unfaithful to the core. We inhabited an adulterous world in which the idea of an affair had assumed an aura of normalcy. Alexis had grafted herself on to Walter's life, just as I had grafted myself onto Carlos. We knew the ice age had arrived and to wait was to perish. It had crept in slowly, inexorably overtaking us while we went about the chilly business of conducting our affairs.

The night I decided to leave Walter, I met Carlos for an early dinner at a little restaurant not far from the hospital. It was a place where we often met. The menu suited him. He was very particular about food. He never touched red meat. He could not stand the taste or smell of garlic. He always ate his salad after a meal, and drank only the best wines. He made a point of ordering sparingly, and ate slowly and with great precision, wielding his knife and fork like surgical implements.

In truth, he was very fastidious about many things, always paying close attention to details.

He believed, for instance, that you could instantly judge a restaurant by the extent and quality of its dessert menu.

He thought hotels could likewise be judged by the sort of clothes hangers they provided their guests.

He believed a fountain pen was as intimate an instrument as a toothbrush, imprinted by its owner and never to be lent, even temporarily, to anyone.

I hadn't understood the particulars about red meat and desserts, hangers and garlic and fountain pens. But he soon educated me in these matters, as well as many others.

He had introduced me to art, by taking me regularly to museums, and helped me to see the beauty in a Giacometti bronze, the energy of the Fauvists, the brilliance and utter superiority of Cézanne. He tutored me in politics. He brought me into the world of philosopical ideas. He gave me new authors to read—Sartre and Sakharov, de Beauvoir and Genet and Camus—books which we then would discuss at great length. My own unformed self was fertile ground for his subtle and continuous imprinting, just as his had been in another time. I am referring, of course, to his so-called "dark period" and of the stain that had surely been left on his psyche as a result of certain experiences in Germany during the war.

I often wondered about those days in the Hitler Youth, but after his initial confession that day after skiing, he had never mentioned the subject again.

As we ate dinner that night, we discussed, as we had so many times before, the predicament in which we found ourselves. He understood we could not go on the way we were, meeting each other in clandestine moments, checking into motels at odd hours only to part a little while later, constructing stories to cover our weekends in Chicago or New York City. We were at a point where we were convinced our only possibility for happiness lay with each other, but each time we contemplated, *seriously* contemplated, taking the steps to end our marriages in order to begin a new life together, huge and intimidating obstacles seemed to rear up and block our path.

The greatest obstacle of all was his children. Guilt had already begun to accrue at the thought of leaving them. Guilt and love— such a deadly combination. The former almost always erodes the latter, and already I could begin to feel his ambivalance growing like a fatal tumor that had attached itself to his conscience.

Why we never thought of Justin as an impediment, I don't know, but he was never an obstacle when we thought of a future together. It was assumed Justin would stay with me, with us, as if he rightfully belonged somehow to us—to me for having given him birth, and to Carlos for having saved his life.

What I did know was that I had reached the end of my capacity for maintaining the sort of life I was leading, as I told Carlos that night. I was leaving Walter. It seemed terribly dishonest—not to mention damaging to both of us—to go on pretending the way we were.

When I announced this, Carlos stopped eating and grew eerily quiet. He brought his hand to his mouth and cupped his chin in his fingers, as he often did when pondering something, and stared at me for a long while.

"But what will you do?" he said finally. "Where will you go?"

"I'll go home," I said. Home meant returning to live with my parents until I could figure out a new life for myself. I had no money. No education. I was twenty-one years old. What other choice did I have? I wasn't sure my parents would want us, Justin and myself. But I was counting on their not turning us away.

I said, "I'm doing this for myself, Carlos, because I must. Don't think I'm trying to pressure you into making a decision."

"Lucy, Lucy," he murmured. "Must you leave?"

"If I go home, my parents can help me, at least until I get on my feet."

"But I could help you," he said. "I can easily afford to support you, to pay for an apartment. That way you could stay here, you could take classes at the university—"

"Do you think I want to be supported by you while you live with your wife and children? I think I would end up despising you, and despising myself even more."

"I won't try to dissuade you from your decision. But please, don't simply cut me off. Will you promise me that you'll give me time to work things out?"

" 'Time'? Of course I'll give you time. You'll always know where to find me." I hesitated, and then added, "I'll be waiting for you."

We left the restaurant without ordering dessert, the little ritual with which we always concluded a meal. I should have seen it as an omen, an indication we would prove ourselves incapable of bringing anything to a full conclusion.

I know that my leaving Minnesota was not the end of it. For a long while Carlos and I remained caught in the orbits of each other's desire. Distance did not diminish my longing for him. If anything, he assumed an even greater importance to me as I struggled to make a new life for myself.

He came to visit me a few months after I'd returned home to live with my parents. I was working as a secretary for the local county planning commission. The office to which I reported each weekday was in a building that also served as the county jail. My nights were mostly sleepless. Each day I sat on the same bench in a little park, sharing my sack lunch with pigeons. I had no money and no future, and no discernible options. I was often weary from the long days at work, the sleepless nights, and from the weight of the depression that frequently overtook me. I was lucky I had my parents to help with Justin. I wasn't up to the job alone. Sometimes I closed my eyes and daydreamed after I ate lunch, lying faceup on the grass in the park, indulging certain fantasies about the future in which Carlos always figured. When I opened my eyes and looked up, I often saw the faces of inmates peering down at me from the third-floor jail, their eyes framed between the iron bars.

That first visit, we stayed the weekend together in a motel at the edge of town. My parents came to meet him one night, and we ate dinner together in a dark, cool restaurant that served Mexican food. My younger brother Arnie was there, too. My younger brother and my parents. Justin was staying with my sister for the night.

They were waiting for us, sitting in a booth in a corner of the restaurant when Carlos and I arrived. My younger brother was wearing his Future Farmers of America cap, and he had pinned all his scout badges to his shirt, as if wishing to display all his accomplishments at once.

"Very pleased to meet you," my father said to Carlos, shaking his hand heartily and indicating he should sit down next to him. My mother looked up shyly at him and murmured, "Hello."

"Now—should I call you Dr. Cabrera, or Carlos?" my father said. I think he hoped for an instant camaraderie, as he did with almost everyone he met.

"Carlos, please."

"This is my brother Arnie," I said. "He's the only one left at home now." I smiled at Arnie. He was a sweet, awkward boy who liked science projects and farm animals and wore thick lopsided glasses held together with adhesive tape. My mother had had him late in life, when she was almost forty-five and probably thought she never have another child. So Arnie was a lot younger than the rest of us, and was sort of a special kid.

"Hello, Arnie," Carlos said, and then he read the lettering on his cap out loud. " 'Future Farmers of America.' Does that mean you're going to be a farmer when you grow up?"

"I dunno," Arnie said. "I'm either going to be a farmer or an astronaut."

Carlos laughed. "That covers the high and the low of it."

We ordered, and while we waited for our food, Carlos listened politely while Arnie told him all about the hog he was raising for his FFA project.

I was feeling a little nervous and ordered my second beer rather soon after quickly consuming my first, ignoring my mother's disapproving look (my parents did not drink, and did not care for the fact I did). My mother and father thought Carlos was separated from his wife. That's what I'd led them to believe. At one point my mother said to him, "You have three children, don't you?"

Carlos said, "That's correct."

"Do they live with you, or your wife?"

Carlos looked a little perplexed, and I answered for him. "They split their time, don't they, Carlos?"

"Right," he said.

My mother wanted to know his children's ages and names and he gave them, but I could see he did not wish to discuss his children with my mother, and yet it was one of the few subjects she could warm to—chileren, family—and when it was dropped abruptly, she looked a little lost.

Suddenly, my father said, looking at me, "This gal here, she was a lot of trouble as a kid, but I guess she's straightened up, hasn't she?"

"Not really," I said, not waiting for anyone else to offer an opinion.

"I would have to agree with that," Carlos said, smiling at me, "but fortunately it's the sort of trouble I don't mind."

I don't know what my parents thought of us that night, but I remember having a good time with them at dinner. They were polite, no doubt curious. I think they were a little awed by Carlos. By his doctor-surgeon-savior-of-Justin aura, the aura they themselves willingly supplied. I don't know how they really felt about Carlos coming to visit me, but I was glad they met him. I wanted them to. It made me feel better knowing that they knew about us, that I'd introduced them to Carlos, as if this legitimized our affair a little more somehow, or gave it a reality, a firmer place in the universe. I know afterward—after that night at dinner—they did not openly approve or disapprove of my affair with him but tolerated it the way they had tolerated other irregularities in my life, as a matter better left uninvestigated. In their minds, I suppose, there was always the hope we'd get married one day. It was a hope not so different from my own.

The next day—the day after the dinner with my parents and Arnie—we drove up into the mountains above town and had a picnic setting beside a little lake. Justin came with us, and Carlos played with him while I spread out our picnic on a blanket in the sun. I felt such happiness, and I believe he and Justin did, too. Anyone seeing us at that moment would have thought we were just another happy little family, spending the day together in the mountains.

Later, while Justin played at the edge of the water, Carlos and I sat in the shade of a tree and talked. He said that life had been unbearably difficult in my absence, and that he and Isabella had been discussing the possibility of a divorce. They had agreed on a trial separation: she was leaving for Europe for a month, and taking the children with her. When she returned, they were to make a decision about their future?

"But why is she leaving now?" I asked. "Why couldn't she have decided this earlier?"

"I don't know," he said. "Things have become quite strained between us, to say the least. The current situation is, I think, rather unbearable for both of us."

I sensed a cruel irony in her decision, a wish to punish him by isolating him now that I was far away, for she knew I had moved back home. Perhaps she thought that by taking the children to Europe and leaving him alone for a while she might gain the advantage; he would see how much more intolerable life could be without them.

He left early the next morning. At the airport he clung to me for a long while, and then kissed me, and held me close again before turning to leave. As I watched him walk away, I wondered whether I would ever see him again, whether or not this might be the last time we'd ever meet. I loved him as I had never loved anyone before. More than I thought possible. And I desperately needed him; I needed him to give me strength, and hope—a belief in a better future for myself. I wanted to run after him and tell him to leave her. I wanted to say to him, clearly and firmly, We must be together. But I didn't. He disappeared through a door, and I turned and walked away, listening to the sound of a meadowlark drifting through an open window.

Carlos wrote often, and occasionally we talked on the phone. His letters sustained me, made me believe that all was not lost, yet they were filled with indecision and torment. In one, he tried to explain his feelings:

> My dear Lucy,
>   Since our last phone conversation—somewhat unilateral—I have been thinking quite a bit. I was trying to unravel what made us both fall in love. The surrounding circumstances were certainly not propitious, and from a purely cerebral point of view, much too complex. On the other hand, "falling in love" is not quite appropriate either since there is a consideration of passivity—but despite its implications, it was an active act, one that we both were aware of and welcomed. It's also true that beyond the initial phase of idealization and overeroticism (if there is such

a thing), we have maintained our initial sentiments of recognition of each other's individuality, respect for ideas, attitudes, etc. In short I think we have preserved an ill-definable capacity to love. I have a difficult time conveying the essential message that I am absolutely honest and true in these feelings—that it never crossed my mind to be unfair or to exploit. Selfish, yes, for this is the essence of our problem. You always say that we are waiting for somebody else to make our decisions. I am writing these very difficult lines not only with tears in my eyes and a feeling of compression in my throat, but also without knowledge of Isabella's final decision. She and the children returned from Europe last week. Without trying to dramatize my situation, I would have to say that I am making a truly sacrificing effort to maintain a status quo at the present. Isabella and I are coexisting in a strained sort of relationship which of course cannot continue. We seem unable to face the fact that everything has changed between us, or make any sort of real decision about our future. I know you'll think me weak. But don't forget that you had a long time of a similar pseudomarriage.

You must believe that all of me aches for you. I see you in my dreams and constantly before me whenever I have the slightest moment to myself. Physically, I am also dependent on you. Even if I wanted to, I don't think I could make love to anybody. On the other hand, just thinking of you arouses me. Often, I have been determined to cancel my entire local commitment and join you. But then I go home and my children cling to me, chatter away about their day's observations, etc., and my intention suddenly weakens, and so far I have continued in the emotional dichotomy. For the first time I feel lost and indecisive. Give me time, my darling.

Besos y amor, Carlos

Time I gave him. Because I, too, still believed in what he had called our "ill-definable capacity to love."

And yet it did not escape my attention—the implication of that one sentence in his letter: "I am writing these very difficult lines . . . without knowledge of Isabella's final decision." They seemed fatal to me, these words, loaded as they were with the admission of his own passivity. Perhaps without quite realizing it, he had assigned our future to Isabella's decision.

Yet I saw no other choice except to wait for that decision to be made. So I waited. In a state of quiet despair and abject misery, I waited. Through a long winter, a spring, and into another summer.

I remember once we met at the ski resort Alta in the depths of the winter, the winter after I left, and we stayed in the old Rustler Lodge, in the only room that was available to us. It had a single bed. In the afternoons, after skiing, we lay in the narrow bed and made love. We ate dinner before the fire with snow falling outside the window. He sunburned his face badly one day skiing, and we spent the rest of our time together sequestered in our room, playing out our love. Even then the disease that would later rob his skin of pigment was beginning to manifest itself. A small white patch had begun to form, in the shape of a little anvil, high on his cheek, and a white streak had appeared in his hair. This was the first time I'd noticed it, lying next to him in the little narrow bed in the room in Alta.

There were other rooms where we met, in other distant places, over the months that followed. Once we waited out an all-day thunderstorm in an old hotel in a mining town in Colorado, in a room where the rain had stained the ceiling and left fantastic watermarks in which—lying on our backs and looking up—we saw the shapes of all sorts of wondrous creatures.

Another time, in Aspen, we watched *The Treasure of the Sierra Madre* together one night and afterward ate a memorably romantic dinner in a quiet restaurant. Later that winter we met again in Park City. We seemed drawn to ski resorts, returning to the love of that sport that had initially brought us together.

Then we would part and I would return to my life, my lunches in the park with the pigeons and the inmates looking down from their cells and the house I shared with my parents and Justin, and he would go back to St. Paul, to his children and Isabella.

In time, I came to see that nothing would change. Only I would grow wearier. And I would come to understand that nobody ever got all of what they wanted, but took what they could, the little piece that was offered, and tried to make something of that. But I began to think the little piece that was mine was eroding under the weight of daily life; I felt it growing smaller and smaller until it seemed there was nothing left of it—or at least nothing I felt was real.

I began going out to bars at night. I met other men. I started sleeping with some of these men. It had nothing to do with passion, or desire. It was a diversion from loneliness. A way to drain my tired heart of its last pockets of hope.

I had my first affair with a woman. I didn't find it so different from the affairs I had had with men. I began drinking a little too much. My behavior grew increasingly erratic. I stopped answering Carlos's letters, which in any case had become less frequent and were filled with a growing indication that his life with Isabella would go on unchanged. I entered a long downward spiral in which everything seemed increasingly meaningless and bleak. I lost my faith, what little I possessed, in my ability to make a life for myself, and so I simply drifted on prevailing currents, moving from place to place with Justin in tow—Provo, Pocatello, Ogden—funny towns and in some ways depressing—forever searching for some meaning which eluded me.

Many years would pass before I would emerge from this period of unsettledness, of simply surviving. By then, Carlos was long gone. Yet he would reappear often, not only as a character in my fiction when at last I began writing, thinly disguised as one lover or another, but also in my dreams, which he haunted with the most bittersweet effect, for a very long time.

THIRTEEN

I'm sitting here at the window this morning, looking out at the parking lot of the Tally Ho, waiting for Joycelle to arrive. She's gone off to run some errands and has promised to be back by noon. I bumped into her at the pool last night and asked if she might like to go for a drive this afternoon. I thought we'd head up to the Valley of Fire, a state park thirty or forty miles north of here, where I've been told there are some very nice petroglyphs.

Her response amused me. She said, "Honey, I'd love to have a date with you."

Nobody, except my father, has ever called me "honey."

It's got a nice ring to it. When she said "honey," I felt a certain lightness, a sweetness descend that I hadn't known in years. It took my back to the times when my father used to call me up on the phone every day, during those early days of Justin's life, and say, "How's my honey doing today?"

I'm old enough to be Joycelle's mother, and yet I feel increasingly dependent on her for some sort of insight into myself. Perhaps not exactly dependent. More at her mercy.

I'm thinking of what happened last night.

We were lying out by the pool in the fading desert light. She was asking me about my life, where I lived, whether I minded living alone, when suddenly she looked over at me and said, "You're afraid of getting too close to anybody, aren't you?"

We were stretched out next to each other on towels laid on the cement at the edge of the pool. My eyes were closed and the sunset glowed orange on the inside of my eyelids.

"Why would you say that?" I asked, pretending nonchalance.

"It's like you've got a fence around you. I can see you. I can hear you. I know you're in there. But I don't think I could ever touch you. I don't think you'd like that."

"Go ahead and try," I said.

She reached over and ran a finger from my hairline, across my forehead and down the bridge of my nose, over my lips and chin, and then she let her finger drop into the hollow of my neck and continue tracing its line until she stopped abruptly at a point between my breasts. I felt her lift her finger away and yet I could still feel her touch, as if her finger hadn't moved.

"There," she said. "Did that bother you?"

"It depends on what you mean by *bother*."

"Did you feel anything?"

"Yes . . ."

"What?"

I opened my eyes and looked at her. She had turned onto her side and her face was close to mine. Her skin was so perfectly smooth. A pouty little mouth. An innocence, combined with some sort of playful mischief evident in her eyes. She looked quite beautiful at that moment.

"It tickled."

"Were you scared?"

"A little, perhaps." I couldn't lie. And yet the truth came out of me with the greatest reluctance. I felt suddenly in danger—of what, I'm not quite sure.

"Have you ever made love to a woman?"

The question stopped me cold, and I took a moment to reply.

"Why do you ask?"

"Just answer me."

"Yes."

"I actually prefer women," she said.

"But you said you thought they made crummy friends."

"Did I say that?"

"Yes."

"Well, I've had better luck making friends with men, but I've enjoyed women more as lovers."

I closed my eyes again. I could feel my breath coming a little short.

"I've always felt there was a lot of competition between women," she went on to say, "you know—that kind of rivalry that makes it hard to really trust one another. On the other hand, men always want to dominate you, and in the end you're nothing but a fantasy projected in their heads."

"Do you think so?"

"Yeah. I've made a living off men, but I've really only loved women. That's been my solution to the whole male-female thing."

"I suppose that's one answer."

"I can see you're not sure."

"I'm still thinking about it."

A few moments later some kids came down to the pool and began splashing around in the water, yelling and being generally obnoxious, and I excused myself and returned to my room, but not before I'd invited her to go for a drive with me today.

I'm still thinking about what she said as I sit here waiting for her this morning.

What I'm really thinking about is how right she was to say I'm afraid of getting close to anyone.

I believe it goes back to Justin, when he was taken from me

only moments after his birth and who remained so precariously sick for so long—so sick that it seemed I could lose him at any time. Even after he was well, I think I kept a certain distance between us.

As he got older, I used to feel afraid for him. He was such an affectionate child. He loved to put his arms around me and give me kisses. He used to climb up on my lap and cuddle against my neck and whisper that he loved me. I never refused him, but I remember feeling a certain stiffness at such moments, as if a part of me couldn't accept so much love. Later, when he was a teenager, he would still indulge in these displays of affection—coming up behind me, for instance, at the kitchen sink and holding me in a long embrace—and I began to worry then about the appropriateness of a boy, now coming into manhood, being so physically affectionate with his mother. I regret this now.

This is only part of the story, I know. I'm not certain I ever fully recovered from my affair with Carlos and the pain with which I was left when it ended.

I don't think I ever opened myself up to anyone again in quite the same way. It wasn't that I didn't *want* to. It wasn't that I didn't *try*. I just never found that it was possible to allow myself to have the depth of those feelings again.

When Carlos disappeared from my life, I suppose I thought I had acquired some experience or skill at love, like an athlete who has developed muscular prowess, and that this would enable me to *feel* those feelings again. But time and again I would end up rejecting a lover or else I would find myself rejected and I would think it was because I had not cared enough. Often, I think I was unconsciously measuring these later lovers against my memories of Carlos, and inevitably they wouldn't measure up. Is there in every person's life one consuming passion against which all others, however subtly or unconsciously, are later measured? Someone who claims that emotion so completely that any future experience of it will be referential, and every love that follows will unconsciously swell in its shadow, will grow and yet only partially fill the space that has already been hollowed out by the deepest, the most profound, emotion.

"It's like you've got a fence around you," Joycelle said last night. I could have replied: It's actually more like a double fence. There's the first fence I constructed, the old one that went up in my twenties. And then there's the one I've thrown up more recently, the wall I put around me when I stepped off that boat.

It's a little after noon when I see her car pull into the parking lot. I watch her get out, and something strikes me that I hadn't really noticed before. And this is how thin she is. A thought crosses my mind: Could she be anorexic? It seems possible, given the way she picked at her breakfast the other day. There's a certain fragility to her that seems unhealthy. Maybe it's just the cold she's been fighting. Or maybe she's one of those lucky women who never gain weight."

She certainly seems full of energy when I open the door and let her in.

"Hi, honey," she says, and plants a kiss on my cheek. "I was going to kiss you on the mouth, but I didn't want to scare you."

"Thanks," I say.

"So, you ready to roll?"

"Just let me get my camera."

"Oh, good, we're going to take pictures."

I grab the camera, and then suddenly I notice her shoes.

"You're not going to wear those shoes, are you?"

"What's wrong with them?" She looks down at her feet, at the bubble-gum-colored high heels peeking out from the bottom of her skinny jeans.

"We're going to be walking around on dirt trails."

"So? I've perfected the art of walking on anything in these things."

I ask her what size her feet are, and when she says seven and a half, I retrieve an extra pair of sneakers from my closet.

"Do me a favor and put these on."

"Like I said, you'd make someone a very nice mother," she says, rolling her eyes, but she does as I suggest and changes her shoes.

"You, on the other hand, look like Elizabeth Taylor." She looks me up and down as she ties her laces. "I mean Elizabeth Taylor before she got fat. What do you call those pants? Jodphurs or something?"

"Yes. Jodphurs."

"Totally cool. And I like the boots, too. It's like having a date with *National Velvet*."

We hit the freeway and begin driving north, under a clear sky with the top down on her car. The world feels larger and more accessible in a convertible; everything's a little nearer, a little brighter, a little sharper. The car pops and rumbles ominously, occasionally backfiring so loudly that it alarms other drivers. They react as if someone has just fired a gun next to them and scowl at us as we speed by.

"It seems to me you might need a new muffler," I say.

"Mufflers are for wimps," she replies, yelling to be heard.

"I thought they were for exhaust control."

"Control. Exactly. That's the part I don't like."

"But you could set off a grass fire with a spark. It could be dangerous."

"What's life without a little danger?"

I shake my head at her, and she reacts by pinching my cheek.

"Let's get off at this exit and get some beer, whaddya say?"

"Beer makes me sleepy in the middle of the day."

"So—we'll take a nap later!"

She rolls down the exit ramp and pulls up in front of a convenience store and runs inside. A few minutes later she comes out with a six-pack, a bag of potato chips, and a copy of the *National Enquirer*.

The beer tastes good and I begin to feel a sort of reckless happiness, driving down the freeway with my hair blowing in my face and the sun on my shoulders and the car rumbling like some growling beast. High above us, jets from the air base nearby are flying in unison and leaving trails so thick and white they look like streaks of shaving cream against the sky.

The jets roll to one side and then disappear behind a ridge. I find myself thinking of my father and how he used to delight in pointing out various planes and identifying them for his children. His years of working on an air base had given him a sharp eye. We'd be in the car, driving along a highway, or standing out in the backyard, and he'd look up and point his finger at something and say, "C-119 . . . a flying boxcar." It seemed a kind of magic to be able to give a name to a speck in the sky.

"Look at that," she says, pointing to the cover of the *Inquirer*, which is partially tucked down into the seat to keep it from blowing away. "ELVIS SIGHTED: KING COMES BACK AS TRANSVESTITE. I thought he looked like a transvestite when he was alive."

"You're too young to remember Elvis."

"Doesn't matter. I wasn't around for the Beatles either. But I can see their faces as clearly as if they were sitting right in this car with us. They may be dead and gone, but their legend lives on. Yeah!" She raises a fist in the air, and I chuckle at her outburst. "I was nuts for the Beatles when I was growing up."

"Where did you grow up?"

She shoots me a disapproving look. "No way am I going to start talking about my past," she says. "We've already been through that. It's not a happy subject. I prefer to live in the present. Okay?"

"Fine with me."

For the next few miles we ride along in silence. I realize her mood has changed and I regret having asked her anything about her past. Yet I can't think of anyway to undo the effect of my question, so I simply let the silence hang between us and stare out at the dry hills which are completely devoid of vegetation and appear brown and desiccated, wrinkled by deep ravines.

We pass a sign saying we are entering the Moapa Indian Reservation. At the turn off for the Valley of Fire, there's a Moapa Indian trading post, and when Joycelle sees the sign SMOKESHOP AND FIRE-CRACKERS, she grows suddenly brighter.

"Hey, let's stop at the trading post and buy some firecrackers."

"Firecrackers?"

"Yeah. I haven't lit off any firecrackers for a long time."

It doesn't seem like such a good idea to me, but I don't want to dampen her spirits again.

The inside of the trading post is one big room with rows of cigarette cartons, firecrackers, liquor, and Indian merchandise—key chains and tiny leather moccasin coin purses, lots of beadwork and carved sculptures, turquoise and silver—some of it cheap-looking, some of it nice—all hanging behind the counter and spread out in glass-topped display cases. The place is busy, full of tourists who've pulled off the freeway and are milling about. The Indians who man the cash registers look bored and stare off into the distance as if purposely avoiding one's eyes.

There's a huge assortment of fireworks, and Joycelle begins loading up on cherry bombs and rockets and fizzing snakes and thick packets of ordinary firecrackers bound together by their woven fuses—as well as things called Mammoth Peonies and Hit Men. She picks out so much stuff she has to give me part of it to carry up to the cash register.

The Indian man behind the counter begins ringing up our purchases without saying a word.

Joycelle stares at him for a minute and then says, "Nice day, huh?"

He nods, but doesn't speak.

"What's your name?" she says.

He looks up at her briefly and says, "Tonto."

"Hey, Tonto. Great name. You guys have the best sense of humor."

He smiles faintly, and then asks, "What's your name?"

"Dale Evans."

"Funny, she doesn't look like Roy," he says, gazing at me.

"Roy had a sex change a few years back. Came out pretty good, don't you think?"

"Not bad. Coulda fooled me."

"How much wampum for all this stuff?"

"Ten bucks."

"You mean ten Indians, or ten dollars?"

She wins him over with that one and he laughs. "What you got, white girl?" he says. "You got ten Indians hidden somewhere?"

"Wish I did," she said. "I'm sure I could have a lot of fun with ten Indians. But I guess we'll have to give you the cash instead."

"Cash is fine."

"What's the biggest firecracker you've got?" she asks suddenly.

"That would be the Silver Salute."

"Then what?"

"The M-50, and the M-80. These are strictly firecrackers."

"Why don't you show those to me, Tonto?"

She follows the clerk down an aisle, disappears for a while, and comes back holding a single silver firecracker the size of half a roll of pennies, with a stiff wick sticking out of the top.

"Silver Salute," she says, holding it up for me. "A deal at eighty cents. That brings us to ten-eighty. Do you mind footing the bill?"

I get out my wallet and pay for the stuff. At the last minute she says, "Hey, Tonto, give me a pair of those mirrored sunglasses and one of those nice beaded hair ornaments."

"White woman big spender, huh?" he says.

"How do you think we won the West?"

"With booze and guns," he says. "And a little smallpox."

"Too bad about the last two."

She winks at him as we're leaving and says, "Catch you later, huh, Tonto?"

"Not if I keep moving, Dale."

It takes about a half an hour to reach the Valley of Fire, and by then we've each had another beer and have to stop once to relieve ourselves behind some rocks. We get back in the car and drive along a narrow two-lane road that winds through an increasingly pretty landscape. Cacti are blooming and the tall ocotillo are tipped with bright scarlet flowers. Then we crest the ridge of a hill and the Valley of Fire stretches out before us.

It's a broad, beautiful valley, carpeted with new green growth and little patches of wildflowers. Purple lupine and yellow mule-ears and Indian paintbrush spring up everywhere. Red rock formations rise up in fantastic shapes and cast black shadows. We park at a trailhead and begin walking up a narrow ravine with high rock walls on either side. The first petroglyphs appear, the stippled shapes of a goat, a sun, and a spiral, etched into the rock.

"Totally cool," Joycelle says, running her fingers over the markings. "Imagine somebody taking the time to do this. Chip some pictures in rock. I guess everybody likes to leave their mark. Even Bob and Mary." She points to some names that have been painted on a rock nearby: BOB + MARY = TRUE LOVE.

"I kind of doubt it, don't you?" she says. "Bob and Mary are probably history now. He married his secretary and she's trying to raise two kids on welfare. So much for true love."

"Have you always had such a dismal view of romance?"

"Occupational hazard," she says. "Anyway, I've never had a relationship that lasted very long. Have you?"

Instead of answering her question, I tell her to stand over by the petroglyphs so I can take her picture. We take a few photographs of each other, and then we set the camera up on a rock and take a picture of ourselves together, using the timing device that releases the shutter automatically. Just before the shutter snaps, she puts her arm around me and draws me close so our cheeks are pressed together.

"Don't worry. I only did that to make sure we were both in the picture," she says.

"I'm sure." I say this looking into her eyes.

"Besides, I *like* you," she says, and runs the backs of her fingers along my cheek.

With that, she turns and makes a little beckoning motion with her hand, then heads off up the trail.

We follow the path, stopping now and then to look at more pet-roglyphs, until it leads us back to the car. By that time Joycelle is a little out of breath, even though we haven't walked more than a mile.

"Are you okay?" I ask.

"I'm just not much of a nature girl, you know. I'm a little out of shape. Let's sit down here and rest."

We stretch out on the sand in the shade of a big rock, and she lights a cigarette and immediately starts coughing.

"I think you should see a doctor about that cough."

"Aren't you sweet," she says, staring up at the sky. "Why, I've never had anybody show more concern for me. You better be care-ful or I'll start forming an attachment. And who knows where that could lead."

"I'm serious, Joycelle."

"That's one of your problems, honey, if you don't mind my say-ing so. You're just too darned serious. But I think I'm beginning to have an effect on you. I really do. I can see you loosening up right before my eyes. I'm taking full credit."

"What'll it take to get you to see a doctor?"

"Let's set off some firecrackers," she says, and then she's on her feet and rummaging around in the car. She comes back with the firecrackers and the last of the beer.

"Come on. We'll light them over by these rocks."

I feel put out with her and refuse to get up.

"Look," she says, sitting down next to me, "if it makes you feel any better, I saw a doctor and got some tests at the free clinic in town. I'm going in again later this week. There. Are you happy now?"

"Happier," I say. "But I think it's a bad idea to light firecrackers out here. This is a state park. We could get arrested. There has to be a park ranger around somewhere."

"There you go again," she says, throwing her hands up in mock exasperation. "How are we supposed to have any fun together if you keep acting like this?"

She rolls on her side and faces me, and I move closer to her and enter the shade cast by an overhanging rock, where it is suddenly cool and refreshing, and with our bodies pressed together, we kiss. It only lasts a moment. And then we roll away from each other.

"A little prelude to the real fireworks," she says, smiling at me.

I felt something dangerous and reckless and wonderful about her, something that seems to challenge me to let go of all my restraint and sadness—and because I want to let go of all of these things, because I want to enter into a world that is lighter and unbound by rules, I give in and smile at her, and then we are on our feet, setting off rockets that erupt in beautiful showers of sparks; we're racing away from the fuse of a Silver Salute sizzling dangerously and holding each other as it explodes with an incredibly loud boom; we're watching black snakes rise in oozing and twisting columns; and we're setting off whistles and bangs, igniting blue rockets and red rockets and white rockets, until only the cherry bombs are left. For our grand finale we construct a pyramid of beer cans and sticks and light two cherry bombs under them, then stand back and watch as the whole thing blows sky-high.

About that time we see a jeep in the distance, driving down the road toward us, and we hardly have time to gather up the evidence, all the spent rockets and mutilated beer cans, and stuff everything into the trunk of the car.

The ranger pulls up just as we're finishing our work.

"Good afternoon, ladies," he says, looking at us out of the window of his Jeep.

"Howdy, Smokey," Joycelle says.

"You guys lighting off fireworks over here?"

"Hell, no," Joycelle says, "we're just trying to get this old heap of a car to start. Darned thing just keeps backfiring."

"Sounded like a little more than a backfire to me."

"You've never heard Myrna before."

"Myrna?"

"That's my car's name," she says. "I reckon Myrna's about the loudest ole car around. And tempermental. Whew-wee! Just like a woman." I can't help noticing how she's adopted an accent for this exchange. She sounds like a cross between Dolly Parton and Ma Kettle. She's also leaning down now in order to speak directly to the ranger through the window of his car, and exposing a good deal of cleavage in the process. This has a noticeably disconcerting effect on the ranger, whose eyes keep wandering.

"It's illegal to set off fireworks in the park," he says.

"And highly dangerous, I would think. Wouldn't you think so, Lucy?" she asks, turning toward me. She gets off a big wink.

"Highly," I say.

"I think there was more than backfiring going on over here."

"We were smooching, that's about all."

He looks as if somebody has smacked him in the face with a wet pancake.

"Just kiddin', Smokey. Well, we got to be goin'. I'd love to stay around and let you look down my blouse some more, but I got other things to do."

She straightens up, backs away, and raises her hand in a little wave.

The ranger starts his car. He looks totally perplexed, as if he'd like to say something but can't figure out what.

"Now, go out there and get some real criminals," she calls out to him. "Go find Bob and Mary and tell them to stop writing their damned names on these rocks!"

As he drives away, Joycelle mutters, "Jerk. I just can't stand to see anybody in a uniform."

She pulls the keys out of her pocket and hands them to me.

"You mind driving home? I feel a little pooped. I think I'll just close my eyes."

The air is much cooler on the drive home. By the time we reach the trading post and the on-ramp for the freeway, the sun is beginning to set. Joycelle is stretched out on the front seat, her head on my lap.

137

I stop only once to get a blanket from the backseat in order to cover her up. She murmurs a thanks and then falls immediately back to sleep.

It's a pleasant drive through the fading desert light. The hills become black silhouettes in the distance. Myrna wanders a bit, pulling strongly to the right, and I have to keep my hands firmly on the wheel in order to keep us on course.

I think back over the years to the time when I didn't have much more to my name than an old car like this. Sometime in the mid-seventies, when I finally left Utah for good and headed for Los Angeles, it was in an old Ford that broke down twice on the way to California.

I had never let go of the idea, first instilled in me in those classes I had taken in Minnesota, that I might become a writer myself, and it seemed to me that Los Angeles was the place where I needed to be. I wanted to be in a city, to meet people who were doing something with their lives. And yet I discovered it wasn't easy living in a city like L.A. Or to make such a big change. My first apartment was a place near Western Avenue and Beverly Boulevard, in a building where I was the only person who didn't speak Spanish. I understood for the first time how it was possible to feel like a foreigner in your own country.

I remember once not long after I arrived in Los Angeles, I went to a department store on Wilshire Boulevard to buy a few things I needed and the clerk wouldn't take my check because it was out-of-state. She was rude to me and I made the mistake of arguing with her until I'd gotten myself thoroughly upset, and then when I went out to the parking lot, my old car wouldn't start, and I discovered I didn't have any money, not even a quarter for a phone call, not that I knew anyone at that point who I could call for help. I was supposed to pick Justin up from school and I was already a few minutes late. I began to panic, thinking of him waiting for me. He was only nine and I was sure he didn't know the city well enough yet to find his way back to the apartment, and in any case, I didn't like to think of him walking home alone.

In desperation I decided I had no choice but to take a bus, although I didn't know the bus system yet and I wasn't even sure whether I could get a bus that would take me near his school, even if I'd had the fare, which I didn't. I stood in front of the department store for a while, watching the buses come and go, and then I got up my courage and I began asking passersby for change. I thought it would be easy to come up with a dollar once somebody heard my story—my car broken down, my kid waiting for me at school, my money left at home—but it wasn't. Person after person walked away from me, usually not even bothering to listen until I'd finished my story. I saw how cruel and indifferent people could be, and how you could so easily be taken for a liar. I must have asked two dozen people before an elderly woman gave me a dollar and a short lecture about how I shouldn't spend it on drugs.

When I got to the school, Justin wasn't there. I began to panic. All my shortcomings as a mother became glaringly clear. I began running down the street and, a little while later, arrived at the apartment, out of breath. There was Justin, sitting on the front steps, playing with a neighbor's dog. "My god," I said, "how did you get home?" "Easy," he replied, "I just walked."

I met a man named Richard Taylor, who like Carlos was older than me. He used to come into the café where I worked for his morning coffee, and we'd end up chatting. He was a writer and he worked in the film business. When he mentioned the movies he'd written, I took pleasure from the fact I had seen some of them.

He was a very decent man—kind, generous, intelligent. And he was funny. That, in many ways, was the thing I like most about him: he could, and did, make me laugh.

I had been writing some stories in the evenings after I'd gotten Justin to bed, and when Richard Taylor discovered I had an interest in writing, he persuaded me to let him see some of these stories. He liked them, he said they showed promise, and after that he began encouraging me. Sometimes he offered suggestions about how I might change something to make a story stronger. He became my mentor, in a way. And then he became my lover.

It lasted only a few years, the relationship with Richard, but everything changed during those years. Justin and I moved into his house in the Hollywood Hills, a Spanish-style villa surrounded by beautiful gardens, with a pool that looked out over the city.

I quit my job at the drugstore, at Richard's insistance, and also at his urging I began devoting myself full-time to my writing. I began meeting people—writers, artists, actors—interesting people who led interesting lives.

I began publishing a few of my stories in small magazines. Many of these stories featured a much older lover, sometimes of foreign nationality, or a sick child or a girl raised on a farm at the edge of a lake. I think Richard assumed he was the model for the older man in these stories, and I never let on that he wasn't, although the passion, the longing so evident in these stories, was not quite the same as what I felt for him.

I traveled to Europe with Richard, spent a summer living in Ireland, returned and wrote more short stories, which were eventually published as a collection the next year and which enjoyed a moderate success. Then I finished a novel, *The Invention of Light*, about my childhood and early marriage, and which drew heavily on Carlos for the portrait of an aristrocratic, older lover who changes the course of the heroine's life and brings her into a different consciousness of the world, only to discover an incompatibility he finds insurmountable. *The Invention of Light* was eventually made into a film. Suddenly, I found I had an income of my own, as well as a new identity. I began to feel more independent, more capable, less dependent on Richard not only for the necessities of life but also for a sense of myself. Perhaps this was the beginning of our troubles.

Eventually, everything between Richard and me just sort of fell apart—not with bitterness, but with a kind of benign understanding that we were not absolutely suited to each other, though we might care about one another deeply—and I moved out and found a place for Justin and myself in an old apartment building in West Hollywood.

The new few years weren't easy for me, but I think they were even more difficult for Justin. I moved again, this time to a cottage in Santa Monica Canyon, near the beach. By then, he had changed schools three times in six years. He was tired of making new friends. He felt a little lost, and more than a little lonely. I tried to make it up to him with trips to Disneyland, with presents, and surprise visits to see his grandparents. But what he really wanted was more of me. What he really wanted was a home life, and a real family, and a mother who didn't go out so much in the evenings. And that I wasn't able to give him.

Joycelle turns her head to one side on my lap, rolling her face up toward me, and I expect her to wake up, but she doesn't. Her hands, which have been folded beneath her cheek, have left the imprint of a ring on her flesh. I study her face, then look up at the road, then gaze down at her again. For a while, I drive along this way, alternately watching the road and stealing long glances at her sleeping face.

It's almost dark by the time we reach the edge of Las Vegas, which appears as a raft of brilliant lights floating on a vast black sea. Not until I pull into the parking lot of the Tally Ho and turn off the engine does Joycelle wake up.

"Where are we?" she mumbles.

"We're home," I say, and smooth the damp hair from her brow. She's been perspiring, even though the air has grown cooler.

"What time is it?"

"Eight o'clock."

"Oh God. I'm supposed to be at work in an hour. I just don't think I can do it."

"You shouldn't go anywhere tonight except to bed. Why don't you go upstairs and call in and say you're not feeling well? And I'll go out and get you some soup."

"Don't bother about the soup. I don't have any appetite. I just want to go to sleep."

We climb the stairs to our rooms and say goodnight to each other, kissing gently on the lips. She unlocks her door, and before stepping inside she turns and says, "Lucy?"

"Yes?"

"It was a nice day, huh?"

"Very nice."

"We'll do it again sometime?"

I nod, and say, "Yes, definitely we'll do it again," and then she smiles at me and shuts the door behind her.

FOURTEEN

The night after I left Carlos in the bar, a storm arose at sea, and
the *Oceanus* rolled and pitched through the darkness of a
moonless night. I couldn't sleep for the sound of the storm around
me. Gale-force winds buffeted the ship. The doors rattled, the
wooden jambs creaked, and from the walls came a low moaning
sound. The very room around me came alive with a soughing,
muffled noise as the ship rose and fell, caught in the tempestuous
cadence of the sea.

The shuddering motion continued well until dawn, which
broke muted in a dreary suffusion of metallic light to the east. A
heavy rain was falling, driven by high winds. From the porthole of
my cabin I could see how the sea formed deep troughs running at
an angle to the ship.

At eight o'clock the captain's voice came over the intercom an-
nouncing there would be a practice lifeboat drill at 10 A.M. All passengers were to put on their life vests and assemble at staging areas
near their cabins. The drill was a routine procedure, the captain

stressed. But he advised everyone of a severe storm warning at sea.

We were entering the area of the Atlantic where the Gulf Stream met the colder Arctic waters. High winds and rough seas were predicted throughout the day, possibly continuing through the following night. Passengers were advised to avoid walking on the decks, and to spend as much time as possible safe within their cabins.

Nausea had begun to overtake me during the night, and as I showered and dressed, trying to ignore the queasiness in my stomach. In the face of the continuing storm, my seasickness showed no signs of diminishing. I remembered a doctor was available aboard ship and decided to set out to locate him at once.

A line had already formed at the ship's hospital, where shots for seasickness were being offered free of charge. As I took my place at the rear of the line, Dr. Ramirez stepped out of the doctor's office and spotted me across the room.

"Ah," he said, crossing to where I stood, "I see I'm not the only one with a sensitive constitution!"

"I'm afraid not. Do you think these shots will help?"

"Absolutely, they're very effective. But be prepared for some drowsiness later."

At that moment, the shipped rolled suddenly, and I was thrown against Dr. Ramirez, who caught me in his arms and held me there as we both struggled for balance.

"Sorry," I said, as soon as I had managed to get my feet under me. "I had no idea the crossing would be this rough."

"Nor I."

"I didn't think I'd feel anything on such a big ship."

"Apparently, this storm is unusually violent," Dr. Ramirez said. "I spoke with a petty officer in the bar last night who told me this is the last crossing of the season for the *Oceanus*. The Atlantic becomes too rough, and the crossings are suspended until spring."

"Have you done this before?" I asked him. "I mean, taken a boat to Europe?"

"Never!" he said, laughing. "And I wouldn't have done so now except I felt obliged to accompany Dr. Cabrera, who as you must know has an aversion to flying."

I looked at him, surprised. "I've never known Carlos to be afraid of flying," I said.

"I believe it's a recent development," he replied. "After his wife's death in a plane crash, I don't think he's felt safe flying anymore."

"His wife . . . ?" I looked at him, incredulous. "You mean Isabella?"

"Yes. I thought you knew."

I turned away from him abruptly, not wanting him to see my reaction to this news. I felt stunned. How was this possible? Who had I seen yesterday out on the deck of the ship if it wasn't Isabella?

"When did this happen?" I asked, still gazing away from him.

"A little over a year ago. Isabella was on vacation, traveling in South America, when her plane went down in a storm over the Andes. In the beginning there was hope she might have survived. Several weeks passed before a search party located the plane. Then the news came that everyone aboard the plane had perished."

I sat down on a chair, feeling suddenly unsteady. "Forgive me," I said to Dr. Ramirez. "I didn't know anything about this."

"I'm sorry to break the news to you in such an abrupt way," he said. "I assumed Carlos had told you."

"It's been many years since we've seen each other. We've been out of touch."

"She was a remarkable woman, Isabella," Dr. Ramirez said. "Did you know her well?"

"No," I said quietly. "In fact, I didn't know her at all."

I had conjured up a ghost, unwittingly mistaken a stranger for the woman who had once haunted my life. It was as if some great obstacle had been rolled away from the tomb of my past, and now the chamber was emptied, leaving nothing inside but the dank and dusty sarcophagus where the body had once laid.

"For a long while after her death, Carlos simply wasn't himself," Dr. Ramirez went on to say, sitting down in the chair beside me. "It was as if some part of him died with her. He stopped going out in the evenings, refused all invitations. He kept up his usual schedule of surgeries during the day, but otherwise he kept to himself. He became a recluse. For years we'd played tennis together twice a week, but after Isabella's death he refused to continue our games. He underwent a great change. He seemed to age overnight. But recently he seems to have come around. Now he seems more like his old self. Perhaps it's normal to go through a period of grieving, and then one day simply emerge, ready to go on with life. In any case, he appears to have gotten over the worst of it."

Now I understood why Carlos had appeared so aged, so different from the man I had known.

It was my turn to see the doctor, and so I parted from Dr. Ramirez, who was still gazing at me as I turned away from him.

"I'm looking forward to your reading Thursday night," he called after me.

"Yes, thank you. I'll see you then."

The doctor, who chatted away while giving me an injection, assured me I would feel better within a few hours. He couldn't help noticing how pale I was, and how my hands shook slightly when I stood up and tried to fasten my belt, struggling to accomplish this simplest of tasks. He assumed it was the seasickness that caused me to appear so shaken.

"Are you sure you feel well enough to return to your cabin?" he asked. "You could rest here for a while if you'd like."

"Thank you, but I'm fine."

I didn't return to my cabin but made my way to the restaurant on the upper deck. The Milwards had finished eating and were leaving just as I arrived, which made everything immeasurably easier since I wished to be alone. I had no appetite, but I forced myself to eat a light breakfast of tea and toast, sitting alone at our table near the window. Rain was falling heavily outside, gusting against the window, driven by high winds. It was as if some unseen hands were throwing buckets full of water against the glass, so violently was the storm raging. I felt afraid, not of the storm so much, but of some undefinable emotion coursing through me.

Why hadn't Carlos told me about Isabella? My behavior of the previous evening now embarrassed me, the toughness I had assumed in his presence, the way I had rejected his request to see me during our time at sea.

I no longer even knew what I felt toward Carlos after all these years. I had no wish to be cruel to him, or rude, and yet I had been.

My thoughts were interrupted by the captain's voice, coming over the intercom, advising all passengers to return immediately to their cabins, put on their life vests, and assemble for the lifeboat drill.

When I unlocked the door to my cabin and stepped inside, I noticed a little envelope lying on the floor, with my name written on the outside. My first thought was that it was a note from Carlos, and I opened it hurriedly. But it wasn't from Carlos. It was an invitation to join the captain in his cabin for drinks the next afternoon.

The last thing I wanted to do just at that moment was attend a lifeboat drill. As I began looking through the closet for my life vest, my thoughts were still very much absorbed with Carlos. It seemed to me that it was in the remembering that we found ourselves pulled down into the abyss of sorrow. The little errors and gestures, the longings of the past, were like straws in the wind, meant to blow away, to dissipate with time. Yet weren't we always betrayed by the very things we wished to conceal? With Carlos I had wished to conceal all the bitter disappointment still locked in my heart, and in doing so I felt I betrayed those other, hidden feelings, if only to myself.

By the time I'd found my life vest and joined the other passengers on the upper deck, I'd begun mentally to compose a note to send Carlos as soon as the drill was over.

I had to force myself to pay attention to the instructions offered by a clean-cut petty officer in the event of an emergency evacuation of the *Oceanus*. As he spoke, the storm pounded against the ship with a thudding and defiant force, as if to remind us of its power. He explained how to locate our assigned lifeboats and, once inside, how to inflate the collars of our life vests, how to activate the little blinking lights that might guide a rescuer to us in the night, and how important it was to remember the correct *number* of one's lifeboat, for we would not be allowed to enter any other boat than the one to which we were assigned.

By the time the drill had concluded, I was perspiring and anxious to escape the stuffy and crowded room.

Back in my cabin, I stowed my life vest away again beneath the floorboard of the closet and took out my pen and a piece of paper and began to write Carlos a note.

When I'd finished, I called for a steward, instructing him to deliver it to Carlos's cabin immediately.

As soon as the steward had gone, drowsiness overtook me. I fell into a deep sleep, punctuated by a dream in which I was floating in a dark and stormy sea, unable to discern any shape in the black and unfathomable darkness, which was complete and all-engulfing and endless, both below and above me, black water, black air, with nothing to guide me, nothing to hold on to, nothing, absolutely nothing all around me except the endless darkness and the wild and roily sea, which dragged me down, down into its inky depths.

FIFTEEN

My tiny bathroom window at the Tally Ho looks out on an alley, a dusty lane littered with old tires and cast-off automobile parts. Often, early in the morning before the day begins to stir, I see a homeless man sleeping there. He leaves a crimson blanket stashed in the weeds next to a chain-link fence. Usually he is gone before the sun rises and doesn't return until after dark.

This morning, however, as the dawn is just breaking and I stand at the window, preparing to take a shower, I look outside, up the alley, and see that he is still there. He appears to be sleeping, a figure stretched out full-length and still in the morning light. Then I see a movement, a fluttering of his hands, quick and sharp, as if some insect has disturbed him and he's shooing it away. His movement becomes rhythmical, and I look again. Only slowly do I realize that he's masturbating, lying there on his back, faceup in the pale morning light, bringing himself a small self-inflicted pleasure there among the dust-caked weeds.

The sight doesn't disgust me. It's more like empathy I feel, a sly and knowing sense of complicity. I understand well how old urges never die, even in the bleakest of times.

I look at myself in the bathroom mirror. What I see there doesn't necessarily please or displease me. What I find interesting, and ultimately ironic, is the fact that the outside of this person has become so familiar, while the inside remains a mysterious configuration, a soul unprepared for itself.

I am thinking of what happened last night.

I had decided to go out about seven-thirty for dinner. A dry, hot wind was blowing when I set out for a Cuban restaurant just off Sahara Avenue. I got as far as the corner and realized I had left my wallet back in my room, and headed back to get it, when I saw Mr. and Mrs. Patel, standing at the railing, just outside my room. They were arguing about something.

Mrs. Patel's voice alerted me to their presence. In her shrill Indian accent, she was berating her husband. I lingered at the bottom of the stairs, hesitant to interrupt them, listening for a moment.

"I am not having this sort of woman staying here. This is not right that she should be taking advantage of us this way."

"And what has she done that is so terrible?"

"She has not paid, for one thing. For another—"

"She has said she will pay tomorrow. Where is your patience?"

"I am just telling you now that this sort of thing will only bring trouble to us. We are not running a brothel. I am ashamed you would let such things go on in front of your daughter."

"What things are you talking about?"

"Bringing men to her room for sex."

"We do not know that for certain. No one has seen this."

"Then what is this, may I ask? You can see for yourself, right here."

I heard the sound of a paper rattling.

"She is putting an ad in the paper. 'I come to your room 24 hours a day! It doesn't get any better. Call Joycelle.' And here is our phone number! The phone number of our motel in a sex ad! What am I to think?"

"I am not so sure that is her in the picture—"

"Of course it is her. You are not looking at her face."

"It says here she is going to their rooms. She is not bringing them here."

"I did not come to America for this. To have to put up with this sort of thing!"

"She is not your daughter. And this is not your house. We are running a business here. Am I having to remind you of this over and over? Do we have so many customers that we can turn them away? You are always making problems where there is no problem. This is what you are doing again now, stirring things up. Just like your mother."

"May you be forgiven for saying such things about my mother."

"Mind your own business, that is what I say to you and your mother. I will see to things myself. Now go find Sushila. Tell her to come to the office immediately. I am having too much to do this evening. She can watch the desk. I must see why the television in 206 is not working."

I heard Mr. Patel hurrying away. As I climbed the stairs, I bumped into Mrs. Patel, coming down.

"Ah, it is you, Mrs. Patterson. Good evening."

"Good evening, Mrs. Patel."

I looked down at what she was holding in her hand, a free throwaway guide to adult entertainment. Quickly, she dropped her hand and hid it in the folds of her sari.

"So hot tonight, isn't it?" she said. "I am hardly breathing in this heat."

I could smell the oil she used on her hair, which lay plastered flat against her head and seemed to release its odor more fully in the heat of late day.

"Yes," I said. "It is terribly hot."

"I cannot get used to this sort of heat. My husband is telling me he does not find it as hot as Bombay. But it is a different sort of heat, I tell him. Here everything is so dry. I feel my skin will crack."

At that moment a car swung into the parking lot. It was Joycelle's old Chevy. She parked below us and got out. When Mrs. Patel saw her, she let out a low clucking sound.

"Problems, always problems, Mrs. Patterson. When one runs a business, there is no end to the problems. Excuse me, I must be finding my daughter now. Goodbye. Have a pleasant evening."

She hurried away as Joycelle approached.

Joycelle shuffled as she crossed the parking lot. Her appearance was disheveled, as if she'd just gotten out of bed. Her hair hung in limp and greasy strands around a pale face. She seemed distracted, drawn inward, as if barely aware of her surroundings. I think she would have passed me without speaking if I hadn't spoken up first.

"Hi, Joycelle."

"Hi."

"How are you?"

"I've been better."

"That's good." I thought she meant she was feeling better, though she certainly didn't look it.

"No, I mean I'm not so good. You know . . . *I've* been better. Better than I feel right now. Anyway, forget it."

A nakedly sad look flashed across her face as she met my eyes for a moment.

"What'd that old bag want?" she asked.

"Mrs. Patel?"

"Yeah. Turkey Curry. Ever notice how funny she smells?"

"She's looking for her daughter."

"Yeah, well, I got to come up with some money or I'm going to be looking for a place to live."

"What's the problem?"

"Frank really screwed me."

"Frank?"

"Just this guy I had a business deal with. He owed me some money and now he won't pay. And he left me to pay this motel bill. He just split. That's it." She said this, looking at me with eyes that were glazed, distant, yet red-rimmed and burning.

"How much do you need?"

She screwed her mouth to one side.

"What are you going to do, offer to lend me the money? C'mon."

"If you really need it—"

"And they say whores are good-hearted."

She tried to grin, but suddenly she cracked. Without any warning, she broke down and began sobbing so hard I thought for one moment she was choking. Her legs seemed to weaken under her, and she fell against the railing and began to slide to the ground. I put an arm around her and helped her up to her feet. She did nothing to assist me in this effort. She was so distraught she seemed only to want to be allowed to lie crumpled on the asphalt at my feet.

"C'mon, Joycelle," I said. "Let's go inside."

I got her up to my room and helped her onto my bed. But nothing I did or said would calm her. She just kept crying, doubled over, curled into a fetal position, shaking with sobs. There was nothing restrained about her grief. She wailed like a child. She gave herself over completely to whatever sorrow was working inside her, like one who knows what it is to lose more energy to weeping than to any other act.

I gave up trying to talk to her. I just waited. I sat by her side, with one hand on her back, and waited.

After a long while her crying stopped and she lifted her head from the pillow and looked at me. I thought I had never seen a more wretched-looking human being.

"I can't go to work tonight," she said. Her voice was dull, a little hoarse and weak. "Call them for me? Would you? Just do that for me. Six-four-two, two-nine-seven-four. Just say I'm sick. I'll call in tomorrow."

I picked up the receiver and dialed the number. A man answered.

"Good evening, the Penthouse," he said. I gave him the message. There was a long pause. "Yeah, right, she's sick again," he said. "Who's this?" "A friend," I said. "Yeah, well if you're really her friend you might try explaining to her she's not going to have a job unless she shows up tomorrow. Do that for me, huh?" He then hung up.

The moment I replaced the receiver, Joycelle was on her feet, striding toward the door.

"Wait a minute," I said. "Don't go yet."

"I gotta go."

"Why don't you come to dinner with me?"

"Not hungry."

"I'll bring you something, then."

"Don't. I'm gonna take a sleeping pill. I don't want to be disturbed."

"What's happened, Joycelle? What's wrong?"

"It's bad," she whispered. "It's real bad."

"What's bad?"

She stood for a moment with her hand on the doorknob, as if thinking something over. Then she mumbled something.

"What? I didn't hear what you said."

"I went back to the clinic today. . . ."

"And?"

"To get these results . . ."

She dropped her head and whispered something again.

"I can't hear you."

"I tested positive."

"Tested positive . . . ?"

Before I could say anything else, she was out the door. After a few moments I went to her room and knocked. She refused to answer the door. I knocked again and called her name a few times. Still no answer. I stood there for a while, and then I left.

I saw her face everywhere as I walked around the city. That little bow-shaped mouth painted a lurid red, the long straight nose, the dark eyes looking out from between the thick fringe of lashes. It seemed wherever I turned there was an adult entertainment guide with Joycelle's picture on the front. Joycelle smiling, her breasts like perfect plastic orbs above the caption "A centerfold spread in the privacy of your room." There she was, staring out at me from a row of newspaper vending machines. I found it hard to look at that image, and turned away each time.

After dinner I walked from the restaurant all the way downtown. A plastic gaiety surrounded me, a feeling of fun on the move in a gaudy world. Clusters of tourists streamed past me, clutching their cardboard buckets of coins. The very air seemed to smell of money. The darkness was a distant scrim, a fake ceiling above a riotously illuminated landscape. Everything was moving fast and loud. In a world where clocks were banished and the night and the day were separated only by a running out of luck or by those lucid enough to recognize their own weariness in the smear of a dawn or a blood-red sunset.

I walked for a long time through the pseudonight, past the Lady Luck and the Horseshoe and the Four Queens and the Golden Nugget, past the Mardi Gras and the Palace and the Showboat and Slots-A-Fun. I walked down the strip, aimless, without longing or purpose, sated and empty, burdened with an urgent wish to keep moving, wanting to put off the moment when I would have to return to the solitariness of my room at the Tally Ho.

It was late, very late, when I headed back to the motel. I felt a steely tiredness deep in my bones, and at one point I sat down on the edge of a planter on the sidewalk to rest. As I sat there, I noticed a place across the street. I probably wouldn't have noticed it if I hadn't stopped to rest. As it was, I stood up and walked across the street to the Penthouse.

I don't really know why I went inside. Seeing the place where Joycelle worked, I seemed compelled to enter, as if I might discover something inside that would help me to understand more about her.

The first thing I noticed is how I was the only woman in the room, at least the only one with her clothes on. The man who took my money did so with a lurid gleam in his eye as he said, "Would you like to sit at the runway, or a table?"

I chose a table, a little ways from the long raised platform where a tall, leggy stripper was strutting between the two rows of men seated on either side of the runway. It wasn't her nudity so much that struck me. Nor the way she gathered up money with her breasts, pushing them together to clasp the bills that were offered. Nor even the way she squatted down in front of each man as she did so, spreading her legs briefly, bouncing a few times before moving on down the line. Rather, it was the faces of the men lining the runway that got my attention. Their rapt wonder. The look of absolute, almost holy facination. Each face, though so different, bore the same reverential countenance, an awe so complete it appeared innocent. The men were seated as if at a long table, suspended in awe, their upturned faces beatific in wonder. So pure did they seem in their worship, they appeared as disciples. There were Japanese men, Middle Eastern men, blacks and whites, young men and old men, all types of men and yet for the moment all differences between them seemed leveled by the sexual sacrament in which they were all partaking, with the priestess of the religion to which they all subscribed elevated before them.

When the stripper finished her act and left the stage, only a few men clapped. The others remained fixed in their attitude of awe, unwilling to break their trance.

Then an older man, an emcee, came out and announced the name of the next stripper. "Isn't this the reason you came to Vegas," he cried. "Isn't it? Isn't it? For these awesome ass-ets! And she's got them. Our next girl. Our Samantha. She's been featured in *Hustler* magazine," he said. "She's starred in a dozen porn films. She's a real nasty girl in motion! She reminds me of my first wife!"

He strode up and down the platform puffing on a cigar, the black cord on his microphone snaking behind him. I couldn't help thinking how he must have once believed he'd hit it big. Be a headliner comedy act. But here he was, an old man warming up a crowd for a stripper.

I could feel the men growing restless. They didn't appreciate his patter. They wanted their new priestess. They began heckling him.

Someone yelled, "Get off the stage, Grandpa!"

"Why don't you drink your whiskey, it may be the hardest thing you hold tonight," the emcee shot back.

"Fuck off!"

"Have you even seen an asshole covered in plastic? Look at your driver's license."

"Bring on the pussy!"

"Yeah, where's the pussy?"

A sort of low chant began—"Pus-sy, pus-sy, pus-sy"—a hissing sibilant sound that rose in volume until it filled the room. Silenced, the emcee stood defeated, as he must have done so many times before, the blue smoke from his cigar leaking from around his tired mouth and drifting in a twisted ribbon through the light beaming down from a spot on the ceiling. I'd had enough. I got up and headed for the door.

"Didn't stay long, did you?" the man at the door said as I passed by him.

"No, I didn't," I replied.

"I guess we don't have what you're looking for."

"I guess not."

"Come back again. We get new girls all the time. Who knows, next time we might have something to your liking."

It's only 10 A.M., and already the heat feels oppressive. I sit fanning myself with a rolled-up newspaper. I've place a chair outside, in front of my room, on the narrow second-story balcony of the Tally Ho, where the overhanging roof affords a little shade. I've come out here because my room has become unbearable. The air conditioner stopped working sometime during the night.

Mr. Patel has said he'll come fix it this morning. I'm waiting for him, biding my time. And wondering where Joycelle is. There was no answer when I knocked on her door earlier this morning. And her car, which was in its space when I came in last night, was gone when I woke up.

SIXTEEN

The distant sound of bells broke through my slumber. Drugged by the shot I had received earlier, only slowly did I realize it was the telephone next to my bed, which must have been ringing for some time.

Slowly, I managed to lift the receiver and utter a groggy hello.

"Lucy?"

It was Carlos on the line.

"Yes?"

"I was about to hang up. I thought you weren't there."

"I was sleeping. What time is it?" I had drawn the curtain over the porthole and the cabin was dark. I had no sense of the hour.

"Four o'clock."

"Incredible. I've slept the whole day. It must be the shot the doctor gave me for seasickness."

"Dr. Ramirez told me he ran into you at the ship's hospital. Are you feeling any better?"

"I suppose. I'm too sleepy to tell."

"Listen—I received your note. I thought perhaps we might talk."

"Yes."

"Why don't we meet in the bar in an hour? Is that too soon for you?"

"No, it's fine. I'll see you then."

I dragged myself from my bed, realizing I did feel better. The shot had worked. No trace of seasickness remained, though I felt a little light-headed from the lack of food. I took a long time shower-ing. While I dressed, I had a sense of being rushed and unprepared. I changed outfits twice and then ended up wearing the black dress I had originally chosen. It seemed foolish to feel such nervousness; nevertheless, I did. I glanced hastily at myself one last time in the mirror, and then left the cabin.

I arrived at the lounge before Carlos, and made my way to the table near the window, the same spot where we had sat before. The storm was still in full force, though the winds seemed to have less-ened. It was almost dark. Rain was falling aslant, running against the windows in thick rivulets and stippling the leaden sea beyond the window.

I ordered a drink and relaxed in my chair, facing the room. The band was playing, and I noticed several couples out on the dance floor. Something about the scene seemed odd to me.

All the men out on the dance floor were of a certain age, and they all wore the same outfit—blue blazers and white pants and white shoes. I suddenly realized they must be the gentleman hosts that Gil Rawlins had told me about. Now I noticed a number of single women sitting alone at tables surrounding the little dance floor. These, I realized, must be the "ladies traveling solo." All of the women appeared to be waiting rather eagerly for their turn on the dance floor.

One woman, in particular, caught my attention. She was rather hopelessly awkward and seemed to lack all sense of rhythm; worst of all, she kept her heavy handbag draped over her arm where it bumped against her as she stumbled through a dance, all the while gazing off into the middle distance. Each time one of the gentlemen hosts asked her to dance, I waited, wondering if she might exchange a few words with him or somehow find her rhythm, or perhaps leave her handbag at the table. But none of this ever happened, and soon no one bothered asking her to dance again.

The bar was gradually filling up. The people who came in were dressed for the evening in formal attire. It was odd to see so many men in tuxedos—odd, but strangely pleasing in a theatrical sort of way. The women glittered in jewels, wearing rich fabrics—satin, velvet, brocade—dresses that showed off a long neck, or the pale swell of cleavage. In my black sheath I felt slightly underdressed.

I looked at my watch, wondering what had happened to Carlos. At a nearby table, two couples were conversing in German. Occasionally, someone would break into English. At one point I heard one of the men say, "But that is precisely what I'm saying, Heinrich. The Nazi occupation of France was somehow beside the point when it came to French colonial rule in Algeria."

I looked up to see Carlos enter the bar and watched him cross the room. He apologized for being late. Dr. Ramirez had phoned just as he was leaving his cabin, he said, and he was unavoidably delayed.

He seemed distracted as he sat down at the table across from me. He had dressed for the evening in a tuxedo which contrasted strikingly with his white hair and pale skin. He appeared very elegant in these clothes, as if perfectly at ease in such an outfit.

Almost immediately, he brought up the matter of my note.

"Thank you for sending it," he said. "I don't wish to take exception to what you wrote, but you are wrong to think I was offended by anything you said last night. It's quite understandable that you didn't want to see me."

"It wasn't really that I didn't *want* to . . ."

"I can understand your feelings."

"Can you?"

"Of course."

"Why didn't you tell me about Isabella?"

"The right opportunity didn't seem to present itself. Also, it's still not easy for me to talk about it."

"Even to me?"

"Perhaps especially to you."

"I'm sorry—"

"In any case, these injuries linger," he said, cutting me off. "That much is undeniable. They have a way of surviving everything else." He spoke in a very formal way, as if no intimacy had ever existed between us. I didn't know which injuries he was talking about. The injury he suffered when he lost Isabella, or me? His words had a surgical precision, yet their meaning wasn't clear to me.

"You see, my friend," he was now saying, "I don't think it's quite possible to confine the pain of the past to the past. It has a way of leaking out, of surging forward like a spreading stain and contaminating the present. The best we can do is try to control the flow, by erecting a little barrier here, a little barrier there. I suppose you'll think me cold and unfeeling if I say that's how I've come to manage. It's how I've dealt with Isabella's death. It's how I managed my feelings for you. I simply walled them in. I partitioned myself in an attempt to control the damage."

"I suppose I've managed to build my own walls," I answered, "and yet unfortunately I think I've ended up as the prisoner."

"I think you despise me a little, don't you?"

"Why should I?"

"For what happened in the past."

"*Despise* is a strong word, and not an accurate one to describe what I feel."

"I'm not so sure. I think you have despised me for a very long time and perhaps it's now too late for anything else. I don't say I blame you. But I do think it's the case."

"How serious we suddenly are," I said, and laughed rather nervously. I was hoping to change the course of the conversation, which was making me very uncomfortable.

"You mean, how serious I am. Forgive me, but I think you are not being so serious. I think you're being rather . . . what is the word? Not *capricious* . . . but—*evasive?*"

"The past is the past, Carlos. Does any of this matter anymore?"

"I think it does. And I think you think so, too, or you wouldn't have sent your note. Your attitude in the flesh is something different, however. You seem divided between facing the past and cutting me off when I make any serious attempt to do so."

"I'm sorry about Isabella's death. I hope you got at least that much from my note."

"She was a very intelligent woman—and believe me, an excellent mother." He made a sweeping gesture in front of him with his hand, and repeated, very solemnly—"and I mean excellent."

"I do believe you," I said, perhaps a little too quickly.

"We managed to raise our children and present a solid front, to carry on with dignity after . . . after you and I parted. It's not much of an achievement in life, is it? And yet at times it felt that way."

"It's more than I can say."

"What do you mean?"

"I mean I haven't managed to have any lasting relationship."

"But I had imagined other men in your life."

"There have been. But none so important to me as you."

He stared into his empty glass.

"Shall we have another drink?" I said.

"Why not." We both looked off in the direction of the bartender, and I let my confession hang between us, where it seemed to continue to reverberate like a tiny bell.

It was at that moment that the man at the table near us, the German I had earlier heard speaking to his companions, turned toward Carlos and said, "Excuse me, but don't we know each other?"

Carlos frowned slightly, and said, "I don't think so."

"Ah, but I'm sure I recognize you, although many years have passed since we last saw each other. Aren't you Carlos Cabrera?"

"Yes, I am."

"I was right, then." We most certainly do know each other. I came across your name on the ship's register, and I though I recognized you when you came into the bar, but I wasn't certain until just now when I heard your friend call you Carlos. I'm Josef Himmelfarb. I'm sure you will recall my brother, Oskar. Oskar Schneider, as he was then known?"

At the mention of this name, it seemed as if every muscle in Carlos's body tensed in a subtle contraction. He seemed to visibly withdraw, shrinking back from the man who was now leaning toward our table. A few seconds went by before he said, "I'm sorry. I'm afraid I don't remember you."

"Or my brother? So you don't recall Oskar Schneider?"

"I don't recall the name," Carlos said stiffly. "You'll have to forgive me."

"Ha!" the German cried. "Forgive *you*?"

He began speaking to Carlos in German then, and although I couldn't understand what he said, it was clear that he was confronting him. It was as if he were spitting the words at Carlos, accusing him of something. Carlos said something in reply, and the man seemed to grow even more agitated. His voice became louder. He grew red in the face and flung more words at Carlos.

The German said something with a particular vehemence, and I noticed Carlos reacted with the look of someone who has just been deeply stunned by some piece of news.

He had just begun to say something in reply to the German's angry outburst, his voice low and even, when suddenly the ship rolled violently, pitching abruptly to one side.

The table in front of us tipped over, and we were both hurled from our chairs. The bar was suddenly filled with the sound of glass crashing to the floor and people crying and screaming as they slid from their seats.

The room went instantly dark, except for a soiled gray light leaking in from the window, in which I could barely make out the shape of Carlos, lying on the floor near me.

"Lucy," he said, "My God, are you all right?"

"My leg," I murmured. The table had tipped over and landed on my ankle. I reached for the table, but the ship rolled violently for the second time, tilting further on its side. Carlos grabbed my hand as we both slid into the wall and were held there by the weight of a couple who were thrown against us.

It seemed as if the whole room had been lifted and turned sideways. There was an enormous crashing sound as the piano suddenly broke loose and hurtled across the room, smashing into the far wall. The entire contents of the bar seemed to slide across the floor at once, bottles and glasses commingling their sounds of falling and breakage.

I believed then that this is how I would end my life, with my face pressed into the hollow of Carlos's neck, our bodies joined as a single weighted entity about to be swallowed up by the sea, which even then seemed only moments away from bursting through the groaning walls of the ship and sucking us into its depths.

But almost as quickly as the ship had tilted, it righted itself, and then swung briefly in the other direction, so that the bodies and bottles, the tables and chairs, the piano and the drums and cymbals and assorted band instruments were sent sliding again across the wooden floor in a strange cacophony of sound like some crazy experimental piece of music in which atonality and chance were the dominant aspects being tried out. I clung to Carlos and held on until we stopped moving. Then suddenly the room grew quiet.

In the hardening dusk, the sea seemed to swell monstrously, crashing into the aft deck, and water pounded against the windows, which seemed to bulge with the weight of the sea. In the bar people groped and struggled to gain some purchase in the darkness. Someone stepped on my leg in an effort to stand up. I realized it was the German who had spoken a few moments earlier to Carlos. In the dim light I looked down the length of my body at him, and, meeting my eyes, he rolled away from me.

Suddenly, the lights came on once again and flooded the room, revealing a scene of chaos. No one seemed seriously injured. No one was dead. But among the elderly passengers, there were those who appeared to have sprained limbs or broken bones that prevented them from moving from the places where they had landed when the ship had suddenly rolled.

"Is there a doctor in the room?" someone said.

I looked up to see it was one of the gentlemen hosts who had spoken, the one with the full beard who looked like a sea captain. "Do we have any doctors in the room?"

Almost immediately Carlos was on his feet, identifying himself as a doctor. He went to help a man who laid nearby, crying for help, his leg bent at an improbable angle beneath him, and began speaking to him quietly.

A few seconds later the captain's voice came over the intercom. He asked for calm. He explained that we seemed to be out of any immediate danger. The ship had been hit by a sneaker wave, he said. A rogue wave. A wave that had come out of nowhere and slammed into the *Oceanus*. He said that although we seemed to be clear of immediate crisis, he advised all those able to return to their cabins to do so immediately and have their life vests ready. The injured were to report to the ship's hospital. If any of the injured required assistance in reaching the ship's hospital, they were advised to stay put until a stretcher team arrived to transport them. He asked for help from any doctors on board. He requested they identify themselves to the staff, or report to the infirmary at once.

As people struggled to their feet and the bar began emptying out, I propped myself up on a chair and waited for Carlos, who was busy calming the injured. I felt dazed, aware of a throbbing in my ankle, and in the dry fear, the aftermath of shock, I tried to believe what the captain had said, that the worst was over, although every nerve in my body told me this wasn't the case.

I discovered, lying near me, a half-empty bottle of gin that had somehow miraculously survived the upheaval. The gin tasted of juniper. I held the taste in my mouth. As I did so, an old childhood memory welled up, of a cat I had once discovered beneath a juniper busy, an elastic band wound so tightly around its neck it was close to death. Maggots had already infested the suppurating wound around the elastic. The taste of juniper, the hapless cat, its slow death, the maggoty wound, the moans of the injured—it all filled my mind with a single feeling of horror, and I couldn't stop trembling. I suddenly felt cold. The woman with the handbag who had danced so awkwardly was lying against a wall near me. She began crying. I forced myself to go to her and help her sit up. She clung to me and shook with sobs. It did not seem to me that she was so much injured as frightened.

"It's all right," I said, patting her back. "Just sit quietly. Don't try to move."

"My handbag . . . where's my handbag?"

I found it for her and placed it in her lap. And then someone came to help her, and I moved quietly away, still clutching the bottle of gin.

When the last of the injured were taken away, Carlos came over to me and drew me up from my chair and held me close against him. We left the bar together, with the ship still shuddering and pitching beneath our feet, and made our way down a narrow corridor and up the carpeted stairway to his cabin in the Luxury Class section of the ship.

My sense of chronology during that night is unclear. Did we finish the gin before we made love, or after? When was it that I turned to him in the darkness, with the storm roaring outside, and said, "Oh God, I'm scared," and he replied, "It's all right now, try to sleep, Lucy, it's all right."

When did I wake to find him watching me in the midst of an eerie quiet and realize the storm had diminished and moonlight was breaking through the clouds, falling in a marbled pattern through the porthole and landing on the whiteness of the sheets? Was it then that I whispered, "You killed everything in me, you know," and he replied, "Stop talking and kiss me, dear Lucy."

I know that at one point during the night, in one of the talks that punctuated our moments of wakefulness, I brought up the matter of garlic. I said to him, "I could never have married you, you know, I couldn't have made a life with someone who didn't eat garlic."

"Be serious," he replied.

"But I am. I remember you telling me it was the soldiers during the war. The soldiers who marched through the little German towns with garlic hung around their necks. How they chewed the cloves and reeked of it. How you couldn't stand the smell of them. You said they repelled you."

"What nonsense you remember."

"It was easier that way. Easier than remembering the other more important things."

"I doubt very much that garlic would have posed a problem for us."

"I began to feel that it was an indication of snobbishness on your part. A matter of class difference."

"What nonsense! It's a matter of taste, that's all."

"Tell me about Justin," he had said a little while later. "I want to know what happened."

"Why do you want me to talk about it now? It makes me sad to talk about it."

"Then I won't force you."

"Oh, what's the point . . ."

"The point . . . ?"

"Perhaps I should talk about it more. But I don't like to. It's a forbidden subject, all my friends know that. You know his body was never found?"

"No, I didn't know. All I know is what you told me in the letter. That he'd become a Mormon missionary in Guatemala and the place where he'd been living had been bombed and he'd disappeared."

"At first they thought he'd been killed in the bombing, like everyone else. They found his shoes. His bicycle. They expected to find his body. But when they sifted through everything, they didn't. Only the bodies—or what was left of them—of another missionary, named Henderson, and the old woman who worked as the cook at the mission home."

"Did they discover who was responsible for the bombing?"

"No. No one knows, or rather they're not saying. We still don't know what happened. Not to this day."

"But there must be some theories?"

"Of course. Lots of them. The Army blamed the rebels. The rebels blamed the Army, accusing it of fomenting attacks on Americans as a way of justifying their presence in an area where they weren't wanted."

"Either theory could be correct, I suppose."

"Of course. Quite a place, your Guatemala. So exquisitely corrupt. What rotten fruit you come from, darling."

"Forgive me, but it's a rather apt choice of words—rotten fruit. Who do you think helped make it that way, Lucy?"

"Spare me the politics. I lost my son."

"Sorry, darling. But it is the truth."

"Truth! I think the truth is so obscured in your country it doesn't exist anymore."

He kissed me lightly on the forehead. "It's rather foolish for us to argue this way. Please. Go on. What else do you know about Justin's disappearance?"

I sighed. "Not much. There was another theory . . ."

"Yes?"

"That the bombing was the result of tensions between the Catholics and other religious groups—the evangelicals, Mormons, Pentecostals—what have you. A lot of people resent the religious invasion by North Americans."

"A strong possibility."

"In any case," I sighed, "Justin disappeared. Someone kidnapped him, for some reason. Maybe he wasn't actually at the mission home at the time of the bombing but came back just as it was being carried out. Maybe he surprised whoever did it. And they took him away with them. And then . . ." I couldn't bring myself to finish the sentence.

"The thing about grief is it's so dark, and the darkness lingers, spreads. It does leave stains, doesn't it? I lost my faith, you know, when I lost you. And then again when I lost Justin."

"How can you lose faith twice, dear Lucy?"

"I don't know. But I did."

"Perhaps it wasn't faith you lost, but something else."

"I think he would have preferred a different kind of mother. I went through a period where I drank too much. For so much of the time it was just the two of us, you see. There should have been someone else there, someone he could have looked to and relied on, someone who could have *comforted* him. But there was only me. And I was preoccupied for so much of the time."

"Preoccupied? With what?"

"With myself. My writing. My work."

"You mustn't feel badly about that. You had every right—every obligation, one might say, to pursue your calling."

"But how could I have forced so many changes on him? Denied him a more stable life? How could I have let him go to . . . to such a bloody, violent place?"

"I think you are being too hard on yourself."

"When he told me he wanted to be baptized into the church, I couldn't believe it at first. I thought he was joking. The irony of it all!" I closed my eyes and I could see the inside of a church—a large, sterile room with plain wooden pews and folding chairs placed at the back of the room to provide extra seating, with the page numbers of the hymns set in black letters in a box on the wall: rows of men and women and children face the front of the room, where teenaged boys in white shirts and hand-me-down suits are standing in a line, preparing to pass the sacrament—the little bits of Wonder bread piled up on a silver tray, and the tiny pleated cups of water.

"Do you know how hard I have worked—how I have struggled my whole adult life to free myself from the influence of that religion?"

"Has it been so difficult?"

"Yes. It wasn't easy to throw it off. And then, my God, my son—my *son* decides to claim the very thing I've rejected!"

"But surely you know that one's children can't be expected to make the same choices as oneself?"

"Of course I know this. But it hasn't made it easier."

He stroked my hair gently. "No, I don't imagine it has."

"At least he believed in something," I said, gazing out the porthole. "That's more than I can say for myself."

I looked up at him then. I had been lying in the crook of his arm, staring into the darkness. But now I wanted to see his face. I wanted to believe that once again I could trust him and rely on him. This is what I think I wanted above all else. I wanted to think that there was one person on earth in whom I could confide, and who would hold me and comfort me and tell me all the things I wanted to hear in order to be relieved of the burden of carrying everything alone, and I found that person looking back at me. I was not disappointed. Right or wrong, I knew that I had come to a place where I wanted to be.

SEVENTEEN

This morning I went down to the office to ask whether Joycelle had checked out of her room. I found Mr. Patel, busy cleaning the glass on top of the registration desk. The smell of ammonia, mingled with the rich odor of curry wafting from the apartment next to the office, greeted me as I entered the small space.

"Good morning, Mrs. Patterson," he said with his usual cheerfulness. "What can I do for you this fine morning? I hope the air conditioner has not broken again."

"No, the air conditioner is fine. I'm wondering about something else. Have you seen Joycelle?"

"You mean the young lady in room 208? No, I have not seen her for several days. In fact, between you and me, Mrs. Patterson, I am having a problem with this lady. You see, she has not paid for her room. She promised to bring me the money several days ago, but she has simply disappeared?"

"She hasn't checked out?"

"No."

"Are her things still in her room?"

"My wife tells me her belongings are still there. She went there just this morning and found everything undisturbed."

"I'm wondering, Mr. Patel, if I might have a look in her room. I'm rather worried about her. She was very upset the last time I saw her. I think it's unusual for someone to simply disappear and leave behind all their belongings, don't you?"

"Do you suspect foul play, Mrs. Patterson?"

"I really don't know what to think."

"Perhaps we should call the police."

"I don't think that's called for. I mean, she may be perfectly fine. She might have taken a trip somewhere." I didn't really believe this. But neither could I imagine what might have happened to her.

"I wouldn't ask you to let me see her room if I didn't think the situation was rather urgent, if I didn't believe it was important. And there's another thing. I'd like to take care of her bill. Perhaps you could tell me how much she owes you?"

Mr. Patel hesitated before he replied. His head bobbed slightly as he said, "*Acha*. I am sure your intentions are very noble, Mrs. Patterson. For this reason I am making an exception for you." He produced a key from the board on the wall and handed it to me.

I don't know what I expected to find in her room. As I unlocked the door and stepped inside, I was greeted by a faint, cloying scent of something sweet—cheap perfume mixed with stale air. The room was identical to my own, but everything about it felt different. Strange how in such a short period of habitation we leave our imprint on a place.

Joycelle's room resembled the quarters of a sexually precocious teenager. Several stuffed animals had been left propped up on the bed. Items of clothing were strewn about—mostly underclothes—a red corset, a garter belt, some fishnet stockings. A pair of pink high heels sat on the floor in front of a chair, as if she'd just stepped out of them. The *National Enquirer* featuring Elvis as a transvestite lay next to a pack of cigarettes on top of the nightstand. The vanity below the mirror was crowded with makeup—tubes of lipstick, creams, mascara, and several pairs of earrings, all gaudy and oversized.

But the item that drew my attention immediately was a photograph wedged in the bottom corner of the mirror between the glass and the frame.

It was a picture of Joycelle with a child, a little girl, perhaps two years old. The child bore an unmistakable resemblance to her. The photograph had been taken on a beach somewhere. The child and Joycelle knelt beside a sand castle, smiling for the camera, the surf rolling in behind them. In the background an older woman sat beneath a beach umbrella. I couldn't tell whether the older woman had any connection to Joycelle and the little girl, or if she was simply part of the background scene, a figure caught up in someone else's picture.

I took the photograph down and looked on the back. Someone had written "Nicole, age 2, Venice Beach" in a childish scrawl. I turned it over and stared at the front again. Something I hadn't noticed before now came into focus. The child had a harelip. One side of her mouth was puckered and drawn up into a little knot of flesh. In every other respect she was an exceptionally beautiful child, so that even this slight deformity appeared as a tender, rather endearing imperfection.

The quiet in the room was ominous. I felt very much like a trespasser. I wouldn't have known what to say if Joycelle had walked in at that moment. Quickly, I opened the top drawer of the dresser and looked inside. More lingerie, a pair of handcuffs, leather straps. When I gently moved these things aside, I discovered a little plastic bag of marijuana, some rolling papers, and a pipe.

I opened another drawer, and then another, both filled with ordinary clothing—T-shirts and jeans and shorts. I was feeling quite guilty about looking through her things and was about to leave the room when on an impulse I crossed to the nightstand and opened the top drawer.

Inside was an address book, a letter, and a bottle of pills. I looked inside the address book. It was almost empty. Only a few names had been penciled in, five or six at the most. Otherwise, blank pages. The little book seemed indescribably sad to me.

Having gone this far, I could see no sense in stopping, so I took the letter out and read it.

Dearie:

Daddy is out working in the fields this morning, a bright pretty day. If the weather holds he should get the hay crop in this week. Bobby has been helping him. He came back home just for the haying, then he and Gertie are headed back to the coast to look for work. Bobby sure is a good worker. Your daddy couldn't have got through without him. He ain't up to running this place alone and you can't get seasonal help no more.

I put up two dozens jars of peaches this morning and they look real pretty sitting here on the kitchen counter. I got another bushel to do before I quit. The arthritis in my hands slows me down. I wish you was here to help me. I remember what a good little helper you always was at canning time. Now you're so far away and I miss you. Do you think you might be able to come home this fall for a visit? Daddy and I figure once the hay is sold we could come up with the money for an airplane ticket for you. We'd come visit you except you know there ain't no way I'd ever get Daddy on a plane. Why don't you ask your boss if you might have a week off? Surely waitresses get vacations like everybody else. It sure would make us happy to see you again. Drop us a line when you can.

Your ever loving Mom

I looked at the name and return address on the envelope: Mrs. R. C. Johnson, RFD, Route 4, Wilton Corner, Iowa. The postmark indicated the letter had been mailed two weeks ago.

I replaced the letter, then picked up the bottle of pills and read the label. I recognized the prescription, a common antibiotic. The prescription was made out to Joycelle Johnson. It occurred to me that I hadn't known Joycelle's last name until that moment.

Outside, the light seemed harder. The asphalt looked very black. I could hear the wind and the rustling of the palms, a sound like that of the sea. Why had she lied earlier and said her parents were dead? Sand was in the air. It was something I felt beneath my shoes as I headed for the office.

Mr. and Mrs. Patel were both waiting for me. I laid the key to Joycelle's room on the counter and said: "All her things are there, just as you said. I didn't really find anything to suggest there's any problem. I'm sure everything's all right, that she's just gone away for a few days and she'll be coming back. But thank you for letting me have a look around."

"We cannot be keeping a room for a person who does not pay her bill," Mrs. Patel said shrilly. "This we are not in the business of doing."

"As I told your husband, I'll be happy to settle her account if you'll just tell me what she owes." I took out my wallet in anticipation of receiving her bill. But they both just stood there, staring at me, as if I owed them some further explanation, or as if they were preparing to deliver some unpleasant news.

Finally, Mr. Patel, looking quite uneasy, said, "My wife is thinking it would be better to simply remove the young ladies' things from the room and keep them in boxes for her until she returns, so we can let the room to someone else."

"This would be best," Mrs. Patel said. She stood stiffly behind the counter, her head raised so that her chin jutted out defiantly.

"She is thinking Miss Johnson is not the sort of person who belongs here at our establishment," Mr. Patel said meekly.

"We can hold her things here in the office. I will pack them up myself," Mrs. Patel added in an assertive tone.

The thought of Mrs. Patel packing up Joycelle's underwear, the marijuana and pipe, seemed something to avoid at all costs.

"It seems to me you don't really have so many customers that there's a shortage of rooms." I glanced out at the parking lot, where there were only three cars to be seen, one of them mine, one of the the Patels', and one belonging to a customer.

"Besides," I said, smiling at her, "I've offered to pay her bill. And if you refuse me, perhaps it would be better for me to take my business elsewhere. After all, I might be next."

Mr. Patel began wringing his hands. "Oh dear, this is not what I am wanting to happen. I have been telling my wife to mind her own business, and now she has made a muddle of things.

"I am in charge here!" he said suddenly, turning to his wife and growing stern with her. "I told you to stay out of it. And now look what you have done! You have offended Mrs. Patterson!"

Mrs. Patel drew herself up stiffly, straightening her back. She gave me an icy look and then flipped the end of her shawl over her shoulder, turned dramatically on her heels, and disappeared into the apartment, slamming the door behind her. Just before the door closed, I caught a glimpse of the old grandmother, peering out disapprovingly at me.

Mr. Patel looked ruefully at me. His head wiggled slightly from side to side, as if it were a ball suddenly set into gentle motion, loosely floating on his neck.

"Never mind my wife, Mrs. Patterson. I apologize for this misunderstanding."

"Perhaps I should be the one to apologize. I'm sorry to have caused any trouble."

"One has to stand up to this woman. Her mother is all the time putting ideas into her head. These women are not knowing how to run a business, I'm afraid. They behave as if we were still in India, living in a little village. Gossip, gossip, all the time it's gossip. This is how they try to rule, these women, from behind the scenes, by making trouble, by planting ideas in one's head."

"In any case, how much does Joycelle owe you?"

He produced a bill. It wasn't very much, considering it represented a month's lodging. The Patels gave weekly rates. It was a sum I could easily afford.

I counted out the money. "Again, I'm sorry for the trouble. I'm afraid your wife is quite put out with me now."

"She will get over it. By tomorrow she will be thinking up some new trouble!" Mr. Patel began chuckling, and I laughed with him. Again, his head wiggled fluidly, almost imperceptibly. There was something so carefree about that gesture, so dismissive of any trouble, that I left the office feeling somehow less worried.

The light is fading now, staining the sky yellow, casting a warm glow in the room. I sit in a chair near the window, nursing my first drink of the evening.

I feel very much the loneliness of this place tonight. It seems the most foreign, the most spent, the *saddest* spot on earth. A little while ago a car pulled into the parking lot, its radio playing so loud I could feel the bass reverberating in my chest. Then the car drove off, and the thumping faded, receding slowly. Yet I can still feel a ghostly pounding in my heart.

I stand up and go to the window and lean gently against the glass. Now I can see the Luxor far down the strip—the new hotel-casino, built in the shape of a pyramid; the sharp outline of a pure, colorless beam of light emerges from the top of the great black triangle, a cold, eerie light shooting far up into the darkening heavens above the city. Strange, but this sight—the perfect black pyramid and the perfect beam of white light emerging from its apex—never fails to move me: it's as if I am witnessing both the past and the future at once, and heaven and earth are connected. The effect is no doubt heightened by the fact that it's that rather extraordinary time of evening in Las Vegas when desert sky turns indigo, and the lights begin coming on, transforming the bleached-out desert city into the jeweled nocturnal oasis.

I leave the coolness of my room, and step out into the dry heat and the faint breeze, which feels sensuous tonight, lovely and gentle against my skin. I know before I even set out where I'm headed this evening.

Out on the Strip, the golden light of sunset is limning the blue. The sidewalks teem with tourists dressed in rumpled shorts and leisure outfits. I pass a fountain and smell the ionized air, an odor of heat and brackish water trapped in the fine mist descending on the plaster gods in front of Caesars Palace.

When I arrive at my destination, I find the same man standing at the door, with the same lascivious smile on his face.

"Table again tonight?" he says.

"Fine." I think of asking him right then and there about Joycelle, but instinct tells me he's not the one to ask.

The barmaid is topless and nearly bottomless as well and not all that anxious to take my order.

"What can I bring you?" she asks without looking at me.

"A scotch and water," I say, and then quickly add, as she starts to turn away, "and there's something else. I'm looking for someone, a friend named Joycelle Johnson. Is she working tonight?"

Now she does look at me, long and hard. I try to appear friendly, unthreatening. I keep my eyes locked on her face, ignoring her bare breasts, which are too large for the rest of her body, like false appendages that have been added on as an afterthought.

"Joycelle? You're a friend of hers?"

"Yes."

She seems to doubt this. She stares at me. I hold her gaze. Out of the corner of my eye I can see a woman entertaining a man at a nearby booth. She kneels on the banquette beside him, lifts her breasts in her hands, and brings them close to his face.

"Joycelle's not working tonight," the barmaid says finally.

"Was she here last night?"

"I wouldn't know."

"Who would know?" I say, not willing to give up.

"I try to mind my own business here," she says. "I don't get involved in disputes."

"Disputes?"

She looks around her, as if to make certain no one is within earshot, and then she says, "Listen, Joycelle got fired. That's all I know."

"Do you know where she is now?"

"I don't. But Cindy might. She's pretty good friends with her."

"Do you think I might talk to Cindy?"

"She's upstairs in the penthouse," she says. "But I could tell her you want to see her. Maybe when she gets a break, she can come down."

"Thanks. I'd appreciate it." I slip a five-dollar bill onto her tray, just to let her know I really do appreciate it, and she smiles at me, suddenly friendlier, as if I have just learned to speak the lingua franca.

Time passes, and no Cindy appears. But the barmaid brings my drink.

"By the way," I ask her, "what's the penthouse?"

She smiles and looks a little embarrassed, like a parent who's been asked how babies are born.

"Oh, you know—it's all private rooms up there. You pay a little extra and you can, you know, request things, dance with the girls, stuff like that."

"I see. I was just wondering if I should go up there rather than wait here—"

"I wouldn't go up there," she says. "You wouldn't feel, uh, very comfortable, I don't think." She offers this as friendly advice. She's on my side now, she's talking to me, one woman to another.

"I already told her you wanted to see her. Just wait here."

So I wait. I wait, and I watch, and I am fascinated, shamelessly so, by the scenes unfolding around me. It's as if I've lived in the world of women all my life and yet never understood there is another world of women, heretofore unseen by me, that intersects so baldly with the raw world of men. I manage to shrink and draw myself into an inconspicuous place. I catch things out of the corner of my eye. I see without appearing to see, and soon I begin to feel that I am in fact becoming almost invisible.

A girl is sitting with a man in a booth, holding her own breasts, offering them up with her own hands to him. She has him in her power. Clearly, he's longing to touch her, but maybe the rules here are *no* touching. Maybe everything *but* touching. He has paid for her company, but she's in control. She choreographs the moment. He tucks some money beneath the garter that encircles her thigh. The bills look like leaves clinging to the slender trunk of her leg. She straddles him now, but there's airspace between them. Her back is toward me. However, I can see his face. So rapt, so intense, so serious. This is serious business for him. For her it's a lark, nothing serious about it. She pushes her breasts close to his face, then backs off, stands up, moves around in front of him, dances a little. She gives him not what he wants but only what she's willing to concede. She's all action, he's totally passive. He looks. She moves. She bounces up on the banquette next to him again, swings a leg over his lap, so she's kneeling above him now, on top, but still not touching him. Then after a while I see her stand up and in one choreographed movement, as if she's done this many times before, she produces a towel from nowhere, like a magician, and discreetly hands it to him while shielding him from sight with her body. It all happens so fast that one can't be certain anything has happened, and yet I know it has, and I turn away, just in time to see a statuesque, beautiful black girl walking toward me.

"You looking for me?" she says.

"Cindy?"

"That's me," she says cheerfully.

"I'm really looking for Joycelle, but I understand she's not working here anymore. I thought you might know where she is."

"Why you looking for her?"

"Because I'm worried about her. She's a . . . friend. I'm staying at a motel out on the Strip, in the room next to hers. She hasn't been around for almost a week. The last time I saw her, she was pretty upset. I'd just like to make sure she's okay."

"She's okay." She folds her long arms in front of her, not so much to hide her nudity, it seems to me, but rather to solidify her air of casualness. There something loose and assured in her attitude, in the way she stands over me, looking down with the glance of someone self-confident and satisfied with herself.

"She didn't seem okay the last time I saw her."

"Well, it's been a pretty rough time. She hasn't felt well. And then getting fired. She hasn't gone back to the motel because she doesn't have the money to pay her bill."

"Where's she's staying?"

"I don't know if I'm supposed to tell anybody."

"You can trust me."

She laughs. "You wouldn't believe the number of people who say that and don't mean it."

"I mean it."

"But how am I supposed to know who you are? She never mentioned knowing anybody where she was staying, except those Indians who run the place. She's been trying to figure out how to get her stuff out of there without them seeing her."

"You can tell her that I paid her bill today."

"You paid her bill? What are you, like a fairy godmother or something?"

"Hardly."

"People don't let go of money unless they got a reason. So what's your reason?"

"Sometimes you don't always understand why you do things. Let's just say I want to help her."

I notice a little change in her attitude now. "I'm going to tell you this even though I probably shouldn't. Joycelle's been staying with me. She got real sick a couple of nights ago. Started running a high temperature. Had a lot of pain in her chest, trouble breathing. Yesterday she went to see the doctor and he put her in the hospital. She's got pneumonia."

"Which hospital?"

"The one out by the airport."

"Thanks for telling me. Do they know how long she might be there? Or how serious it is?"

"It isn't just pneumonia she's got."

"Yes. I know that. She told me."

"I don't know who you are, but if you can help her, she needs it. At this point she needs all the help she can get. She's been sick for quite a while. I gotta go now."

"Thanks again, Cindy."

"Sure. Like you say, we do things for all kinds of reasons. I got a feeling you're okay."

I head back to my room, and sit at the window in the incandescent moonlight. Of all I've witnessed this evening, nothing seems as harsh, as depraved, as cruel, as the thought of Joycelle lying in a hospital room alone.

It's impossible to sleep. At 1 A.M. I get up and sit down at the table I've fashioned into a desk for myself. A packet of old letters from Carlos is lying to one side. I'm drawn to them. I select one and begin reading:

> Dearest Lucy,
>
> I just received your letter. I am so happy you can meet me in Aspen next week, happier than I can possibly say. I've already booked our accommodations. I followed your advice and bought new ski poles (the right size) and shall hopefully get some new ski pants à la mode so as not to embarrass you by appearing too old-fashioned. The fur jacket I am also abandoning. I leave it to the younger generation like yourself. By the way, I read a book on Adolf Hitler and Eva Braun recently. One of the many interesting aspects is that members of the Braun family emigrated to Utah early in this century, to your hometown, I think. Do you know any Brauns there? Perhaps you yourself have some Bavarian red cells circulating in your arterial tree—

which would explain part of your toughness, high-strung temperament, etc. Fortunately, whatever other mixture there might be, superimposed upon these characteristics are a most attractive physique, a keen intelligence and sweetness (p.r.n.), and a special disposition to make out of you the most lovable, desirable and perfect individual on this earth—at least for me.

Te amo, Carlos

What did he mean about my sweetness (p.r.n.)? What did those initials stand for?

If I ever knew, I've now forgotten.

EIGHTEEN

There were no birds in the middle of the Atlantic, no visible signs of life as I looked out beyond the railing. What life there was lay beneath us, swimming in the dark sea, the hulking shapes of whales cruising through a perpetual darkness, the swift fishes in their scaly solitude—all unseen, all life cast deep within the ocean, creatures turning in watery beds while above them we churned our own friable wake, parting the surface of the water briefly and leaving behind nothing as the sea closed again over the evidence of our passage.

All morning the sea swung up lazily and let us down again, as if the events of the night had exhausted not only the passengers aboard the *Oceanus* but the ferocity of the storm that had tossed us about. We lay side by side on chaise lounges, on the lee side of the ship, where we were protected from the wind. Every once in a while the clouds parted briefly and sunlight flooded the deck, falling on our faces like a blessing.

Carlos was reading, his head bowed toward the book he held in his hands, his thin body covered by a plaid blanket drawn up to his chest. I was also reading, a book of Conrad's stories that I had taken out of the library earlier. Occasionally, I glanced up at him, quietly studying his face, and he, looking up briefly from a page, held my eyes for a moment. There was something at once familiar and strange about the experience of lying next to him this way, out on the deck of the ship, like a couple who had passed their years in intimacy and had long since established a quiet routine. After a while, I noticed he had fallen asleep, and I drew the blanket covering him up a little higher on his chest.

Earlier that morning we had parted after spending the long night together. We left each other after agreeing to meet again out on the deck at noon. I had returned to my cabin and showered and put on fresh clothes, after which I lay on my bed for a long while, thinking about what had transpired.

During the night he had held me and whispered endearments, comforting me as the storm raged outside. He had made love to me with great feeling, as if some deep desire had long been stored inside him, and I had opened to him completely, just as I had done in the past. Afterward, he had listened carefully as I revealed to him the details of Justin's disappearance and my own troubled journey to Guatemala in search of some trace of him. I had buried myself in the whiteness of his arms, and smelled the sandalwood scent of his skin as I poured out my feelings. Later I had fallen asleep again and then awakened abruptly, somewhat disoriented in unfamiliar surroundings, to find him still holding me in the semidarkness, studying my face as I emerged from sleep.

But with the coming of the first light, falling through the porthole in a softly rounded beam, a change had come over him. The brisk rather businesslike manner which he adopted as soon as I awoke seemed to erase, or at least mute, the passion that had passed between us during the long hours of the night.

There was a studied air in the way he got up and stood at the

mirror in his silk dressing gown, brushing his hair, then crossed to
the phone and ordered breakfast, speaking formally in a clipped
voice as he gave exact instructions regarding the preparation of
the eggs and toast—even how he wished the grapefruit sliced. I
couldn't help noticing how neatly his belongings had been arranged
in his cabin, and the air of luxury, of costliness, that clung to each
item—the silk dressing gown, the expensive leather slippers, the
monogrammed shirts and the custom-made tuxedo, even the set of
tortoiseshell brushes, and the matching leather suitcases which sat
in the corner of the room.

He appeared subdued during breakfast, which we ate in his
cabin. I began to feel uncomfortable with him. Did he perhaps regret our spending the night together? When I asked him if there
was anything wrong, if he was upset about anything, he became serious and furrowing his eyebrows, he said, "Wrong? What do you
mean? Of course there's nothing wrong," and with a precise, delicate movement tapped the top of a boiled egg with the tip of his
knife, carefully removing a segment of the shell before spooning
the first taste of yolk into his mouth.

When later I left him and made my way back to my cabin, I
began to feel a certain anxiety—the anxiety of not knowing
whether intimacy with him wasn't doomed to be more painful than
rewarding. We had been thrust together the night before by
chance. I couldn't help wondering how, or if, we would have found
ourselves in the same bed, making love again after all these years, if
the storm had not acted like a catalyst, literally tossing us together.

What I had felt for him when I was a young woman of twenty
was still present in some muted, preserved form, but it seemed to
me these emotions were accessible only in the way certain artifacts
in museums are accessible—as something appreciated, perceived,
but somehow lodged safely out of reach, like a painting guarded by
a golden cord and set behind protective glass.

An old bitterness still colored my feelings toward him. Or was
it simply fear? The fear of being seduced again by him, only to find
myself once more rejected.

Now he looked so peaceful, sleeping there beside me out on the deck of the ship, but I couldn't help notice once again how age had settled on his features. The sea breeze gently stirred his white hair while he slept, oblivious to my gaze. In spite of the many years that had passed without our seeing each other, I thought perhaps I knew more about this person than I knew about anyone else. My trust in him had once been so deep that I had revealed myself more fully to him than I had to any other human being, and I couldn't help thinking that this was also perhaps the case with him.

From the very beginning, when I had stood beside him after that first day of skiing at Magic Mountain, I had sensed his *otherness*, the almost magnetic quality of foreignness he exuded and which drew me to him like the silvery flakes of snow had been drawn to his fur jacket. As he stood beneath the circle of light cast by the streetlamp, I had felt his deep sensuality as something brilliant and yet somehow dangerous—as something *unrefusable*.

I remembered a story he once told me. He was living in Germany with his grandmother and mother, who was by then divorced from his father. He was fourteen years old. His mother was still a young woman, barely thirty, whose circle of friends included an upper-class coterie of well-bred men and women, some powerful generals and politicians, and a few bohemian writers and artists.

His mother had a friend, a stylish woman in her thirties, who had always had a particular affection for Carlos. One day, when this friend was visiting, his mother had gone out for some errands. While she was gone, this woman had seduced Carlos. It was his first sexual experience. He had been initiated by a woman more than twice his age, in his mother's own house, and by one of her closest friends.

When he spoke of the experience later, it was with a certain frankness and wistfulness. He had not been prepared for her advances. Initially, he had felt shy and awkward and uncertain. But his mother's friend was so skillful, so tender with him, that the experience had proved to be a perfect beginning to his erotic life. He told me had had liaisons with a few other older women among his mother's circle of friends. He had also experimented with boys at the school he attended. The sensuality I had recognized in him early on must have been present in him from the time he was very young.

When he first told me these stories, I hadn't felt any jealousy. On the contrary, I felt envious of him. My own sexual awakening was marred by guilt and the usual ignorance of teenagers, and complicated by the strictness of my religion. I could mark the moment when this innocence was lost.

I was perhaps fourteen—the same age Carlos had been when his mother's friend seduced him—when Bruce Larkin, one of the boarders who lived with us, first came into our household. He was a schoolteacher, a bachelor in his thirties, and that in itself was unusual in a town where most men were married at that age. There was a predatory air about him. I felt it in the way he sometimes tried to get me to sit on his lap, cajoling me, grabbing me suddenly and pressing me against him as if to begin an innocent game of wrestling. But it never felt innocent to me. I felt overpowered, intimidated, and fearful of him.

One Sunday morning he cornered me in the kitchen shortly after he had returned from a priesthood meeting. He said that he had heard things about me and he thought he should warn me about what the boys were saying. The moment he said this, panic began rising in me, commingled with the fear I always felt in his presence.

"I'd like to know what you've been doing up in the foothills with those boys," he said.

Cornered, his body looming over me, I stammered, "I haven't been doing anything."

"That's not what I heard," he said, leering at me. "I overheard some boys talking this morning before priesthood meeting. They were talking about you."

"What boys?"

He named a couple of boys my own age I rode horses with sometimes, one of whom was named Joel and whom I had begun to think of as my boyfriend. I had let him kiss me. Sometimes we went further and he laid on top of me and pressed himself against me until I felt his hardness rising. It had become a game with us, these little sexual forays, a game which brought pleasure and which somehow seemed indistinguishable from the other games we played, the races we often challenged each other to on horseback.

"They said you're playing dirty up there in the hills," Bruce Larkin said to me. "They said you let them do things other girls don't."

Shame burned in me and made me speechless. I was struck dumb by the phrase *playing dirty*. What had seemed harmless and mildly exciting now seemed terribly wrong.

"I ought to tell your parents," Bruce Larkin said. And then smiling down at me, as if he were some beneficent blond god granting me a temporary reprieve from damnation, he added, "but I won't. I won't tell them because I think I'll give you another chance. But you must tell me what you let the boys do to you. You must tell me everything."

I ran out of the kitchen, fleeing from him, and hid in the woods for the rest of that day, terrified of returning to the house, filled with shame and a sense of guilt. I didn't know whether he would tell my parents. I was angry at my friend Joel for what I imagined he had said for Bruce Larkin to overhear. I felt betrayed and black-mailed, and I began to feel that I hated men and I would always hate them.

When I finally returned in the evening, Bruce Larkin acted as if nothing were wrong. I could tell he hadn't told my parents anything. But for a long time I lived with the fear that he would. For a long time afterward he held me hostage. And I understood very clearly, for the first time in my life, what sort of terrible power another person could hold over you, and how swiftly sensual feelings could become the sullied realm of secrets.

I believe I married when I was so young in order to escape the repression of such a household. I thought I'd found a way out. Instead, I discovered what a dull and routine business sex could be, how it could result in a dryness of heart, how it could leave one feeling used and unfulfilled and yet incapable of naming the thing that was missing.

Carlos changed all this. I came to understand what infinite erotic possibilities existed in this world. It was as if some part of myself had been waiting to find its counterpart, waiting in a state of excruciating longing to be freed from the darkness that had begun to engulf me on that Sunday morning when Bruce Larkin had cornered me and twisted my unformed self into a state of shame and guilt and confusion.

With Carlos I had managed to release myself from this dark past. My erotic life began, that first night, in the Paul Bunyan Inn, in a bed stained with blood, and it continued, unfolding in new and wondrous ways as we pursued our desire over the months and years that followed, surviving even, in some muted form, the passage of time, all the years and events that had separated us for so long and then suddenly, without warning, brought us together again in the insular world of the *Oceanus*.

Wouldn't it be strange, I thought, if I were to fall in love with him again? If I were to fall in love with the same man, with the same utter abandon, twice in my life? It seemed at that moment, looking at him lying beside me, a thing quite eminently possible.

He opened his eyes suddenly, as if startled by something.

"My God, I fell asleep. A sign of my growing decrepitude. What time is it?"

"Almost one-thirty."

"Are you hungry? Shall we have lunch?" He extended his hand to me.

"I'm starving," I said. "And I'm also quite cold."

"Poor thing," he murmured, and drew me close and kissed me.

"'Poor thing' yourself," I murmured, and kissed him once more.

"Poor *old* thing, you mean."

"Oh yes, poor *old* thing."

I had hoped that we might eat alone, just the two of us at our own table, but when we arrived in the Queen's Room, the maître d' escorted us to a table where four people *were* already finishing their first course. The only person I recognized was Dr. Ramirez, who stood up as Carlos and I approached.

"Ah, Dr. Cabrera, there you are!" Dr. Ramirez said. "And you've brought someone. Excellent! I'll ask the waiter to bring us another place setting."

There was a brief moment of confusion as chairs were shifted and a place was made for me at the table. Then Carlos introduced me to everyone, beginning with an elderly woman named Dr. Hannah Ettinger, and then a robust, florid-faced man named Dr. Eric Lappin and his wife, Marie, all of whom, Carlos informed me, were traveling together in order to attend the same medical conference in England.

I had hoped to sit next to Carlos, but to my dismay, I found myself accommodated in a space between Dr. Lappin and Dr. Ettinger, with Carlos seated across the table from me.

"We were just discussing the storm last night," Dr. Ettinger said when we were all settled in our places. "The so-called *rogue* wave. I don't believe I've ever been more terrified in my life!"

"We were just getting ready for dinner when it hit," Marie Lappin said. "Eric was getting out of the shower. I was standing at the sink. The entire cabin tilted to one side, everything went dark, and the next thing I knew Eric and I were both thrown into the next room!" Her eyes grew wide in mock terror.

"I believe it was worse for Dr. Ramirez," her husband said. "You were trapped in the library, weren't you, Ricardo?"

"Perhaps not exactly trapped. They just couldn't get the door open for a while. I was lucky not to have been hit by any falling books."

"Imagine being crushed by the collected works of Conrad!"

"Or felled by *Moby Dick*!"

"What about you, Carlos? Where were you?"

"In the lounge."

"The lounge? How frightful," Dr. Ettinger said. "That's where some of the worst injuries occurred. I heard the piano broke loose and slid across the room."

"It did. It was quite terrifying."

"Someone could have been killed!"

"I think it's rather remarkable no one was."

"For once," Dr. Ettinger said, "I was glad to have a television to watch. I do not ordinarily watch TV," she said, turning toward me, "but I was most happy to have the distraction last night as I waited out that storm."

"Where were you when it happened, Lucy?" Dr. Ramirez asked.

"In the bar with Carlos."

"Ah. In the eye of the storm."

"Dr. Ramirez has praised your writing very highly," Dr. Lappin said. "He says we must all read your book *The Invention of Light*. And of course we trust his recommendation. Dr. Ramirez is the intellectual in our group."

"No, no," Dr. Ramirez protested. "I'm afraid that honor must go to Dr. Cabrera."

"Well, I would say that sheer *age* gives me an edge in these matters," Carlos said.

"I'm afraid you can't claim seniority on the basis of age. I believe I am the oldest member of this group," Dr. Ettinger insisted.

"The oldest, and undoubtedly the wisest," Carlos replied.

"No, no, no—"

"Ah, yes, yes, yes!"

"You'll have to get used to a certain level of verbal competitiveness if you choose to join our group, I'm afraid," Dr. Ettinger said, turning toward me. "Doctors can be the strangest company. We know so much about so little."

"Ah, please excuse me," Dr. Lappin said to the elderly Dr. Ettinger. "But what can you possibly mean by that comment?"

"I mean we have spent our lives delving into cells and tissue, opening arteries and examining poor diseased hearts, about which we have come to know very much indeed. But a certain absorption with our profession has perhaps excluded a fuller examination of life—that is to say, a familiarity with the world of literature, or music, for instance. Our profession consumes not only our time, but seemingly all the available imaginative space."

I was struck not only by what she said, but by the way in which she said it. And I felt instantly drawn to her.

"Ah, I see!" said Dr. Ramirez. "We're essentially learned dullards!"

"You have such a way with words, Ricardo," Dr. Ettinger said to Dr. Ramirez, again in that gentle tone of voice. "But let's not be reductive. I'm simply speaking a truth which I think you, of all people, fully recognize."

"What do you think, Lucy?" said Dr. Ramirez. "Are doctors dull?"

"I'm afraid my familiarity with doctors is rather limited." I cast a glance at Carlos as I said this, and he returned my look with a rather bemused smile on his face.

"You needn't be circumspect in this group," Dr. Ramirez said.

I laughed. "Actually, I was thinking of something as you were talking. One of the things that struck me about Dr. Cabrera—Carlos—when I first met him many years ago was his views on the education of doctors."

"My God," Carlos said, laughing and interrupting me. "This woman has an encyclopedic memory. Unfortunately, the mundane seems to get included as well as the more profound bits of learning she has managed to store away!"

"Let her finish," Dr. Ramirez exclaimed. "Go on. What were Dr. Cabrera's views on the education of doctors?"

I cast another glance at Carlos, who seemed amused, and interested in hearing me out, as if he, too, were curious.

"Carlos used to hold the view that his residents should be able to converse with familiarity about a wide variety of subjects. He said he often brought up political issues with them, and encouraged discussions about ethics, philosophy, literature. He felt that young doctors should be encouraged to view medicine as only a part of their education, to avoid becoming narrow human beings. Just as I remember him telling me how he stressed they should learn to eat with both the right and the left hand, and perform other tasks the same way, so as to become ambidextrous and thus become more skillful surgeons."

"Excellent!" Dr. Ettinger exclaimed. "That's precisely what I was talking about. Pity such views aren't promoted more vigorously today. But I suppose, in the era of ultraspecialization, things have moved in quite the opposite direction."

Marie Lappin, who, I couldn't help notice, was staring at me with rather bald curiosity, spoke up. "How long ago was this? I mean when you first met Dr. Cabrera?"

"Nineteen sixty-seven," I said.

"That of course accounts for a good deal," Dr. Lappin said. "We who are younger forget what a radical time that was, in many, many ways. If I remember correctly, you trained under Dr. Waggenstein at the University of Minnesota, didn't you?"

Carlos nodded. "Along with the others. Christiaan Barnard. Norm Shumway."

"Christiaan Barnard!" Marie Lappin said, rolling her eyes. "What a playboy he turned out to be."

"On the contrary," Carlos said, turning serious. "He was a very good surgeon, an excellent surgeon with a first-rate mind, who could also, by the way, write rather well. It was his books as much as anything else that brought him recognition—well deserved, to my way of thinking."

"I just meant he became such a celebrity, you know, hobnobbing with all the beautiful people." As she spoke, she flicked her blood-red nails in front of her, as if showing off her impeccable manicure.

"There's no question he became a celebrity," Dr. Ramirez said.

"But it was an era when heart surgery itself was very glamorous. Now it's become rather commonplace, I'm afraid."

There was a slight lull in the conversation as the waiters arrived with the main course and distributed the plates among us. I couldn't help noticing the murals on the wall, the images of nymphs and satyrs frolicking in pastoral scenes.

It was at that moment, as I was looking around the room, taking in the rather genteel atmosphere, that Marie Lappin spoke up and asked a question of me.

"How *did* you and Dr. Cabrera meet?"

"We met in Minnesota where I had taken my son for open-heart surgery."

"Your son had a heart defect?"

"Yes. Dr. Cabrera operated on my son."

Dr. Ettinger exclaimed, "How very interesting! What sort of defect did your son have?"

"He was born with a transposition of the great arteries."

"A transposition!" said Dr. Ramirez. "A very complex problem, I would think, in those days. I don't believe anyone had even begun to attempt to deal with transpositions much before 1960. However, I assume the surgery was successful?"

"Yes, it was."

"You were very lucky to have had Dr. Cabrera as the surgeon!"

"Very lucky," I said, gazily levelly at Carlos, who had grown quiet.

Dr. Ettinger said, "I assume the corrective operation was a Mustard procedure?"

"Yes," I said.

"And did your son have a Blalock-Hanlon procedure as a palliative measure before the Mustard?" she inquired, showing a very real and concentrated interest in the subject.

"Yes," I said. "That was performed in Utah, where my son was born, when he was just three weeks old. He was two-and-a-half when Carlos performed the second operation." I kept thinking these technical questions were really Carlos's provenance, not mine.

But he showed no inclination to interrupt. Instead, he methodically, and very quietly, continued to dissect the fish on his plate into tiny portions, which he then guided, with great precision, onto his fork with his knife and lifted to his mouth.

"We're talking about the dark ages of heart surgery!" Dr. Lappin exclaimed.

"Really, Eric," Dr. Ettinger said, frowning. "You make Dr. Cabrera and myself—pioneers of such surgeries, if I may say so without sounding too immodest—sound like we're dinosaurs."

Carlos looked up and said drolly, "I may appear to be as extinct as a dinosaur, but I myself prefer Dr. Ettinger's view of things. *Pioneer* is a much kinder word, and it describes precisely what we were about in those days."

"Of course!" Dr. Ramirez said. "I think Eric was paying you a compliment, weren't you, Eric?"

"It's true. I can't imagine the difficulty of dealing with such complex problems using such primitive procedures."

"Primitivism is a relative concept," Carlos said. "In those days, I assure you, the Blalock-Hanlon wasn't primitive. Nor was the Mustard. They were the most radical methods imaginable."

"The interesting thing to me," Dr. Ettinger said, "is that we managed to be successful in as many cases as we were, given the newness of the surgical techniques available to us. But I'm curious, Lucy. How is your son now? Is he able to lead a relatively normal life?"

Looking steadily at Dr. Ettinger, hoping to gain courage from the kindness so evident in her face, I said: "My son lead a very normal life until the time of his death. He died several years ago, in Guatemala, not from any medical complications with his heart, but because he was in the wrong place at the wrong time. He was part of a religious group. The house where he was staying was bombed and although his body was never found, it's now presumed he was also killed."

For a moment no one said anything. Dr. Ettinger's face underwent the subtlest, and yet most profound change as she returned my look. I saw there such understanding, such deep sympathy, it seemed as if she could communicate a perfect understanding of my loss without so much as moving her lips.

"That's just *awful*," Marie Lappin said—a little too loudly, and too suddenly, as if she felt compelled to break the silence and relieve the shocked atmosphere at the table. "Poor thing."

Her husband added, "Terrible."

I felt I needed to say something, to steer things away from the obvious need each person at the table must feel to offer further condolences.

"Yes, it was terrible, most of all a terrible waste of a life that had been so hard-won. Justin—my son—had grown into such a strong young man from such a troubled and difficult beginning to his life. For that I have to thank Carlos, of course, for giving him as many years as he had."

"But if they never found his body, maybe he's still alive," Marie said. "I mean, it's possible, isn't it—?"

"I wish it were. In Guatemala the disappeared don't return." I sighed, and tried to smile, though my face felt stiff.

I looked at Carlos, who was watching me very closely, one hand supporting his chin, his elbow resting on the table. His eyes were slightly hooded, as if he had retreated into some very private sphere.

"Do you remember, Carlos, how we didn't think he would be able to ever be active? How it was then thought that children with transpositions—even after surgery—would never be able to engage in any sports, would have to lead a sedentary life?"

"That was the prevailing view."

"At the time, someone said that the most Justin could expect was to perhaps be able to do a little ballroom dancing. And I believed it at the time! It seemed so strange—a little ballroom dancing! But as he got older, I could see him growing stronger, and I felt I shouldn't tell him what he could or couldn't do. I didn't want to limit him. I decided to simply let Justin decide what he could and couldn't do. Of course, I watched him very carefully. But he seemed so active, so strong, and soon he began doing all sorts of things—riding a bike, then skiing, hiking, playing tennis, all things we did together. And after a while I forgot he had any physical limitations. And so did he. He grew up like a normal little boy. There was nothing to indicate he shouldn't. It was a relief to both of us, to be able to go on, to forget the past. And that's what we did."

Dr. Ettinger reached across the table and placed a hand on my arm. "I'm so sorry you lost your son. So very sorry."

The meal had ended, and somehow Dr. Ettinger's words released us all from the necessity of continuing the conversation. It remained only for someone to make the first move toward departure to wind up our little luncheon.

"You're reading tonight, aren't you?" Dr. Ramirez said.

"Yes."

"Splendid," he said. "I look forward to it very much."

Dr. Lappin and his wife both murmured that they, too, would be there at my reading.

Dr. Ettinger said: "Then we'll all attend, with great pleasure. And perhaps afterward you'll do us the honor of joining us here for dinner? That is, if Dr. Cabrera has no objection to sharing you with us again."

"Do I have a choice?" he said.

"No!" everyone answered in chorus, laughing.

"Ah! Just as I thought. Once again I'm being ruled by committee, even here in the middle of the ocean. Apparently, there's no escaping these things."

"Apparently not," I said. "I'll be happy to see you all later." I stood up to leave.

Carlos rose and came to my side and, holding my elbow gently, steered me passed the nymphs and satyrs looking down at us from the walls, until we were at last clear of the room.

Once in the hallway, I glanced at my watch. I was expected in the captain's cabin for drinks before my reading. And already I was feeling very tired.

"Shall we go back to my cabin?" he asked.

"I'm afraid I have to leave you," I said. "I've agreed to meet a few people, and then I need to prepare for my reading."

"When will I see you?"

"I don't suppose before tonight."

He leaned down and kissed me lightly, and I murmured "Goodbye," and then I turned and walked away from him, wishing very much at that moment that we did not have to part.

NINETEEN

The Tally Ho is unnaturally quiet this morning.

On the table before me is a hand-drawn map—not of any country one would recognize—but a map of an imaginary world called Treewaken. Elevations have been noted in concentric, wavery circles; mountains, rivers, and plains are named and shaded in contrasting colors, and distance is indicated by a graph coverting miles to inches.

In the bottom right-hand corner, the mapmaker has carefully printed his name: JUSTIN MARK PATTERSON.

As a child, he would look for hours at maps of South America, or Africa, and lose himself in imaginary travels. He would put his finger on a place and say, "When I grow up, I'll go there." The South Pole, I remember, was one of those places. And if I said to him, "It's very cold there at the South Pole, Justin," he would draw back and look at me with unnatural solemnity and say, "I know *that*, Mother," as if he were trying to say his knowledge of the world already far outdistanced mine.

He used to quiz me on the names of state capitals. Or he'd challenge me to name the longest river in the world, the highest mountain, the desert with the least rainfall. Geography became his passion. He committed the world piece by piece, continent by continent, to memory. He was drawn to extremes by his fascination with globes and atlases, road maps, seafaring charts, maps of the heavens, maps drawn by early explorers—any sort of map. Soon he seemed to exhaust the possibilities of the real world, and he began creating his own maps of imaginary countries with names like Treewaken, Balderland, Sing-Soo, and Offmore.

I wonder now if he wasn't simply trying to create worlds with a greater sense of order than he found in the one I offered him. Looking at his little kingdom of Treewaken, the only map of his I have managed to save, I can't help thinking that even then, at the age of eleven, he was somehow trying to escape the limitations of the world in which he found himself.

In the years since his disappearance, I have tried to visualize what might have become of him. I've imagined things I've never wanted to imagine, had visions of unspeakable horrors. Much worse than my recurring nightmare of him calling out to me for help, and being unable to either locate him, or to reach him. I imagine the faces of the people who took him, faces heavy with menace —soldiers, guerrillas, ordinary peasants—figures with an immunity to violence written on their features. I try to imagine what they might have done with him. More often, I try not to.

I cannot think of him now without seeing that country in which he disappeared, a land so lush, so green, so fertile. And so twisted by an omnipresent terror, a constant fear which seemed to lurk everywhere, even in the eyes of the soldiers who stopped me not once, but several times during the weeks I spent in Guatemala. Each time they demanded to see my passport. Each time they looked me over carefully, as if to read my hostile thoughts. Or reduce me to an object for their eyes. So often these soldiers were only boys themselves—boys who had been taught to handle their weapons as menacingly as their superiors, and make the same sort of threatening remarks.

I kept running into Mormon missionaries who were there—just like Justin was—trying to convert people to a religion that believes it has something to offer, a means of saving their souls, and giving them a firmer grasp on some notion of goodness.

I'd be walking down the street in a little village that was so poor the children were shoeless and sick and had hair the color of carrots from malnutrition—villages ravaged by disease and war and death and poverty—where men sat drinking some clouded liquid from filthy recycled Jim Beam bottles, drinking until they appeared senseless and dazed, and the women seemed sad and broken by their harsh lives—and I'd look up to see two blond young men walking down the street toward me, wearing white shirts and ties with little name tags pinned to their pockets identifying them as representatives of LA IGLESIA DE JESUCRISTO DE LOS SANTOS DE LOS ULTIMOS DIAS. Of course, I knew who they were even before they got close enough to read the name tags. They stood out among those poor, dark-skinned villagers like aliens dropped down from another world. And of course I was also looking for them. I wanted to find someone who might have known my son, who might even have been his companion for a while. But soon I didn't even have to look.

I came upon them everywhere—these boys—in Panajachel, in Cobén, in Quiché. One day, in Guatemala City, I passed eight Mormon missionaries on the street in one afternoon. I seemed drawn to them, or they to me, and of course I would always stop and speak to them. Sometimes I confessed to being Justin's mother. Other times I did not.

In Chichicastenango, I met two boys one day, an Elder Romney, and his companion, Elder Waters. Elder Romney was a farm boy from Utah; Elder Waters came from a small town in Idaho. They looked so dispirited, so out of place with their cropped blond hair, their blue eyes and white shirts and dark ties, wandering among the villagers—the children with distended stomachs, the thin, dark men, the barefoot and pregnant women, all clothed brilliantly in contrast to the sterile outfits of the Mormon boys. They were happy to talk to me. I could see they were lonely. I could tell how difficult it was for them in this country. They had been in the village only a short while, they said, and hadn't had much success in making converts. They rented a room from a family of converts. They had no superiors nearby. Their Spanish was limited, and sometimes, they said, they talked for an hour to a prospective convert before realizing their listener spoke only an Indian dialect and hadn't understood a word they'd said.

I invited Elder Romney and Elder Waters to a restaurant and bought them a soda. They instantly opened up to me. They spoke to me as if I was the first person who'd understood their language in a long time. They said American tourists were sometimes unkind to them, berating them for being in a country where they didn't belong. "Why don't you go home?" one woman had recently said to them as they strode through a marketplace. "Why don't you leave these people alone?"

They said that when they'd first arrived in this village, the Army had been conducting a campaign against the rebels. One day the water supply had been cut off. No one could figure out what had happened until someone checked the village well and found a number of mutilated bodies. The bodies had clogged the pipes, cutting off the water. The bodies were removed, but for days, Elder Waters said, bits of flesh had turned up in the drinking water.

"These people—they are like Lamanites, the dark-skinned people described in the Book of Mormon," Elder Romney said. "In fact, they are the direct descendants of the Lamanites. They have no respect for life anymore. They have fallen into darkness, just like the ancient tribes." He took the Book of Mormon out of a backpack he carried and began to read to me a passage concerning the atrocities committed by the Lamanites against the tribe of Israelites—the light-skinned Nephites—as recounted by the prophet Mormon to his son, Moroni:

"My beloved son, I write unto you again that ye may

know that I am yet alive; but I write somewhat of that which is grievous. For behold, I have had a sore battle with the Lamanites, in which we did not conquer and we have lost a great number of our choice men. And now behold, my son, I fear lest the Lamanites shall destroy our people; for they do not repent, and Satan stirreth them up continually to anger one with another.

Behold, I am laboring with them continually; and when I speak the word of God with sharpness they tremble and anger against me; I fear lest the Spirit of the Lord hath ceased striving with them. It seemeth me that they have no fear of death; and they have lost their love, one towards another; and they thirst after blood and revenge continually.

The Lamanites have many prisoners, which they took from the tower of Sherrizah; and there were men, women, and children. And the husbands and fathers of those women and children they have slain; and they feed the women upon the flesh of their husbands, and the children upon the flesh of their fathers; and no water, save a little, do they give unto them. Many of the daughters have they taken prisoners; and after depriving them of that which was most dear and precious above all things, which is chastity and virtue—and after they had done this thing, they did murder them in a most cruel manner, torturing their bodies even unto death; and after they have done this, they devour their flesh like unto wild beasts, because of the hardness of their hearts. O my beloved son, how can a people like this, that are without civilization, whose delight is in so much abomination—how can we expect that God will stay his hand in judgment?"

Elder Romney closed the Book of Mormon, leaving his hand resting on its cover, and said, "That's how it is now. Just as it was then. These people are without conscience. They no longer know right from wrong."

I looked at him, thinking, This is where my son spent the last months of his life, in this brutal, sad, country, among boys like this boy who really believes he is here to save souls from such abomination and darkness.

I asked myself: How could I have let him come to such a place? What could I have done to stop him? But I knew it was pointless to think this way. He *believed* in it all. He felt he had a calling. He was driven by his faith to spread the Word. Like Elder Romney and Elder Waters. He was convinced he was doing the Lord's work, as he said in his last letter to me:

> The people here are more humble than I could have imagined. They are ready to accept the gospel, and with it, the joy it can bring into their lives, as well as hope. I sometimes feel sorry for them, they have so little in the way of worldly goods. I see them walking everywhere—always walking, sometimes miles everyday just to get from their little *aldeas* in the mountains to the towns where they sell their crafts—and I realize that never in their whole lives will they own a car, or even a horse or mule, and I wonder how can anyone accept such a meager existence? But then I see how rich they are in spirit, how ready they are to accept the Lord and serve Him, and then I wonder how I ever could have thought them poor.

"The church is growing rapidly in these countries," Elder Romney said. "Almost a third of our new members worldwide come from Latin America."

Elder Waters spoke up and said to me, "We're the new religion for these people. We're what the Catholics were to them four hundred years ago."

I wanted to say to him, Don't you think those Catholics have done enough damage to last at least another millennium without adding fresh confusion? Don't you think it's time for the New World spiritual inquisition to end? But I didn't say anything. I saw no point in offending them. I looked into their blue eyes, and I felt nothing but sympathy for them, and a deep, deep sadness.

Before I parted from them, I asked them the question I had been waiting to ask them. Without letting on that I was Justin's mother, I inquired if they had known Elder Patterson, the boy who had disappeared after the bombing. Of course, they know of him, but it turned out that neither of them had ever met my son. They arrived after the bombing. But they had heard certain things. They knew, for instance, that his problem with flat feet had confined him to a desk job at mission headquarters for a while. They knew he had broken the rules by setting off alone that day without his companion. Missionaries were never to go out alone but only travel in pairs, like creatures of the Ark. No one knew why he'd gone off alone, or where he'd been that day, only that he wasn't in the house when the bomb went off but must have been nearby, since his shoes had been found, and the bicycle which he used to travel from village to village. They knew that the village where he'd been transferred was one of the most dangerous areas of the country. They knew he had converted a few people before he died, and that because of these converts, the glory of God would be upon his head forever.

"That's what they said to me: *"The glory of God will be upon his head forever."*

As we prepared to leave the little restaurant where we'd been sitting for over an hour, sipping warm sodas and swatting flies away from our faces, Elder Romney tried to give me a Book of Mormon. He reached into his knapsack and took out the book and thrust it toward me with both hands, saying, "Take this book, I want to give it to you, it's free."

I stared at it for a moment—and briefly considered taking it, just to please him. It was a small blue paperback. A picture of a golden angel blowing a long golden trumpet adorned the cover. Pointing to the figure on the cover, he said, "That's the Angel Moroni, who appeared in a vision to a young farm boy named Joseph Smith, in 1820 in upstate New York, and told him to go to a place called the Hill Cumorah. He dug a hole and discovered the golden plates that he translated into the Book of Mormon."

He didn't know, of course, that this was a very old story to me—perhaps the oldest story of my life, one I'd been told since language first became a part of my being—the most powerful myth, one might say, of my early consciousness. And what a story it had been. Full of secrets and mystery, magic, and buried treasure: the boy, the angel, and the golden plates lying like a pirate's booty in the bottom of a hole.

He did not understand that I'd been raised in the church—I had intentionally neglected to mention this—and of course I knew that he felt compelled now to try and convert me before we parted, for this was his job, his raison d'être, the thing for which he had been carefully trained. He said if I would read the book and pray about it, the truth of its message would be revealed to me. He said it truly was a record of the ancient people who had once lived here in this land—a wicked people who had eventually destroyed the Nephites—who were a white and delightsome people.

"White and delightsome?" I said, trying not to sound too incredulous.

"Yes," he answered. "But no one is beyond redemption," he added, and I could not help feeling he was speaking quite directly to me.

"That's why we're here," Elder Waters said. "We want to restore the truth of the gospel of Jesus Christ to these people." He said that when he gave the Book of Mormon to the Mayan Indians, he told them, "This is a letter from your grandfather; read it carefully."

"Please, take this book," Elder Romney said to me again, extending it further toward me. "It holds the keys to your happiness."

I thanked him for the offer of the book, but said I had no wish to read it.

I left them, feeling I had come as close as I ever would to understanding what had happened to my son. Not why he had disappeared, but why he had been there in that country in the first place.

They were so young, so far from home. They seemed to take some disproportionate pleasure from the fact that I'd listened to their stories, spoken their language, treated them to an hour's conversation over a sickly sweet drink in a dismal restaurant, as if for a brief while their immutable loneliness had been lifted from them. I felt some kindness had passed between us. I wanted to believe someone might have shown a similar kindness to my son.

We walked out into the street together. The light was falling. Villagers were packing up their goods, closing up the little stalls in the marketplace, wrapping up their wares in brightly colored blankets, creating impossibly large bundles which they hoisted upon their backs and carried away, bent over beneath their burdens. I shook their hands—Elder Romney and Elder Waters—and wished them well. I cannot deny—not then, and not now—that I felt some deep connection to them, this sense of being *of the same tribe*, and that at that moment my son and I were also once again united, drawn into the shadow of the circle into which he had stepped and from which, I realized, I would never fully escape.

TWENTY

When I arrived at the place where I had been instructed to wait for Gil Rawlins, who was to escort me to the captain's cabin, I found an empty room. Apparently, I had arrived too late, and everyone had gone on without me. In a sense, I was relieved. I would much rather spend the afternoon with Carlos. I was about to head back to my own cabin and call him, when Gil Rawlins burst through a door.

"There you are!" he said. "We'd about given up on you. You're just in time to join us for the tour of the bridge before drinks in the captain's quarters. Come along and I'll show you the way."

He guided me up a narrow stairway, to a door marked ENTRY PROHIBITED! PERSONNEL ONLY. The door had an airtight seal. As it closed behind us, I was aware of a sucking sound and the tremendous force with which the door snapped shut. We climbed another stairway, and another—narrow passageways barely wide enough for a human to pass—until at last I found myself standing in a large room filled with instruments on the uppermost level of the *Oceanus*—the bridge from which the ship was piloted.

The captain was a large, beak-nosed Englishman who towered over everyone and wore a crisp blue suit, trimmed in gold braid, and a matching cap—an altogether imposing figure who stooped slightly, as if to diminish his extraordinary height. Various officers were attending to the ship's controls, while the captain was busy explaining different instruments to a small audience composed of two couples. I instantly recognized one of the men as the German who had spoken to Carlos in the bar the night before.

Gil Rawlins interrupted the captain briefly in order to introduce me to everyone.

"Lucy Patterson, our guest writer, this is Mr. and Mrs. Josef Himmelfarb from Germany, and Mr. and Mrs. Ralph Bevins from Australia. Mr. Bevins you may recognize as the internationally renowned stage actor. Herr Himmelfarb and his wife, who are making their tenth crossing with us, are the owners of the publishing house Verlag Himmelfarb. And this of course is Captain Ross Jacobs."

Josef Himmelfarb fixed his eyes on me with a particular intensity. When I shook his hand, he said, "Aren't you the person I saw sitting with Carlos Cabrera in the bar last evening?"

I said that I was, and I saw a look cross his face, a look that was somehow disturbing, as if he were peering deep into my face in an attempt to assess my character. But we were immediately distracted by the captain, who drew our attention to the view from the bridge.

We were suspended high above the ocean in a cubicle surrounded with glass, overlooking a homogeneous watery world where light was the only distinctive feature. It was a world quite perfect in its sameness. In a fine straight line of a horizon extending a full three-hundred and sixty degrees, the sky met the sea, creating a full circle which seemed to drop off slightly in a gentle curve, revealing a slight roundness of the planet, with the ship placed exactly in the middle. I had never had such a sense before of being precisely in the center of the world. The ship's wake, stretching away in a lacy path of whiteness, was the only clue suggesting we were part of a moving entity. Otherwise, it seemed the *Oceanus* was a stationary behemoth, suspended above, and not on, the water.

We made our way to the captain's cabin, where drinks were served by white-coated Filipino boys who stood rigidly at attention, lurking in the background, occasionally stepping forward to refill a glass or pass a bowl of nuts with white-gloved hands.

The cabin itself was rather ordinary, an anteroom lined with wood and decorated with maps and charts, brass lamps, and various nautical instruments. The captain sat in a chair, facing his guests, who sat on leather sofas placed opposite each other. The talk centered on the storm the night before, which had, the captain said, caught everyone by surprise.

"A very freak event—that sort of rogue wave," he said. "It came from the aft. We had no warning, I'm afraid. A most unfortunate thing."

"The injuries seem to have been minimal," Herr Himmelfarb said.

"It could have been much worse, of course," replied the captain. "We treated a number of broken limbs, a few minor concussions, but nothing more serious, thank God."

"It scared the devil out of me," Ralph Bevins said. "I said to my wife, 'I think I'll take my chances on a bloody plane next time.'"

"One must never underestimate the power of the sea," the captain replied. "Even in the age of supertankers and computerized guidance systems, the sea is still the sea, formidable and unpredictable. And I'm afraid we're in for some more weather tonight."

"What interests me," I said, "is how few people choose to travel by boat anymore. I suppose people just don't have the time. Or they think they don't. But it wasn't so long ago that it was the only way to cross the ocean."

"Correct," said Captain Ross. "Commercial transatlantic flights really didn't get going until the nineteen-fifties. In less than forty years the patterns of travel have changed completely. Airplanes have made sea travel practically obsolete. What's strange is we somehow forget this—that flying, I mean, is so very new. To most

215

people flying now seems rather boring. In a way I think sea travel never was."

"You've got the cruise ships now, don't you? Sort of like Las Vegas at sea, eh?" said Ralph Bevins. "*Fun* cruises. No one really intends to get from point A to point B on those things, do they? The whole idea is to have a floating party for a few days."

"I wouldn't be too critical of the cruise ships," the captain said. "I'm afraid without them most shipping companies would be out of business. And most people would have no opportunity at all to experience an ocean voyage."

"There's a certain tranquility to be found at sea, a sense of timelessness," Herr Himmelfarb said in his thickly accented English. "That is, unless one encounters some reminder of the past to throw everything into turmoil." He looked directly at me as he said this. "However," he added, changing his tone, "I have lived long enough to know that time is an elusive thing, and history, though dead to some people, is a living subject for others."

Captain Ross said, "One thing is certain and that is that everything is constantly changing. Still, as long as ships sail the seas, I'll be a part of this world. I can't think of any occupation for which I would be fit other than piloting a ship."

The conversation shifted then to how the captain had begun his career at sea. As I listened to his stories of his early adventures, first as a boy working on his father's trawler in the North Sea, later about his commission in the Royal Navy, I wondered why we had been invited for this strange little occasion. Clearly, we had each been included because we were celebrities of sorts—a writer, a publishing magnate, an actor—and this was a way of honoring our presence on board. But it was an odd group to have thrown together.

It wasn't long before the captain thanked us all for joining him, and brought our brief little cocktail party to an end. Although I had consumed only one drink, it was a stiff one, and as Gil Rawlins ushered us from the cabin, I realized I felt pleasantly light-headed.

"We're all looking forward to your reading tonight," Gil said.

Herr Himmelfarb, who had been walking a few steps ahead of me, stopped so abruptly I almost bumped into him.

"You're giving a reading this evening?"

"Yes," I said.

"I assume Dr. Cabrera will be there, too?"

"I imagine he will."

"Has Dr. Cabrera had a chance to mention anything to you following our conversation last night?"

"No, he hasn't."

"I didn't think so. He pretends not to remember me or my brother. I would advise you, if you really are his friend, to tell him I intend to refresh his memory before this voyage is over. If he wishes to discuss the matter with me in private, I'd be willing to do so. If not, assure him that I will choose the right moment to expose him publicly."

With that he turned and walked way from us, leaving his rotund wife to trail off a few steps behind him. I was left standing with the Bevinses and Gil Rawlins, all of us staring after him in confusion.

"Funny bloke," Ralph Bevins said.

"Who's Dr. Cabrera?" his wife asked, although before I could answer, Gil said, "What was that about?"

"I'm afraid I don't know. I don't know anything about him, do you?"

"Only that he's a very powerful man in his field, a very wealthy businessman. He's an old friend of the captain's. I think I remember the captain telling me that Herr Himmelfarb is a survivor of the death camps. I can't be sure about that. But I do think he mentioned it to me once in passing."

"It's quite understandable how such an experience could leave you unbalanced," Ralph Bevins said.

"But who *is* Dr. Cabrera?" his wife asked again.

"Just a friend of mine."

"In any case, I must leave you now," Gil Rawlins said, clapping his hands together lightly, and then looking at his watch. "Bingo's about to begin in the Grand Lounge and I'm afraid it falls to me to pick the numbers this afternoon."

We said goodbye to him just outside the casino.

"What sort of books do you write?" Ralph Bevins asked as we strolled together between the slot machines.

"Novels," I said. "Short stories."

"And what will you read from tonight?"

"I usually wait until the last minute to decide."

"Funny, but I imagine you could read anything aboard this ship and no one would know the difference. I mean, it's not the most sophisticated audience, is it? I've been struck these last few days by what I've noticed people reading. Sydney Sheldon, Danielle Steele—romances, thrillers—that's all I see in people's hands! Whatever happened to the great books? No one reads dead authors anymore, just the latest best-sellers. I dare say you could choose any great author, purloin his work, read from it tonight, and no one would know the difference!"

He chortled at his own preposterous idea. I, on the other hand, grew very still and rather serious. What if I were to read a passage from Conrad tonight? Would anyone recognize it?

"Will you join us in the bar for another drink?" he said.

"Thank you , but I think I've had enough. One more drink, and I might not be up to a reading tonight."

I parted from the Bevinses, who assured me they would see me later at my reading.

Immediately, I went to Carlos's cabin, but there was no answer when I knocked at the door. I searched the bars, the restaurants, the lounge and library. In the library I ran into Constance Milward.

"Where have you been hiding?" she said. "We missed you at breakfast, *and* at lunch today."

"Sorry. I should have sent word to you. I ran into an old friend and I've been having my meals with him."

She raised her eyebrows. "An old friend? I hope he's not too old to still have fun with."

I laughed. "Fortunately not."

"Wasn't the storm horrible last night?"

"Terrifying," I agreed. "I thought it was the end."

"Can you have a drink with me? I was just headed for the bar—"

"I've love to, but I really can't. I'm reading tonight and I need to spend a little time preparing."

"It's tonight, is it? We'll be there—all three of us. Wouldn't miss it."

"Good, see you then."

I walked the decks, all three levels, thinking perhaps Carlos had fallen asleep again on one of the chaise lounges. But there were very few people on deck, it was far too cold, and he was not among them. The sky was growing dark. A wind had come up and once again the sea was churning, stirred by the oncoming storm.

I checked the movie theater, then returned to his cabin again and knocked, but there was no answer: it seemed he had simply disappeared. Not even Dr. Ramirez, whom I telephoned in his cabin, had seen him. I felt totally perplexed at not being able to locate him. Finally, I gave up and took a short nap in my cabin before showering and dressing and getting ready for my reading.

When I arrived at the ship's theater, just before six, I noticed Dr. Ettinger and Eric Lappin and his wife Marie, sitting near the front of the room with Dr. Ramirez. The Bevinses were visible a few rows behind them. I recognized several of the gentlemen hosts, as well as a number of the ladies I had observed who were "traveling solo." As I stood to one side, chatting with Gil Rawlins, I saw the captain arrive in the company of Herr Himmelfarb and his portly wife. The Milwards entered shortly afterward and came over and said hello before taking their seats. Other people, whose faces were familiar to me, having glimpsed them in passing over the past few days, entered the theater and settled themselves, until almost every seat was taken. Still, one person was missing.

I kept looking for Carlos, who was nowhere to be seen, and a certain anxiety began growing in me that something had happened to him. Perhaps he wasn't coming, but what would prevent him from doing so?

I continued to feel a sense of urgency, the need to tell him about Herr Himmelfarb's threat to "expose him publicly," to at least tell him about our weird conversation. Finally, I saw Carlos enter the room, and pausing only briefly to catch my eye and smile at me, he took one of the few remaining seats, near the rear of the theater.

At that moment Gil Rawlins stepped up to the microphone and began introducing me.

Facing the audience, I said that what I was about to read was a story I had written some years back called "A Desert of Pure Feeling." In a voice that seemed slightly shaky to me. I went on: "The title refers to the sense of purity—a feeling of almost exquisite clarity and separateness that an individual often feels at the moments of most profound emotion. I've always been interested in beginnings, how things start with a minimum of cognizance on our part, and how they can end when we are the least prepared, or least wish them to. The beginning of perception often comes with loss, or absence—with a kind of subtraction of the known. Such a sense of loss precipitates a purer perception. The piece I am about to read is from the opening of the story."

I cleared my throat, took a sip of water from the glass sitting on the podium, and I began to read:

"For some time the road had been deserted, a muddy and rutted expanse of potholes stretching before him under a leaden sky. The rain had ceased, but every once in a while he felt a wayward drop fall out of nowhere, striking him on the face with a faint splash. His shirt, which earlier had become soaked in the downpour, clung to his skin like a transparent rind, a film of whiteness through which his skin showed like a pink stain.

"He guided the bicycle to the edge of the road and braked to a stop. Setting his feet down in the mud, he reached up and loosened his tied and rested. All around him the trees rose green and steaming. From the depths of tangled vines came the sound of birds, a cawing and cracked noise richocheting through the trees.

"He was thinking of the distance he still had to go, and of the pain in his feet. His flat feet had been a problem for him from the moment he had arrived in this country. In the basket attached to the front of his bike was a brown knapsack, made of leather and cracked at the corners. He undid the buckle that held it closed and took out a piece of paper on which a list of things had been written in a thick script. As he drew the paper out, something else fell and landed in the mud at his feet. It was a little lamb, cut out of felt, and pasted to a stiff backing. He wiped it off on his trousers. Then he put it back into the knapsack.

"Brushing his wet hair off his forehead, he stared at the paper and read the first line: *'Jesus te amo.'* 'Jesus loves you,' he said out loud. Then he read the second line, *'Dios no ha fallado.' Fallado*, he said to himself. What was *fallado*? He searched his mind, hoping to turn up a clue to the meaning of the word, but nothing came to him, and after a while he put the paper back in the leather knapsack and buckled it closed, then began pedaling down the road again, dodging the deep ruts, grasping the handlebars firmly to keep the bicycle on course, only once in a while lifting his eyes to gaze off into the distance, which seeped ever and ever nearer. His landmark was the dark cone of a volcano, looming solitarily against a bruised sky . . ."

Although I stood in a room full of people, I had retreated into a world of my own making. There were those in the room who would know that the story they were hearing was not completely made up. Carlos, Dr. Ettinger, Dr. Ramirez, and Dr. Lappin and Marie would recognize the boy in my story, the missionary wandering in the countryside of Guatemala. They would know the identity of the mother. Just as Carlos would recognize the lover, would know that I had reshaped him into my comforter, the man who accompanies me to that far off country, where I discover miraculously that my son has not died after all, but emerges emaciated from the bowels of a jail.

There, in that room aboard the *Oceanus*, I made my life over into fiction—*a perfect lie*. So completely did I roam again among those dead souls of my long-extinct universe, I was united with my lover, as well as my son, each of whom acted out their assigned parts with perfect equanimity, each of whom existed for me and me alone, just as I had wished them to do in life. And when I came to the last page and read the last words on that page, I left the desert of pure feeling as abruptly as I had entered it.

Gil Rawlins stood up and spoke in a loud voice from the place where he stood to one side of the room.

"Perhaps Lucy would be willing to answer a few questions from the audience," he said. "That is, if anyone has any questions."

A few people rose, one by one, and asked the sorts of questions people always asked. I gave the sorts of answers I always gave, keeping my replies short, hoping to end things quickly.

Then someone asked a more interesting question. A tall, gray-haired man rose and asked if there was one book in my life I had read that had changed forever the way I viewed human nature.

I paused only slightly before replying: "Yes, there was. I read it when I was still very young. Hardy's *Tess of the D'Urbervilles* affected me that way. It brought moral questions into a different perspective for me. I found my own life changed in the wake of reading it."

"In what way?" he demanded to know.

"I found myself incapable of making the same easy judgments about right and wrong. Tess was damned because she had a child out of wedlock. She was *immoral,* in other words. And yet to my way of thinking she was an innocent, a good woman, just as her seducer might be viewed not as an ogre, but rather as a sensuous man. It was her seducer who perhaps showed the greatest concern for her, who came to her aid when she was abandoned by her righteous husband. But then we have to say her husband was not so bad either, not really: he did come to her side in the end—of course, it was too late. It seemed to me Hardy was saying there was a larger truth about the real nature of goodness, which takes into account the idea of human frailty. And it seemed to me that he was saying Tess brought her own downfall upon herself, because she was incapable of telling the truth. And so I suppose he was saying that the only morality is truth. Unfortunately, we know what a slippery subject that is."

It was at that moment that Herr Himmelfarb rose to his feet. Pretending not to see him, I glanced quickly at my watch and said, "It's getting rather late, if you don't mind I think that's enough, thank you all for coming—"

"Just one minute!" Herr Himmelfarb boomed. His voice rang out in the room with unnatural force, so that everyone in the audience seemed to turn at once and look in his direction.

"Please, my good lady, just one more question for you."

I sensed that something terrible was about to happen.

"If someone whom you believed to be a moral human being was suddenly revealed to you as a person who had committed a most heinous crime in the past, would you absolve him, based on his later good works, or would you hold him accountable for his earlier sin?"

"I'm a fiction writer," I said. "I'm afraid I'm not in the business of judging that."

"Ah, but I think you are! I think that is precisely your business. What is literature if not an attempt to examine human nature and pronounce judgment?" Out of the corner of my eye, I saw Carlos stand up and quietly leave the room.

Very calmly, I said, "As interesting as your question undoubtedly is, it's not one I feel prepared to answer. And so if you'll excuse me . . . thank you all again, thank you for coming."

I left the room quickly, not wishing to speak to anyone. I expected to find Carlos waiting for me in the hallway, but he was nowhere to be seen.

I made my way to his cabin and knocked. There was no answer. Remembering that we had agreed to have dinner with Dr. Ramirez and the others, I thought perhaps he had decided to wait for me in the dining room, but when I arrived there, I found everyone seated at the table except Carlos.

"There you are, my dear," Dr. Ettinger said, taking my hand. "That was a splendid reading. We all enjoyed it very much. We've

223

just been discussing it."

"Sit down, sit down," Dr. Ramirez cried. "We've been waiting for you to arrive before ordering. Where is Dr. Cabrera?"

"I thought he'd be here already," I said.

"Maybe he's on his way."

"Perhaps. But I think I'll just go have a quick look for him. He may be waiting for me in the bar."

"Tell him to come at once," Dr. Ettinger said. "We're all famished and we can't possible start without him. Or you."

I didn't expect to find him in the bar, but had an intuition where I might find him, and I hurried off in the direction my senses were leading me.

It was cold out on the deck. A fierce wind was blowing and it cut through my clothes and burned against my ears. High waves crashed against the side of the ship. It felt dangerous to be out on deck, as if one could easily be pitched over the railing if one weren't absolutely careful. I walked well away from the railing, staying as close to the wall of the ship as I could.

A three-quarters moon hung in the sky, creating a little light by which I could make my way. When I reached the spot where Carlos and I had sat reading earlier in the day, I could see a lone figure standing at the railing, clutching the railing and looking out to sea. I knew it was him by the way the moonlight illuminated his white hair. He turned his head as I approached, and then looked back again at the sea.

I stood beside him for a moment without speaking, staring out into the night, holding on tight to the railing, my knees flexing to accommodate the movement of the ship. The lights of the *Oceanus* cast little cheerful yellow spots onto the surface of the sheeny, swelling sea. There was only the sound of the engines and of the waves breaking against the hull, a sort of ripping noise, like the sibilant hissing of a thousand snakes.

I reached out and looped my arm through his and drew close to him, wishing to shield my body from the wind and hold on to him. It felt a little vertiginous standing so close to the railing.

"Carlos?" I said. "What are you doing? It's crazy to be out in this weather."

He remained rigid in his pose.

"What am I to do?" he said softly, still facing the sea. "I'm ruined, Lucy. Ruined."

"Ruined? What do you mean?"

He brought a hand to his forehead and rubbed it, bowing his head slightly, then grabbed the railing again.

"That man has the power to ruin me."

"Who? You mean Himmelfarb?"

He nodded. "What did he say in there just now?"

"I didn't give him a chance to say anything. I cut him off just after you left."

Carlos turned and looked at me. He smoothed a hand across my hair.

"You're shivering," he said.

"That's because I'm freezing. Can't we go inside? The others are waiting for us in the dining room."

"I can't possibly go back in there and sit in the dining room."

"But why?"

"I know he's waiting. He wants another confrontation—"

"But you must, Carlos. I don't know what's going on, but it can't be that bad. What are you going to do? Hide in your cabin until we reach Southampton tomorrow? He did ask me to tell you he would be willing to talk to you in private. Maybe that's what you should do. Send him a message. Arrange a meeting."

"Unthinkable," he said.

"But why? Why not talk to him and get it over with?"

"I refuse to."

"He told me he'll expose you publicly. Whatever that means."

There was a long silence, and then he said, "So be it." His face appeared drawn, his mouth set in a tight line.

"What is it, Carlos?"

"It's the past come to haunt me."

"What past? What are you talking about?"

"I had no idea, I assure you, not until yesterday . . ."

"No idea about what?"

"I can't explain now, Lucy."

"Why not? Don't you trust me?"

"It's not about trust."

"What's it about, then?"

"I'll tell you later," he said. "Let's go inside now and have dinner. You're right. I can't hide."

He took my arm, but I pulled back and looked at him.

"Are you sure you can't tell me what's going on?"

"I would prefer not to. Not just yet."

Braving the bitter wind and staying close to the ship's wall, we made our way along the deck. At one point he stopped and, facing me, said: "If anything should happen to me, there's a notebook in the inside pocket of my briefcase. I want you to have it. I don't want anyone else to see it. Here's an extra key to my cabin. Everything you need to know is in that notebook. But promise me that you'll destroy it after reading it."

"But nothing's going to happen to you!" I looked at him, suddenly frightened.

"Promise me, I insist."

"All right," I sighed. "I promise."

I glanced down, feeling a jumble of confused emotions. But he lifted my chin gently in his hand and forced me to look at him.

"Don't ever doubt, Lucy, that I have loved you as well as I was capable of loving anyone." He kissed me lightly on the forehead and drew me against him, pressing my head against his chest, and then very quickly he released me and, turning abruptly, led the way into the bright, warm, waiting interior of the gently rocking ship.

TWENTY-ONE

The hospital is located at the far end of the Strip, near the airport, surrounded by land that has been scraped clean of all growth in preparation for some new development—a ragged and evocative region of nothingness blending into the desert. The sun seems to press upon the parched brown earth with a redundant intensity. Shading my eyes against its glare, I make my way from the parking lot to the main entrance, and step into a world whose old familiar smell never fails to elicit an anxious response. It's the smell of sickness, and of Justin's early years.

Joycelle Johnson, I'm told, is in a room on the second floor, in the infectious diseases ward. I stop at the nurses' station and check to make sure it's all right to visit her. When I mention Joycelle's name, a doctor standing next to me, a young man who has been writing something down on a chart, turns to look at me.

"You've come to see Miss Johnson?" he asks.

"Yes."

"Are you a relative?" Some slight accent colors his speech. The plastic name tag affixed to his white jacket identifies him as Dr. Wytold F. Dusek.

"I'm a friend."

"We were hoping to locate a relative, but she claims to have none."

"How is she doing?"

The doctor hesitates. "Are you aware of her condition?"

"I know that she has tested positive for AIDS, and that she has pneumonia."

"That's correct," he says. "To be more precise, she has acute pneumocystis pneumonia. I'm afraid her condition is quite serious."

"But she just discovered she was HIV-positive. How could she have gotten sick so quickly?"

"I think she may have been feeling ill for some time. That's my guess."

"Yes. I think that's possible."

"It's been difficult to get her to talk with us—to get any kind of medical history from her. Are you close to her? Do you think you could talk to her and get her to cooperate a little more . . . ?"

"I don't know. How long will she have to stay here?"

"There are several tricky problems with her case. One, it's conceivable she'll respond to the treatment for the pneumocystis and can be released in a couple of weeks, when we've completed the full course of the drugs, but she'll have to continue taking medication orally or else she's certain to have a relapse. These treatments require money, of course, and Miss Johnson claims to have no insurance. She was admitted through the emergency room because she required immediate care, but . . ." He doesn't have to finish the sentence. His look conveys everything.

"So what can she do?"

"Does she have a place to live when she does leave the hospital?"

"Yes and no."

"She needs to see our medical social worker, who can help her apply for disability benefits, but so far she's refused to even consider that. There are some drug-trial tests she might qualify for."

I sigh, and look away from him.

"Does she have a job?"

"No," I say. "In fact, I don't think she has any resources at all."

"I'm afraid as a doctor I can only treat certain medical problems. But I can give you the name of several groups that might help her. I know of a group living situation for people with AIDS, if you think she'd agree to that."

"I'll talk to her," I say.

He writes down a few names on the back of his card. All the while he's been speaking with me, I've noticed a certain kindness, a genuine concern behind his words. Now he smiles at me as he hands me the card.

"I'd like to talk with you after you've seen her," he says. "The nurses can page me, I'll be making rounds on the ward. Maybe between us we can find a way to help her."

She's lying in a bed near the window. Her head is turned away from me: she's looking out the window, where the uppermost branches of a tree are visible, the whitish leaves stirring in the wind. Her hands are clasped on top of the sheet, which is drawn up to her chin. A green oxygen tube snakes from an outlet on the wall, across her shoulder, and is affixed to the membrane separating her nostrils. Not until I am standing over her does she turn her head and look at me.

"Hello, Joycelle." I reach down and touch her arm. I feel a hard obstruction in my throat when I gaze down at her.

"I heard you'd been to the club," she says. Her voice is a little weak and raspy.

"Cindy told you?"

She nods. "She said you paid off Turkey Curry. Is my stuff still there?"

"yes. It's all there."

"I'd like to get out of here," she says, and looks out the window, as if drawn to the blue sky and the branches of the trees. "I don't see any point in staying here."

"I spoke to your doctor—Dr. Dusek. He says there's a good chance you can leave in two weeks when you finish the course of treatment."

"They put that stuff in my vein every night at nine o'clock. It feels like I'm being poisoned. Last night it made me feel so sick I thought I would die." She turns back and looks at me, and in a voice totally devoid of all emotion, adds, "But I'm going to die anyway."

"Come on . . ."

"Come on where, Lucy? Where should we go?"

"You know what I mean."

"No. What do you mean?"

"I don't want you to act like there's no hope. This is your first illness, the first real battle you're going to have with this disease, and you can't give up yet."

"I can't? Why not?"

"Because there are certain things you can do to fight it. Things you must do."

"What difference would it make?"

"Dr. Dusek gave me some names of people who might help. There's a group home for people with AIDS—"

"Forget it," she said. "I'm not checking in with a bunch of cadavers. It ain't worth it."

"I guess you're the one who has to decide that."

"That's right, I am," she says defiantly.

"Maybe it's worth it to spend a little more time with Nicole."

Her head snaps up, and she turns and glares at me.

"How did you know about her?"

"When you didn't come back to the motel, I asked Mr. Patel to let me have the key to your room. I found the picture of Nicole. I also found the letter from your mother."

"Great. That's great." She smiles a thin smile. "First you go snooping through my things, reading my letters, looking at my pictures. Now you stand here talking about Nicole like you knew something about this situation. What the fuck, Lucy? What did I do to deserve all this wonderful attention from you?"

I see how hurt she is, and I have to turn away because it's terribly hard to look at her. Neither one of us speaks for a few moments. Then she says, "Hand me that box of Kleenex, please."

The *please* is exaggerated, laden with anger.

She takes the Kleenex without looking at me, coughs into it, folds it over, and then drops it into a waste bag attached to her bed. The bag is marked EXTREME CAUTION: INFECTIOUS WASTE.

I draw up a chair and sit down beside her bed, and without looking at her, with my eyes fixed on a point midway up a blank wall, I begin speaking to her in a low voice: "I'm sorry."

"I think you should be."

"I don't suppose you want to believe that I went to your room because I was concerned—"

"About what?"

"About you, of course."

"And you had to read the letter from my mom because you were so concerned? That was a part of it—of this *concern* for me?"

"I don't know, Joycelle. I was there . . . it was there. I read it, that's all."

"Now I guess you think you know a lot about me."

"I'm sure there's a lot more we don't know about each other. The truth is, we hardly know anything about each other."

"If I'd wanted to tell you about Nicole, I would have brought up the subject myself. That's what bothers me. You don't understand anything about it. You've never even had a kid."

"Yes I have . . ." I lean forward, and place my hand on hers and look into her eyes, half waiting for her to pull away. But she doesn't. She lets me take her hand and hold it, and I go on.

"You once asked me if I had any children and I said no. It wasn't exactly true. I had a son who was killed. Actually, he wasn't killed outright. At least I don't think he was. He disappeared while living in a country in Central America. He's never been found, and there's no question in my mind that he's dead."

Out of the corner of my eye I can see Joycelle is listening to me, her head turned in my direction, listening quietly and calmly to my words, and I go on: "For years I've created all sorts of scenarios about what might have happened to him. I kept hoping—hoping against hope, really—that somehow he might still be alive somewhere. Finally, I've had to accept that he is gone, that I'll never see him again."

I turn and look at her. Something passes between us in that moment—a look that's completely unguarded.

"Sorry," she says. "I didn't know."

"I had no right to look through your things. But I was worried about you. You didn't come back to the motel. And I'm telling you about Justin now not because I want your sympathy but because I want you to understand that I do know what it means to have feelings for a child—"

"It doesn't matter," she mumbles.

"What doesn't matter?"

"Everything. You looking through my stuff. I don't know why I made such a big deal about it. It's all pretty meaningless anyway. Who cares if you know about Nicole? If my parents are really alive? What difference does it make now? You don't beat AIDS. It's a death sentence, isn't it?"

"I wish I knew more about it. I think there are certain drugs that are now available—"

"Come on, Lucy. You know as well as I do what's going to happen to me."

I stand up and walk to the window, where I can look down on the hospital parking lot. What can I say to her? I'm afraid she *is* going to die, and I feel so frightened for her I don't know what to say. The asphalt appears dense and black and oily, like a dark and mobile sea wavering in the heat. I feel incredibly tired, but I think it's really the weight of sadness making me feel this way. In the distance I can see the Red Rock Canyon, ridges the color of dried blood. I realize at that moment that I have a wish to go home, that I want to be back in my valley, surrounded by the inevitable peace and quiet that I know I will find there. In a month or two the weather would be changing, fall coming on. I realize I want to be at the ranch when the leaves change color and the air grows cold. I am tired, and I want to go home.

When I turn away from the window to face her again, she is plucking at her bedclothes. Beads of sweat appear on her upper lip. Her eyes are closed and her face is contorted, as if in pain.

I go to her side and smooth the damp hair from her brow.

"What is it, Joycelle?"

"Pain," she mumbles, not opening her eyes. "Pain in my chest, my back. Even the end of my nose hurts.

"What are they giving you?"

"Darvocet. But only every six hours. It's not time yet for another. They don't bring it for another hour.

"I'll be right back," I say. "I'm going to talk to the nurses."

At the nurses' station, I have Dr. Dusek paged, and when he arrives, he gives his consent to increase the medication. He claims not to have known she was in such pain.

The nurse hurries off to take Joycelle the pain medication.

I speak to Dr. Dusek for some time. I ask him to give me a prognosis for Joycelle—a prognosis for the course of her disease. I ask for his help in beginning to comprehend not only the dimensions of her illness but her options for treatment.

"Do you intend to become her primary caregiver?" he asks at one point.

Instead of answering him, I ask more questions.

She looks so peaceful, almost beatific in her calmness, when I return to her room, and I realize without even asking that the Darvocet has begun to work. Her features have softened and taken on a dreamy look. When her lunch arrives, I help her eat, though she manages only a few spoonfuls of soup and some sips of apple juice.

She falls asleep midafternoon and doesn't wake again until her evening meal is brought. By then, she is ready for another Darvocet. After it takes effect, she manages to eat a little more. And then she begins talking, telling me the story of Nicole.

I sit in a big padded chair, facing her, my hand resting on her leg which is poking out from the bedcovers—rubbing the stubble of dark hair on her shins, massaging her ankles and calves, trying to remember some of the things my favoraute aunt once taught me about the art of foot massage and reflexology.

"I had her when I was seventeen," she says.

I think, So we both had a child at the same age—seventeen.

I never did know who her father was, though I could make a couple of pretty good guesses. I didn't want a baby, you know? But I waited until it was too late to get an abortion. For a while I thought maybe I wouldn't give her up when she was born. But I realized how stupid that was. I knew that life was lot easier when I only had me to take care of. So I went to an agency. These people wanted to adopt her and they were going to pay me a lot of money. And I said okay."

She asks for a sip of water and I help her sit up to drink, and then she goes on.

"Then Nicole's born—but she's born with a harelip, and the people back out. They want a perfect baby. I didn't know what I was going to do. That's when the Painters got in touch with me. They saw Nicole and fell in love with her. The harelip wasn't a problem for them at all. They said they'd take Nicole to see a plastic surgeon when she was older, but that even if it couldn't be fixed, they didn't care. They wanted a baby, and Nicole was that baby. They thought she was just beautiful and they said they'd give her a good home. They're pretty amazing—Mark and Karen. That was Karen in the background in that picture of me with Nicole at the beach. They also said I could be a part of Nicole's life as much as I wanted to, that they thought it was important she knew who her real mother was.

"It's funny. There are times I feel like the biggest loser in the world—the worst person that ever was—because I gave her away.

And then other times I feel like what I did was a good thing, like I gave her a chance at a better life. Not everybody could have done that. I mean, thought of what was best for the child.

"She lives with them in Venice, California, in a nice house real near the beach. She's four now—almost five. I haven't seen her in over a year. It's tough, you know? I...I almost think it's better not to see her too much. It's a lot easier that way, at least for me."

"So you never told your parents you'd had a child?"

"No," she sighs. "My parents. That's another story."

"Why did you tell me they were dead?"

"Haven't you ever wished for something so much that you just sort of begin to believe it's true? My dad abused me when I was growing up, and I hated him. I mean, I really hated him. My mother knew what was going on and she never did anything to stop it—"

The nurse arrives, coming into the room suddenly, and tells Joycelle it's time to start her medication; once the I.V. is flowing, all her energy seems consumed by the struggle taking place deep within her cells. She lies sweating, her jaw clenched, the occasional tear escaping from the corner of her eye. At one point she asks me to turn on the TV, and we watch with feigned interest a program about bats in Mexico. When it is over, she falls asleep again, exhausted, and I sit with her for a while, looking at her sleeping face, thinking things over. And then I make my way out into the night where the carnival has begun anew.

TWENTY-TWO

In honor of our last night aboard the *Oceanus*, Dr. Ramirez had insisted on buying two bottles of Château Margaux, 1964, and undoubtedly the wine had contributed to the high spirits that prevailed at our table. Even Carlos seemed to forget, at least temporarily, his troubles with Himmelfarb. If Carlos was aware of the German's presence in the dining room, he didn't show it, although Himmelfarb sat directly across the room from us. Not once did I see Carlos glance in his direction, though I couldn't help looking over at him occasionally.

As the meal progressed, I gradually began to relax and enjoy myself, and it seemed that Carlos did, too. Dr. Ramirez was especially lively and amusing. At one point he announced: "Our little voyage here has been like a microcosm of *The Magic Mountain.*"

"Explain yourself, Ricardo," Dr. Ettinger said dryly, "for the benefit of those of us who don't know the novel as well as you do."

"I don't mean that we resemble a group of tubercular patients confined to a sanatorium in the Swiss Alps. But there is a sense of an insular world where lives intersect briefly under rather intense circumstances. I can't help feeling this particularly at meal times. You have a cosmopolitan cast of characters, as in *The Magic Mountain*—Spaniards, Germans, French—an array of Europeans with a few Americans like ourselves thrown in—"

"Dr. Cabrera isn't American, are you?" Marie Lappin said. "Aren't you from Costa Rica?"

"Guatemala—but you're close. However, may I remind you I am a naturalized citizen of the United States. You may consider me one of your own." The irony in his voice wasn't lost on anyone.

"In any case," Dr. Ramirez continued, "here we are, all thrown together for this brief time. What do you think, Miss Patterson?" he added with mock seriousness. "What terrible revelations will come to light before this voyage is over?"

"We will all be revealed to be hopelessly naive in our assumptions about each other."

It was the first thing to come into my mind, and I'd said it as a lighthearted comment, but immediately regretted my remark.

"Do you mean to say our secret selves will be brought to light?" Dr. Ramirez asked.

"Oh, how thrilling!" Marie exclaimed. "I've always wanted to know what Eric is really thinking. Now I'm about to find out, darling, and there'll be nowhere for you to hide."

Her husband frowned. "Perhaps I'd better just confess now and save you all the trouble of discovering what a terrible bastard I really am!"

"What about you, Dr. Ettinger? What sort of secret could possibly be lurking in your dignified past?" Dr. Ramirez asked as he carefully refilled our glasses.

She shook her head and laughed, and yet I sensed her discomfort as she tried to ignore him by turning her attention toward her meal, her eyes casting downward toward the tournedos of beef sitting on her plate amid a pool of rich brown sauce.

"Look," I said. "I was only joking when I made that comment. We don't have to be serious."

"Pandora wishes to close the box, but I'm afraid it's too late," Dr. Ramirez said.

"Why don't you begin, then, Ricardo?" said Dr. Ettinger dryly. "I'm interested to see whether my sense of your essentially noble character has been flawed all these years."

Dr. Ramirez hesitated, and I thought I saw a slight flush rise to his face. I sensed a certain eagerness among us, a rather predatory readiness for a confession. But I also sense no one wished to be first.

"This is silly—"

"Perhaps I should be the first to speak," Carlos said suddenly, interrupting me, "since I have something of consequence to tell."

"No, Carlos—"

He held up his hand to silence me.

"I'm very serious," he said. "It's a fact that very well may come to light anyway before this voyage is over. So why shouldn't I be allowed to tell my version of things?"

"My goodness, this does sound serious," Marie said.

Carlos leaned back in his chair and took a sip of wine. He crossed his arms over his chest and straightened his back. Then he began speaking, in his elegant, precise fashion: "As some of you may know, I spent much of my youth in Europe. We are talking about a very long time ago, but nevertheless a time still in this century." He paused to allow a little riffle of laughter to pass through the group.

"I spent most of the Second World War in Germany. I was ten when the war broke out, and fourteen, almost fifteen, when it ended. During that time I was not only a member of the Hitler Youth, I was one of its shining stars—"

A low cry of surprise escaped from Dr. Ettinger's lips. "Is this true?"

"Absolutely," said Carlos with utter solemnity. "I was—if I may say so—a very good athlete as a young man. Physical prowess was all-important to the leaders of the Hitler Youth, and this made me a most attractive recruit. Intellectual ability was actually suspect—it could lead to insubordination. But if you were good at tennis—or

Ping-Pong or skiing . . . I happened to excel at all three. Thus I not only competed successfully, I was actually held up as an ideal specimen of German youth."

"But you weren't German!" Dr. Ettinger cried. "How could they have considered you—a Guatemalan—to be one of their own?"

"Quite easily. I spoke perfect German. I had light skin and blond hair. My genetic roots were impeccably Aryan since my ancestors had all emigrated from Europe in the previous century and intermarried only within their class. I had no difficulty being accepted, I assure you. Accepted and embraced. I might also add that I had little choice in the matter. Children at that time in Germany were driven into complete surrender to Nazi organizations, since without membership in them one could not hope to acquire an education, an apprenticeship, the opportunity for higher studies or a career as an official—not that these were my particular aims, except of course I wished to remain in school.

"A certain pathological desire for uniforms and insignia infected German youth. I found this quite silly, but it did exert a mysterious force—these compact columns of marching, uniformed youths with waving flags—the beat of drums and the singing at rallies. At a rather young age I came to understand the power of crowds, the almost electric charge that accumulates and which has the power to subsume—and I mean completely—the individual consciousness. It's no wonder all the students rushed to join. And although I was not among those fervid for membership, I admit I did like the sense of fellowship—the hikes, the outings to the mountains, the sports competitions in which I excelled."

"But did you know what was happening to the Jews?" Marie asked with what I had come to regard as her characteristic bluntness, an inclination to rush to the heart of the matter, no matter how gracelessly or abruptly.

"Did I know specifically? No. Did a fourteen-year-old boy imagine Belsen, or Auschwitz, or Buchenwald existed? No. But one would have had to be deaf and blind not to apprehend the fact of mass deportations, not to know of the pogroms, the humiliation and persecution, the disappearance of entire communities overnight. Of course I was aware of this. Where were they taken, these Jews? We didn't know. But from the moment the Nazis took control of the school I attended, our courses were altered to include scintillatingly crass lectures on such topics as how to recognize a Jew by his racial characteristics at a first glance. One is taught these things for a purpose, to make unwitting accomplices out of the youngest minds. And I regret to say that is exactly what happened to me."

"I am very sorry—very sorry—our little game has forced such a confession from you," Dr. Ettinger said in a voice laden with sadness. "It seems rather unfair of us."

"On the contrary," Carlos said. "You forced nothing but a revelation whose time had perhaps come anyway. The true question is this—the one that was broached tonight at Lucy's reading. To what degree am I to be held accountable for my participation in these crimes of history?"

Dr. Ettinger spoke up first. "I say this as one who lived in Europe during the time these things were taking place, as someone even older than you, as a woman born in Belgium before the First World War. I have also lived long enough to know that the burden of guilt cannot be placed upon a child, whether that child was German, or Japanese, or American. The atrocities of this century are the work of adults. No one has suffered more than the children. What you have told us in no way affects our esteem for you. I feel confident in speaking for all of us at this table. If anything, we have gained new respect for you as a result of your honesty."

There was a low murmur of assent, though I remained silent, my eyes fixed on Carlos, who showed no emotion whatsoever. As if his mind were still silently churning behind his calm blue eyes.

I felt that he hadn't said everything, that he was holding something back, and that any moment he might began speaking again and tell us the rest of the story that he'd only just begun. But the longer he remained silent, the more I began to think that I was wrong, that there was nothing else to tell. I realized I had been half holding my breath since he'd begun speaking, and now I took a deep inhalation and let it out slowly, as if releasing my anxiety.

The waiter arrived at that moment to clear our dinner plates and hand each of us a dessert menu, which we all fell to studying as if looking for a means of escape or distraction. It was Carlos himself who managed to bring us back to a somewhat normal state by ordering a bottle of champagne to accompany dessert, and then suggesting that we all go dancing after dinner in the Grand Ballroom. His abrupt change of mood surprised me, but everyone else seemed to accept it with relief.

"Eric detests dancing," Marie said, rolling her eyes.

"It's not that I detest it, my dear, I'm simply not very good at it."

"Does that mean that you're going to dance with me tonight?"

"Maybe. If the music isn't too loud and fast. Under no circumstances will I engage in whatever they call it these days where you flail around on your own without so much as touching your partner. I'm of the old school, the days when dancing meant a chance to hold a woman in your arms."

"I remember those days myself," Dr. Ettinger said with a low chuckle. "At Madame Choumette's—the school in Brussels I attended—we used to have regular tea dances in the afternoons. I still remember Madame Choumette circulating among the dancers with her ruler in hand, measuring the distance between us if she thought we had breeched her rule of maintaining at least six inches of air space between our bodies! Later it felt positively, deliciously indecent to attend wartime dances where men held you pressed fast against them and danced cheek-to-check. I enjoyed all this enormously, but I always felt rather nervous, as if at any moment Madama Choumette might appear with her ruler!"

She laughed so merrily at her own story that her cheeks flushed and her normal reserve was completely dispelled. I saw her softness, her femininity emerge, and for the first time the real beauty of her aged face. Her gray hair was swept back in a bun, yet a few wisps had escaped and formed an attractive nimbus against the light—wisps which she now attempted to brush back in place. How old was she? I wondered. Eighty? Perhaps even older. However old, she exuded a vigor and vitality that one occasionally sees in individuals who have remained active, who have continued to work at their professions long past normal retirement age. She was a tall woman who held herself very erect, even when seated. Until this evening I had only seen her in a rather mannish gray suit with a white blouse buttoned to the throat. But tonight she wore a long black gown with a gently scooped neck set off by a simple strand of yellowed pearls, an outfit that suited her and emphasized her rather long and elegant neck.

"Have you ever been married, Dr. Ettinger?" Marie asked.

"No," Dr. Ettinger replied quietly, "though I was once very deeply in love with someone who died during the war."

"Was he killed in action?"

Dr. Ettinger smiled and looked down at her hands for a few moments. She took so long to answer I was afraid she had been upset by the question. But when she lifted her face, I saw she was smiling. A certain radiant look emanated from her face. Her eyes possessed a luminous, gentle clarity, and when she began to speak there was a surety and confidence in her voice.

"I believe it is my turn to make a confession," she said, "although I abhor the idea of the word—my Catholic upbringing, I'm afraid. Also, I find it somewhat bothersome, the current tendency to 'tell all,' at any cost, under any circumstance without regard for propriety. That is the real reason for my hesitation in answering your question, Marie. Yet I am drawn to tell you what I am about to because I think it might possibly lift a burden from me, one I have carried for many years, as perhaps Dr. Cabrera was moved to unburden himself tonight. My lover was not killed in action. She fell from a horse while we were riding together one day. Her neck was broken, and with it, my heart."

She raised her napkin to her lips and gently stroked the corners of her mouth, before going on in the same even voice, as if this little hesitation was her way of allowing us a moment to absorb the impact of what she'd just said.

"I hope I have not embarrassed any of you by telling you that my one true love in life was a woman, not a man. I realize that in doing so I have undoubtedly dispelled an illusion about myself, as Lucy suggested earlier might happen to us here tonight. Are you prescient, my dear?" she said, turning to look at me and laying her hand on my arm. "Did you suspect that I have long had a wish to reveal myself to my friends here?"

"No," I said quietly. "No, I didn't have any way of knowing . . ."

She withdrew her hand and, reaching up to her throat, began turning the string of pearls in her fingers.

"I loathe the saying 'in the closet,' yet I'm afraid it rather precisely describes how I've lived my life. Bigotry and discrimination are all too real in this world. One must remember that homosexuality itself is even now regarded as a great evil. Even now, I find myself trembling slightly at the thought I've breached the wall of silence with you. But truth is noble, is it not, Dr. Ramirez? Surely someone in one of those great books you're so fond of quoting from has said as much, no?"

"Truth is noble," Dr. Ramirez said, gazing at her with great affection. "Noble, and liberating. And I find you an absolutely remarkable human being."

"Bah!" Dr. Ettinger said, pretending to sound gruff, yet looking extraordinarily pleased.

"Gee," Marie said in her slight Southern drawl, "I just don't think I've got a thing to tell you about myself that is anywhere as interesting as what you all have said!"

"Thank god," said her husband dryly, and everyone laughed.

"I believe we've had quite enough revelations for one evening," Dr. Ettinger said. "I propose we have after-dinner drinks in the ballroom, and dance! What do you say, Lucy?"

Before I could reply, Dr. Ramirez exclaimed, "Excellent! Excellent idea! And I claim the first dance with Dr. Ettinger."

Rarely in my life have I felt such happiness in a group of people as I felt that night as we made our way to the ballroom, with Dr. Ettinger flanked by the Lappins, strolling arm in arm, and Dr. Ramirez and Carlos on either side of me. There was a charmed, almost magical quality to our happiness, a feeling of camaraderie that seemed to know no boundaries. I'm sure our mood was boosted by the general atmosphere aboard the ship on our last night at sea. Everywhere one looked, one saw people dressed in formal attire, smiling happily, grouped intimately on the banquettes surrounding the huge dance floor—laughing, talking, drinking.

Dr. Ettinger, Marie, and I settled ourselves at a table surrounded by plush leather chairs at the edge of the dance floor, while the men went to the bar to fetch us drinks. Only one thing marred my sense of complete contentment and that was the thought that this was my last evening with Carlos.

In truth, I had begun to wonder if it would be our last evening together.

Having entered each other's lives again—out of pure chance—what would happen tomorrow when the voyage ended and took us in separate ways? Neither one of us had spoken about this. But in my most private moments I had begun to imagine a scenario, and I wondered if Carlos, too, hadn't begun to have his own thoughts on the subject.

It wasn't that I imagined we would share what remained of our lives together. So much had changed between us that it seemed improbable that we would be together again—that we could claim any sort of real future for ourselves—even if I had wanted that future, which I wasn't at all certain I did. Rather, I simply wanted more time to see what might come of our feelings. Did this mean I was ready—able—to fall in love with him again—in fact was already doing so? I knew that I didn't want to part from him just yet.

I imagined proposing to him that I go on with him to London while he attended his convention, so we could at least spend a few more days together. Perhaps he might even want to come to Cornwall with me afterward. I couldn't help hoping that he would.

Marie and Dr. Ettinger were discussing their plans for getting to London the next day. But soon the men returned, and all thoughts of the future were replaced by a sense of sublime contentment with the present.

"May I have this dance, my dear Dr. Ettinger?" Dr. Ramirez said, as he set down the two drinks he held in his hand.

"Certainly. With all the compliments of Madame Choumette." Dr. Ettinger rose and followed him out onto the dance floor.

Marie stood up. "Come on, honey," she said to her husband. "It doesn't get any slower than this."

She was referring to the music, a treacly sort of waltz that had brought large numbers of people to the floor. Somewhat reluctantly, Eric allowed himself to be led away, leaving Carlos and myself alone.

I slipped my hand into his, leaned back against the banquette, and placed my head against his shoulder.

"Are you all right?" I asked him.

"Fine," he said abruptly, with a slight shrug. "Would you like to dance?"

"In a minute. I'm enjoying watching everyone. Look how happy Dr. Ettinger looks. She's a remarkable woman. I like her very much."

"Ricardo is a good dancer."

"He is."

"I'm not surprised. He's extremely bright—quite gifted at everything he does."

"He's very devoted to you, isn't he?"

"Devoted? I'm not sure I . . . catch your drift, so to speak."

"I mean, he is devoted to you, like a disciple to a guru."

"Perhaps. The guru image isn't inappropriate. He was one of my residents."

"Is he married?"

"Not in the conventional sense. But he has a live-in lover. A young man who is a concert pianist."

"He's gay?"

Carlos smiled at my surprised look. "Ah, another illusion dispelled tonight?"

"Stop it," I said. "I was only joking when I said that about illusions."

"I suppose that leaves only you—and Dr. Lappin and Marie—with secrets unrevealed. What do you think of them? Rather a strange couple, no?"

"Eric and Marie? They seem all right. She's a little vapid. But they seem like a happy couple."

"Really? What if I were to tell you that Dr. Lappin is having an affair with one of the student nurses, and that his wife is a kleptomaniac who's been arrested several times?"

"You're making that up," I said. "You're just trying to shock me."

"Isn't that what we all want? To be shocked? To have someone stand before us, revealed in all their nakedness, to see them reduced to a mere mortal like ourselves—suffering, flawed, full of the anguish of life?"

"I'm really not so interested in gossip, and that's what all this amounts to."

"Then you are alone, a freak in this era of endless talk shows and tabloids."

"Do you mind terribly if I change the subject? There's something I want to ask you."

"Go right ahead."

"Could I come to London with you tomorrow?"

"I had thought of the same thing myself, as a matter of fact—I was going to say something to you."

"We could go to the theater. Take walks in the park. It's been a long time since I've been in London. I know you'll be busy—that's all right, too. I'd be happy on my own."

"But are you sure you wish to be with me?"

"I wasn't asking you to marry me."

"Hmmm, yes."

"Such an old man."

"You ain't kiddin'."

"Is she really a kleptomaniac?"

"Ah, see! You *are* curious, just like everyone else."

"Is she?"

"Hmmm. Yes."

"You keep saying 'Hmmm, yes.'"

"Hmm, yes."

"Oh, stop it," I said.

As soon as we began dancing, I was overcome with old feelings, re-membering other times, other places where we had danced—from that first time in the German restaurant after the day of skiing, to one night in Chicago, at the height of our affair, when we had gone to a supper club and danced until the band had quit and we were left alone on the dance floor. I had worn a gray sheath, sleeveless, with a square-cut, low neck. I could see the table where we sat. The dance floor. I remembered an erection pressing against my thigh on and off throughout the evening, and the feeling of being so exquis-itely in love.

Age had not diminished his skills as a dancer. If anything, he seemed lighter and more agile, still every bit as graceful. It felt so pleasant. Ah. To dance again, and to dance with him.

There was something about dancing with him that was so inti-mate, more intimate, even, in a certain way than sex had been. Per-haps romance is what I'm talking about. It had to do with the open display of our attraction, the way we fit ourselves to each other in such a loving, tender way for all the world to see, no longer caring whether anyone guessed we had once been lovers and, in our own tentative fashion, had become so again. It had to do with the beauty of two bodies moving as one.

With my face pressed against his shoulder, I followed him, and as I did so, I inhaled the scent of his tuxedo, a purely male scent that caused me to think of García Lorca and a passage I had read long ago and which stayed with me because it seemed to describe the mysterious attraction which men's clothes could elicit. In *The House of Bernarda Alba*, Bernarda says: "Women in church shouldn't look at any man but the priest and him only because he wears skirts. To turn your head is to be looking for the warmth of corduroy."

And although his tuxedo was made of wool—not corduroy— the attraction, the deep association with the scent of male clothing—the "warmth of corduroy"—exerted an unconscious pull on my psyche, as it always had, drawing me toward men from the time I was a child and my father gathered me up in his arms upon returning from work and pressed me against his clothes, which were so different in feel and texture and smell from the clothes my mother wore, establishing forever a longing for that comfort, that all-encompassing feeling of safety and protectiveness that would be transferred from man to man in my life, captured in that dusky world of maleness, of napped and thick fabric.

As the evening wore on, we changed partners, and Carlos danced with Marie and Dr. Ettinger, while I took turns with Dr. Ramirez and Eric Lappin. Eric was—as he had said—not a very good dancer, but he tackled the task of leading me across the dance floor with a certain cheerfulness and élan, as if he might actually be enjoying himself, and we had a funny conversation about his devotion to his dogs. Dr. Ramirez was smooth and polished in his movements. I could follow him effortlessly and did so with great delight, aware of his natural elegance.

I also danced with the Milward brothers and Gil Rawlins. I even took a turn with the captain. Then Carlos sought me out again, and I was happy to find myself once more dancing with him, and even happier to think of the days to come, of the days and nights in London that we could now look forward to.

When the dance ended, Carlos and I joined the others at the table. Then the band announced it was taking a break, but would resume playing in fifteen minutes, and continue playing until two o'clock.

It was already just a little past midnight, and I could sense by the way Carlos looked at his watch that he was thinking it was time to go.

Later, I would regret that I hadn't taken his cue at that moment and said our goodbyes and made our way to his cabin. But I wasn't ready to leave just yet. I was feeling happy and I wanted a few more dances, a little more time to enjoy everyone's company, and so when Carlos said he was feeling tired, I spoke up and said, "Wait till the band comes back—just a couple more dances—then we'll leave."

He acquiesced to my suggestion with a little shrug.

"We should all go to bed soon anyway," Dr. Ettinger said, "although I must say, I haven't had so much fun in ages. I'm sure I'll pay for it tomorrow. I sense a spectacular hangover brewing in this poor old head."

It was at that moment that everything changed, and the thing that I hadn't believed would happen did. Later, I would look back and wonder, did I actually see Herr Himmelfarb approach the table, or was he already standing there, beginning to speak when I became aware of his presence?

Himmelfarb got all of our attention as he addressed the entire table with his first remark.

"I am surprised to find you all sitting here so calmly, enjoying yourselves, with a Nazi in your midst."

He spoke loudly, so loudly that the people at surrounding tables ceased talking and turned their attention toward the small, bald man who had spoken.

He shouted, "Yes, Nazi! Nazi murderer! I am talking to you, Dr. Cabrera!"

"Look here," Eric Lappin said, looking up at Himmelfarb, who stood closest to him. "You're either drunk, old man, or demented. In either case, leave us alone. No one invited you to this table."

"I don't need an invitation," Himmelfarb boomed. "Justice doesn't require one." He pointed at Carlos and shook his finger at him. "Why don't you tell your friends here what happened to my brother?"

I glanced at Carlos, who remained absolutely still, his back stiff, his eyes slightly hooded and staring straight ahead.

"You're making a scene, sir," Dr. Ettinger said angrily. "I won't tolerate this sort of behavior."

"Behavior?" Himmelfarb shrieked. "*My* behavior? What about the behavior of your friend here? Or hasn't he told you about his Nazi past?"

"We are very well aware of his past, I assure you," Dr. Ettinger snapped. "Now go sit down and leave us alone or I shall call one of the stewards."

"Call whomever you wish," Himmelfarb said, "I won't leave until I finish what I have to say. He knows he is the murderer of my brother."

"I was not aware, I assure you—" Carlos began coolly, but Himmelfarb cut him off.

"You are a lying bastard," Himmelfarb fumed. "It was you who had my brother sent to the camps. You who killed him! Why don't you tell the truth?" he screamed. "It's the only thing that can possibly save you!"

"Get one of the stewards," Dr. Ettinger said to Ricardo. "Go find someone—anyone. Quickly!"

"Why don't we just throw the bum out ourselves?" Eric said.

"Get the steward," Dr. Ettinger said firmly.

Ricardo started to rise, but Carlos laid a hand on his arm and said, "No. Let him speak."

"But he's crazy—" I started to say.

"Yes, I am mad," Himmelfarb hissed, staring at me. "How could you sit here with him? How could you, a writer—one who is interested in truth—let yourself be tainted by his lies? Or are you so caught up in creating fictions that you are willing to believe in his innocence?"

The room around us had grown very still. Every face was turned toward our table as Himmelfarb said, "My brother was betrayed by him."

He paused, gazing around him to make sure everyone was listening.

"In 1943 my parents were rounded up and sent to a death camp. My brother and myself were spared only because we had been sent to live in the country with an elderly Catholic couple who had agreed to disguise us as their grandchildren, a ruse that worked very well until the day Carlos Cabrera discovered my brother's Jewishness and reported it to the headmaster of our school. I was warned of these events, and was able to escape to another village where I was hidden and not discovered until much later. My brother was not so lucky. He was taken away that same day. Later I learned he had been sent to Buchenwald, where he died. My brother's name was Oskar Himmelfarb. Remember that name! And remember the name of his murderer! Dr. Carlos Cabrera!"

Two stewards, noticing the commotion, had arrived and were standing by helplessly, listening to the last part of Himmelfarb's speech.

Dr. Ettinger now motioned to them. "Remove this man from our presence," she said. "We've heard quite enough from him."

One of the stewards attempted to take Himmelfarb by the arm, but he was shaken off.

"I shall leave now of my own accord," he said calmly, a little smile playing on his lips. "I shall leave you to decide whether I am telling you the truth. But consider this—try to imagine why I would lie. On the other hand, consider the reasons why a man such as Dr. Cabrera would deny what I have just said."

With that he turned and strode away, returning to his table.

People began murmuring at the tables around us, shifting in their seats. Once again the clink of glasses, low voices, began to stir nearby. At our own table an awkward silence prevailed. I believe it was impossible at that moment for any of us to know what to say.

Carlos stood up abruptly.

"Excuse me," he said.

"Where are you going?"

"I must get some air."

"I'll come with you," I said, and started to get up, but he turned quickly and said, "Please. Let me have some time alone."

I let him go, watched him cross the room, as did everyone else who had been within earshot of Himmelfarb's remarks. When he was gone, we all sat in stunned silence. Then Marie said, "That was perfectly awful."

"Dreadful," her husband concurred.

"The rotten bastard," Ricardo added. "I don't believe him, do you? There must be more to the story, don't you think?"

He was speaking to me, but I found I couldn't answer.

I searched Dr. Ettinger's face, looking for some signs of—of what? I desperately needed something, anything, to help me quiet my pounding heart. But she sat very still, saying nothing, simply staring out across the empty dance floor.

"Lucy, don't you think we ought to do something?" Ricardo said.

"Like what?"

"Talk to him? He must be feeling quite wretched. I don't think he should be alone."

"I quite think he wants to be alone," Dr. Ettinger said softly. "I think he might find it rather difficult to face any of us right now. Except perhaps you, Lucy. Perhaps Ricardo is right. Do you think it might help if you were to go to him?"

"What do I say to him?" I asked Dr. Ettinger, searching her face for some clue as to her own feelings.

"That I cannot tell you, my dear. I am rather perplexed myself by this whole thing. I really am not so concerned with the question of guilt as I am deeply disturbed at the thought that anyone—but especially Dr. Cabrera, who has so much to lose by this—should be confronted by events that occurred so long ago. Whatever happened, I have difficulty believing he understood the consequences of his actions fully. You might try to comfort him with that thought—the idea I expressed earlier, that children are made to bear the most terrible crimes during wars. Sometimes, I imagine, they are even a party to them. But surely his young age—the vicious world in which he found himself—is really to blame for whatever happened."

It was as she said the words "especially Dr. Cabrera, who has so much to lose by this" that I began to feel afraid.

"I'm going to find him," I said, and stood up quickly.

Dr. Ettinger caught my hand for one brief moment.

"Good luck, my dear. Let him know, if it seems appropriate, that we are all—" She broke off her sentence, seemingly unable to find the right words, and simply shrugged and shook her head. I pulled away from her and hurried out of the room.

I ran up the two flights of stairs to the door that opened up onto the deck. The night had turned even colder, and the moon had disappeared behind clouds. The ship was shrouded in a light mist that hung on the air like a fine rain held in suspension. Beyond the railing the waves were rising in huge swells. The ship rolled and creaked, and I staggered to maintain my balance. I set off, hurrying, and almost immediately I slipped on the wet deck and fell to my knees, bruising my palms as I tried to catch myself.

I circled the entire upper deck, staying as far as I could from the railing, but I didn't see him. I was just descending the iron stairway to begin searching the deck below when I heard a woman cry, "Help! Help! Someone fell overboard!"

Later I would discover that this woman was the same woman I had seen dancing with the gentlemen hosts that second night at sea, the one with her heavy handbag draped over her arm. Her name was Agnes Bittner, and she was a retired school teacher from Baltimore who had never married and was taking her first boat trip. An unhappy, troubled soul, a lady traveling solo.

She was dressed in layers of clothing, and as she hurried toward me that night, calling "Help! Help!" I had the impression of a small child waddling awkwardly under the burden of her clothes. Even before she told me what she'd seen, her voice verging on the hysterical, her finger pointing into the darkness, I knew what had happened.

I felt my knees go weak. My soul flew out of my body, leapt forward into the darkness as I rushed to the railing and hit my chest against it as I flung myself forward. I peered into the unfathomable, inchoate blackness of an impossibly huge and terrifying void, at waves curling and crashing in on themselves, and began screaming out for him, crying "Carlos! Carlos!"

I did not leave the spot at the railing. It was Agnes Bittner who summoned help, who drew the first person to the scene, a young steward who immediately threw out a large white circular lifebuoy to mark the spot, then alerted the captain, who set about cutting the engines to an idle, although the *Oceanus* continued to slip forward, parting the darkness like a huge bejewelled monster gliding further and further away from the place where Carlos had disappeared. Long before the ship came to a standstill, the rescuers had launched a lifeboat, swinging out over the side of the ship and descending onto the sea to the accompaniment of the sounds of creaking cables, and my anguished, uncontrollable sobs.

By then, they were all there—Dr. Ettinger, Marie and Eric, and Ricardo—and the Milwards, who brought an extra coat and wrapped it around me. Word had spread quickly among the passengers, many of whom came rushing out onto the deck before the captain ordered them back. The crowd had briefly included Gil Rawlins, the gentlemen hosts, Ralph Bevins and his wife, even Himmelfarb—they all pressed forward, full of questions, stunned by the thought that Carlos had fallen overboard. "He seemed to just lose his balance," Agnes Bittner said over and over. "I saw him standing there. One minute he was leaning out over the railing, like he was just looking out at sea and then he seemed to lean too far forward just as the ship hit a wave and he lost his footing and fell."

For the first hour we stayed at the railing, then retreated to a small room inside, high up above the decks, where we could still look out—Ricardo, Dr. Ettinger, Eric and Marie, and the captain— all of us listening to the crackle of the walkie-talkie the captain held in his hand and peering out at an inky, curdled sea on which we could sometimes glimpse, in the sweep of a passing light beam, the perfect white circle of an empty life preserver.

Dawn found the *Oceanus* floating quietly, becalmed on a purple sea, the decks emptied of all but rescue personnel. We had been told to return to our cabins by the captain in the early morning hours. There was never any real hope of finding him alive, never much hope of finding him at all. Did he leap? Or did he fall? Was Agnes Bittner right? Was it really an accident? How did he fall overboard? I believe I do know the answer, though I will never know for sure.

TWENTY-THREE

In Southampton there had been an inquiry into Carlos's death, and I had been summoned for questioning, as had Hannah Ettinger and Dr. Ramirez. Dr. Ettinger had been quite insistent on one point: There was no evidence, she argued, to prove that Carlos had committed suicide. The fact that he had been upset didn't mean he necessarily wished to kill himself. It was equally probable he had lost his footing and fallen overboard, given the fact the sea had been very rough at the time. It was clear to me she was making a final effort to protect Carlos's reputation, to spare him the stigma of suicide and the gossip it would have engendered. In the end, she had prevailed. His death was ruled accidental; a certificate attesting to this was signed in our presence.

I spent the next forty-eight hours in a hotel room in London, drinking as I had not drunk for many years. I felt compelled to hold my own private wake for him. I didn't leave my room, barely slept, or ate. Two days later, suffering from a monstrous hangover, I boarded the train for Cornwall, and during the journey stared blankly at the spindly rock formations rising out of the sea, at the farmland and copses lying beneath a leaden sky, while listening to the high, shrill laughter of the young couple in the opposite seats.

In St. Agnes I checked into the Porthvean, a small two-story hotel overlooking a rocky inlet—very like the place I had imagined before I even set out on my journey. The first night I was overcome with exhaustion and fell into a good sleep. The next morning, before it was light, I set out for a walk. I walked along a country lane, past meadows and fields where sheep were grazing. I startled a pheasant who in turn startled me. I ended up on a high knoll where I could view the countryside—dark ploughed fields, green meadows, a river twisting like a gray ribbon flung down upon the land, and I wept, standing there in a cold, bitter wind, unable to understand why the two people I had loved most in my life had both disappeared.

In St. Agnes, each morning I walked, often taking a path that followed a cliff above the sea, usually stopping at the same bench, which offered a view of a solitary gray rock rising up out of the water. The sea was a living, undulating entity, a body of water that formed not so much waves as gentle rolling swells of mesmerizing beauty. The body of the sea and my own body seemed connected by certain rhythms, unseen forces. A strange little circular eddy occurred some distance from the shore where a pool of white bubbles had formed on the surface. From where I sat, I could see dark shapes of rocks and sea grasses growing on the ocean floor, which sometimes appeared frighteningly human in form. All around me little purple and yellow flowers, gorse and heather, grew out of the rocky soil. Lone seagulls sailed by, buffeted by the wind, resembling paper airplanes set on a lurching course. The solitariness of the rock and the seagull, and the monotonous wrinkling of the sea, were the physical embodiments of my own interior moods. When the cold became too much to bear, I'd return to the hotel and sit by the fire, nursing a drink, and allow my thoughts to take their own dark course.

In the evenings I watched the local news, which began to feature regular reports about the "Beast of Bodmin Moor," a large cat-like creature that had attacked a woman as she was out walking on the moors. The woman reported that she had felt something approach from behind and spring upon her with inhuman force, knocking her to the ground where she lay unconscious for some time. When she came to, the thing had disappeared, leaving only muddied prints on the surrounding ground. The following night it killed and badly mutilated a number of sheep. The creature, whatever it was, was thought to be some sort of large cat—a tiger or panther that might have escaped from a private zoo and was now terrorizing the countryside. Night after night, there were fresh reports—a sighting of a large black creature near Tintagel, a cow killed in its stall, discovered ripped to shreds, a cold brought down in the middle of the night and half devoured by the time its owners came upon it the next morning. The police advised local residents to stay indoors at night. During this time, the Beast of Bodmin Moor loomed large in my mind, incarnating an unidentifiable sense of menace and evil.

One night, after I had been at the Porthvean for almost a week, I took out the small black notebook and settled into a chair near the fire. For a while I simply held it in my hands, admiring the expensive leather cover, which suggested the taste for fine things that I had always associated with its owner. A faint odor clung to it, the smell of fine leather, of new paper, and something else, which I quickly identified as the smell of Carlos, which was the odor of sandalwood soap. Carefully, almost reluctantly, I opened it and began reading.

The first part of the notebook contained pages of hasty scribblings, scrawled in uncharacteristically messy handwriting, quite likely a part of the speech he had intended to deliver at the conference in London. These notes were almost indecipherable to me, couched as they were in the jargon of his profession, containing statistics and terms that were meaningless to me. But a little further on, I came to a page with my name written at the top.

My dear Lucy,

I have not felt at peace with myself since last night, in the bar, when I had the misfortune to encounter a figure from my past. You cannot have been aware of what was happening, since what was said between us was spoken in German. At the time, I was glad this was the case. Now I think it has made things more difficult for me. If you had been privy to what was said, perhaps I would have less now to explain, or at least it might be easier to know where to begin.

The man who confronted me in the bar last night is named Josef Himmelfarb. By the time you read this—if in fact you do read this—you will no doubt already be aware of his name, and perhaps much more as well. I lied to him when he asked if I remembered him, or his brother, Oskar.

Oskar was the smartest student in my class—a class in which I had held that honor until he arrived, one fall, limping badly as he entered the classroom, and took a seat directly next to me. The limp was a result of an early child-hood accident. It was his only flaw—physical or other-wise— and for a long time it was his saving grace as well, as it kept him from participating in sports, and with it, the communal scenes of nakedness that occurred in the shower room.

I admired Oskar more than I had admired anyone in my life up to that point, outside of my immediate family. In Oskar I found the brother I had always longed for. He was handsome, quick of mind; he had a droll sense of humor, and an uncanny ability to judge character; he was sensual, almost feminine in his beauty. In time, I developed other feelings for him, of a more carnal nature. He became the object of my most profound longings. It is no secret to you that I experimented sexually with boys in my youth. Oskar was not the first to stir such feelings in me, though he resisted my advances for reasons I couldn't understand, for in every other way he led me to believe that he was attracted to me in the same way I was to him.

I think it fair to say I became obsessed with him, finding every excuse to be with him, inviting him to spend the weekend at my grandmother's house—invitations, by the way, which he never reciprocated. I knew only that he lived with his elderly grandparents and his older brother on a small farm outside of town. In the beginning I thought perhaps he was embarrassed by the difference in our backgrounds and that's why he refused to invite me to his home. I tried to play down that difference, but it wasn't easy to do. He could see for himself that I existed in a realm of privilege, since a chauffeur delivered me to school each morning and came for me in the afternoon. The inequality in our lives was blatant.

Yet on another level, we were perfect equals, in our love of learning, in the delight we took in reading philosophy and poetry, the books we shared, the long discussions that took place those few times when he came to stay with me for a weekend. We were united by a contempt for the coarseness of the "revolutionary" ideals, the complete surrender we sensed in our fellow students, who seemed cowardly and incompetent and stupid in their devotion to Hitler and the cult of militarism. As I became more active in the Hitler Youth, a rift began to develop between us. He could not understand why I didn't resist participation in the sporting events and weekend hikes organized by the SD. Initially, I suspected he was jealous of my physical ability. I tried to explain that my love of sports was quite separate from the larger ideology espoused by the organization which sponsored these events, but he would have none of it. In time, a bitterness arose between us, feelings that were inflamed as he began to shun me in favor of another friend, whose company he began to keep. And I in turn developed terrible feelings of jealousy.

Neither my mother nor my grandmother approved of my friendship with Oskar. From the beginning they let it be known they considered him common, beneath us, a boy unworthy of sitting at our table or sharing our meals. It became more difficult to gain permission to see him. And in any case he had begun to avoid me, leaving me distraught.

This was the climate that existed at the time I discovered his secret. I was allowed to invite one guest to my birthday dinner, and I invited Oskar, much to my mother and grandmother's dismay. They acquiesced only after I made a terrible scene in which I threatened to not attend my birthday dinner if I couldn't invite whomever I chose. At first Oskar refused my invitation, but I pleaded with him, and then I bribed him, offering to give him certain books he'd admired in my grandmother's library if he would come and spend the night with me.

And so he came. The dinner was tense, quite awful, really. My mother had invited a few of her friends who proceeded to drink too much and make disparaging remarks about the ignorance and stupidity of the local villagers, even though they were aware Oskar came from one of these families. My mother behaved shamefully toward him, and although he maintained the perfect composure he was quite capable of displaying in any situation, I could sense his humiliation.

He spent the night, however, sleeping in a room adjoining my bedroom. I had tried to get him to stay in my room with me, but he wouldn't consider it. The two rooms, however, were connected by a bathroom, and in the middle of the night, I noticed a light on in there. I crept to the door and opened it slowly, so slowly, and so quietly he didn't see me for some time. In any case, he was preoccupied. I had caught him masturbating, seated on the edge of the tub, his eyes closed. He was completely naked. I guessed his secret, from the fact he was circumcised.

When he opened his eyes and saw me standing there, he stopped what he was doing and sat very still. I won't ever forget the expression on his face as it turned from one of intense pleasure to unmitigated fear. He covered himself with one hand. Neither one of us spoke for a long while. During those moments, I realized I possessed an intense power, the power over him that I had sought for so long and which I believed could make him agree to the thing I had desired. And it was this sense of power of the most pure, the most evil kind that led me to say to him what I did: I said, "I won't tell anyone if you'll come to bed with me now."

He took a long time to answer, and when he finally spoke, it was with pure hatred in his voice. "Go to hell," he said. Then he rose and left the bathroom, returning to his room and closing the door.

He was gone the next morning when I awoke. At breakfast my mother said: "What did I tell you? No breeding. The boy lacks breeding. Imagine! Leaving before breakfast, without so much as a thank-you to anyone!"

I betrayed him that very same day.

I never knew what happened to him, only that he disappeared that afternoon. He was taken away. His brother also disappeared. You must believe me when I say that at the time I did not imagine what fate awaited him. Only after the war had ended and the existence of the death camps came to light did I begin to imagine I might have been the instrument of his death.

For fifty years I have lived with this uncertainty about what happened to him, and with the knowledge of my terrible behavior. I never made any attempt to discover whether he had survived the war. Out of pure cowardice and guilt I tried to erase this episode from my memory.

And in this effort, I am ashamed to admit, I was largely successful, until that moment in the bar last night when Josef Himmelfarb confronted me and told me the truth, that Oskar had perished in a concentration camp as a result of my betrayal. That is what he was saying to me as he spoke to me in German.

My entire life now seems cast in shadow. I can no longer pretend to be the man I have let others believe I am. Nothing can excuse me. I have nowhere to hide.

This morning at breakfast I was unable to bring myself to tell you the truth. I know now that I am guilty of the most terrible act, and that for all my efforts to save lives, they count for nothing when compared to my crime.

I do not know what will become of me, now that my past has caught up with me, now that I am in danger of being revealed. I have no honor left, and to live without honor is quite impossible for me. I feel I am making a perilous descent, and having discovered—having been forced, finally—to admit my own capacity for evil, I can see no possible way out of the pit.

I must end this or I shall be late for your reading, which is soon to begin. I do not understand why our lives came together again this way after all these years, but it seems fitting to me that they did. If, on the other side of this, there is life remaining to me, I would like to think I might spend even some small portion of it with you. That is if you do not despise me too deeply for what you now know about me. Forgive me, if you can. Adios, my darling Lucy.

                                        Te amo, Carlos

I closed the little notebook. It rested on my lap for a long while, my hands folded on top of it, my eyes gazing into the fire. In spite of the warmth of the flames, I felt deeply chilled.

A tiredness overtook me, as if I had been running, running, for days, and had finally reached a point of exhaustion. So much of what I'd told myself was a fiction, an invention of someone unprepared to face the truth.

I realized I was not a victim but a coward, and that Carlos was no hero but a traitor. I was as much responsible for the end of our affair as he was. What I knew in that instant about myself was that I had never been abandoned by him: I had given up because I hadn't the courage to have him. And then for years I had made my fate sound unjust with my own stories: I had accumulated my little sad versions of my life, just as he had denied the crimes of his. We shed our illusions so reluctantly, are loath to part with the stories we tell ourselves even when all the evidence points to the wisdom of doing so. I bowed down before my memory of Carlos for years, granting him the love and respect I could not grant myself.

I felt the last vestiges of an old illusion disperse, and I was born again, to a world much colder, much harsher in its colorlessness, a world bereft of the fallacy and the figures of love, a world in which the blazing specter of consciousness would forever make me a witness to its failure.

I picked up the notebook and, page by page, fed it to the fire, which flared up and devoured everything, including the leather binding, which took a long time to burn. It curled, slowly blackened, resisted the flames for a while, until I took the poker and moved it to the center of the fire, where the heat was so intense it finally succumbed, turning into a hardened welt of hide, then dissolving to ash, leaving behind a stench of burnt flesh.

I went out into the night and walked the moors under a full moon, inviting the Beast of Bodmin Moor to come for me, beckoning the power of darkness, tempting him to show his face. I no longer cared what happened to me. I strolled fearlessly among the purple shadows for hours, thinking about the events that had brought me to this place. I could examine my past with a new clarity. I could see my failures as well as my triumphs as nothing more than the drawings of a child on a sandy beach, doomed to be erased by the incoming tide.

I remembered Justin, as a boy, bringing me a map of one of his imaginary worlds, and the look of immense satisfaction on his face as he laid it out before me and began to explain the name of the tribe that lived in this land, their hunting habits, the shapes of their dwellings and the length of their winters, inventing a whole landscape and inviting me to enter it with him.

I thought of the way he used to say to me, when he was eight or nine years old, "Tell me a story about when I was little," and how difficult it was for me to conjure up a memory that didn't involve a hospital or a blue-lipped little boy struggling for his life, and how in the end, sensing how important it was to him, I would invent some little tale about a swan chasing his across a lawn, or the first time he climbed out of his crib all by himself.

The incoming tide was the pull of death, which had already begun to tug at me. It plucked at my sleeves, the hairs on my head, it rode the winds blowing down from remote Arctic regions. It seemed sure to arrive before morning, creeping up, perhaps from behind, to bear me away.

But nothing came to me, except the first light of dawn, welling up from the east, the soft gray infusion of a new day. And in its feeble warmth I made my way back to the hotel.

TWENTY-FOUR

Joycelle is sitting in the living room, staring out the window, when I enter the house. I'm surprised to find her up so early. She smiles when she sees me, and holds out her hand.

I set the antlers down on the floor and kneel beside her and take her hand.

"Where did you find those?" she asks, gazing down at the antlers.

"I took them from the deer that was killed near the mailbox."

"They're beautiful," she murmurs. She lifts her face again and looks out the window. Above the snow-burdened firs, the sky is clear and blue to the south, while to the north, storm clouds are gathering. A clump of snow is dislodged by a magpie landing on a branch and falls to the ground with an airy thump, and then the magpie flies off, chattering and swooping down to a new perch on a fence rail.

"What shall we have for breakfast?"

She hesitates for a few moments, as if thinking over her choices, and then says, "How about eggs Benedict?"

"Eggs Benedict? What a funny choice."

"You know—eggs, ham, muffins, and that sauce that's about a thousand calories a bite."

"You've never asked for that before."

"I know."

"So why did you think of it now?"

She smiles sheepishly and points to a magazine lying on the floor, on the cover of which is a sumptuous-looking plate of eggs Benedict.

"Looks pretty good, doesn't it?" she says. "I just read the recipe. Sounds like something we can pull off."

"Absolutely. Let's get to work."

We set about making breakfast together in the kitchen. She slices the ham and gets out the egg poacher while I begin making the hollandaise sauce.

"Because it's Sunday," she says, "I think we'll have some champagne and orange juice. What do you call that drink?"

"Mimosa."

"Yeah. Mimosa. I always like that word. Sounds like a talking bird."

"Or an island in the Pacific."

"Speaking of islands, I've been thinking about what you said yesterday. About taking a vacation somewhere. Do you really think we could do it?"

"Why not?"

"I think it ought to be someplace where it's warm," she says.

"Yes. Maybe an island in the Caribbean, or Hawaii. Or perhaps Mexico."

"I don't want to go to Hawaii." She wrinkles up her nose and shakes her head. "You can have the surfer and hula routine. I'd rather go to Mexico, I've always wanted to go to Mexico. Is it warm down there now?"

"If we go far enough south. There are some nice beach resorts. I've been to one. Everything's probably changed now. That was a long time ago."

"You went there with Carlos?"

"Yes."

"I've never been anywhere." She turns and looks at me with those dark brown eyes.

I feel a little stab of pain. A tiny spasm of grief shoots through me when I think of the future, how little time there might be.

I take the dishes out of the cupboard to warm in the oven, but when she sees the plates I've chosen, she speaks up and says, "Let's use the good china, huh? After all, it's Sunday."

I do as she says and get down the Wedgwood plates with the intricate pattern of flowers and birds, thinking how she has become increasingly particular in the last little while, very precise in her wants.

In our first months together I found it difficult to get her to tell me what she wanted. Perhaps she felt unworthy of making demands. Or maybe it is only now that she is able to know her wishes clearly. We both are aware of how important this is. There is an unspoken feeling that we should not hold anything back, that every day is precious; there's no reason to deny ourselves anything.

She comes and stands close to me, peering over my shoulder at the hollandaise thickening in the pot.

"Those are very pretty," she says. "Where did you get those?"

I realize she is commenting on my earrings, two small cabochon rubies. This, too, is new, her meticulous attention to certain details around her, usually connected to something I'm wearing, as if things were somehow becoming brighter and more vivid for her.

"A gift from the past."

"Carlos?"

"No. Someone named Richard. We lived together for a few years. During the time I spent in Los Angeles."

"You've never mentioned him before."

"I haven't? He was a nice man—actually a lovely man, but . . ."

"But what?"

"Somehow it never worked out."

"I get a little jealous when you talk about men."

"Really?"

I turn and face her. It's sometimes hard for me to look at her so directly, to see the change in her. Recently, I cut her hair, at her request, since it had begun to grow thin and brittle anyway. Now she has a little cap of short brown hair lying close to her head—what we call the monk's cut. It suits her, I think, though it makes her face appear a little more gaunt and austere.

Now it is not only the changes in her appearance that make it hard to gaze into her face at such close proximity. It's also the look in her eyes. She seems to be looking right through me, trying to penetrate my thoughts, and I see her own vulnerability.

"You shouldn't feel jealous. You have no competition," I say, "not from the living or the dead."

I take her face in my hands and I kiss her, first on one cheek, and then the other.

She murmurs, "I hope not."

As I stand there, meeting her gaze so effortlessly now, I think of that moment during dinner the last evening on the boat, when Hannah Ettinger had said, "Truth is noble, is it not, Ricardo? Surely someone in one of those great books you're so fond of quoting from has said as much." And how Ricardo had answered, "Truth is noble, and also liberating."

So very liberating, I might have added. Like receiving the keys to the kingdom of peace.

Overcome with feeling, I turn back to the stove.

I tell her I think her eggs must be done.

Over breakfast we discuss plans for our trip.

"Let's go for two weeks," Joycelle says suddenly.

"One might be better."

"You don't think I could go for two, do you?"

"It's not that."

"What then?"

"You probably could do it. But you might wear yourself out. It's better to go for one week. Then we'll come back here for a while, and later we'll plan another trip."

She looks at me, and I know what she's thinking: There might not be a later.

"Really, one week will be long enough. You'll see."

"Can we just see how I feel? If I'm doing okay, then, can we stay an extra week?"

"Well . . . I suppose. But promise me that if you start feeling badly, we'll come home immediately."

"But Lucy," she says softly. "I already feel bad."

"I know . . . I do know."

She shrugs. "So let me decide, okay?"

"Let you decide, huh?"

"Yeah, me."

"So I just turn the whole show over to you?"

"That's about it."

"You're getting pretty bossy."

"That's because I'm in charge."

"So what's my role in this whole thing? The travel agent? The tour guide?"

"You can be my companion." She looks smug.

"Your companion? And what sort of duties does that involve? I always like to know what I'm getting myself into."

"Well . . . arranging our travel schedule . . . choosing the right hotel . . . taking care of room service orders—breakfast in bed, that kind of thing. Mixing drinks, of course. Applying suntan oil. Hmmm . . . I'm sure I'll think of a few other things."

She hesitates, and then adds, "Of course, if I croak while we're away, you'll have to see to the funeral arrangements."

"Good God, Joycelle."

"Just joking, Lucy."

"It's not funny."

And suddenly my throat hurts. All around my larynx there's a feeling of constriction and swelling and pain.

"Come on, Lucy."

"I don't like it when you talk like that."

"Lighten up," she says.

"But I really don't."

She taps her fingers on the table and sighs. "Look, you're killing me with this attitude."

"Very funny. You don't let up, do you?"

"What do you want me to do, turn morose?"

"Just don't be so flippant."

"*Flippant?* That's good. I guess I should develop some proper respect for death, huh? Instead of this unhealthy black humor."

I don't say anything.

"Look, maybe we need to do something," she says. "Why don't we drive into town and get a movie?"

And then something courses through me, and it is not so much a thought as an inchoate, cellular feeling that I am—that something is missing, something quite important that I am failing to do, or see, and I feel the need to be alone for a while.

"Let me take care of a few things first." I stand up and quietly begin removing the plates from the table.

"I'm just going into my study for a while and then we can go to town."

She catches my hand and holds it for a moment. "I'll clean up, don't worry about the dishes. But before you go, would you put that music on that you were playing yesterday?"

I put on the tape of Jessye Norman singing Kurl Weill songs. Now the sound of "September Song" fills the room, an almost painfully beautiful sound. Light is flooding through the windows. Even though it has begun to snow again, it's still bright outside. A white winter light.

I leave her standing at the kitchen sink, looking out the window, with Jessye singing to her, and go into my study and sit at my desk.

I gaze out the window. The metal chairs at the top of the garden have blown over and lay on their sides. Dried corn husks are stacked amid the dark furrows of the garden where the snow is beginning to accumulate, flake by flake, in an even blanket of whiteness.

As a child, I had always loved the winters, especially the hours between when school let out and the moment when darkness fell, hours rich with possibility and beauty, when the light waned so slowly, so imperceptibly, that it seemed one moment I was sledding down a hill, wrapped in the soft and woolly gray evening light, and the next I was trudging home in darkness, dragging my sled along a country lane, with the beckoning lights of home in the distance, limpid facets of yellow magnified by the crystallized night air. I felt it was toward some yellow glowing point of the future that I was now headed. A feeling of light was emerging, shining through a tunnel of the days stretching before me.

I feel as if I'm on the edge of grasping something. I have the feeling that for so much of my life I have been caught in the eddying currents that have drawn me constantly, ineluctably toward the dark cave of self-interest. And I can sense now that some fundamental lesson has not been learned.

After a while, what really seems like a very long while but is actually only thirty or forty minutes, I go to find Joycelle.

Who is not in the kitchen, nor the living room.

Who is not anywhere in the house.

Who seems to have disappeared.

The truck is still in the driveway. And so is the car. I begin striding across the barnyard, calling her name. The snowflakes fly into my open mouth and catch on my eyelashes. When I reach the barn, I unlatch the heavy door and pull it open and step inside. In the low light I can see the cat curled in its box, the row of saddles, the bridles hanging on their pegs, the dusty nooks and shelves of tools, the empty stalls. But no Joycelle: she is not here.

She is not in the granary, or the guest cabin, nor is she in the gazebo or the workshop. She isn't in any of the places I expect to find her. It has begun to snow harder. I stand in the center of the barnyard and watch the flakes drifting down around me, large wet flakes that fall so slowly I can see the shapes of the crystals, and I begin to feel afraid.

There is only one place I can think of left to look for her.

I head for the stone steps leading to the top of the cliff overlooking the river. The stones are slippery, and I can't see more than a few feet in front of me. By the time I reach the top, I'm out of breath and stop to rest a moment. From this spot I can see out over the whole valley. The ranch looks like a child's toy set: a perfect barn, neat interlocking rail fences, brown horses and white goats, and in the middle of everything, a little log house with a red roof. The storm causes it all to appear fuzzy and rather ghostly.

Starting off again, I follow the path that leads to the edge of the cliff, moving almost by instinct through the swirling snow.

And then I see her.

She's sitting on top of the rock, her back to me, sitting at the very edge of the cliff, her legs dangling over the edge. I have to force myself to keep moving toward her, and drop down on my hands and knees and crawl the last few feet. I never come this far out on the rock. I hate getting this close to the edge. The cliffs drops straight down to the river, a distance of sixty or seventy feet. And yet here I am, not exactly sitting beside her, but stretched out on the rock on all fours, trying to ignore the fear which feels like an electric tingling in my groin.

"Joycelle?"

She doesn't indicate she's heard me call her name.

"Joycelle!" I call again, and she jumps a little and turns around.

"Jesus, you scared the hell out of me."

"Sorry."

She leans forward a little and looks down at the river.

"Don't do that. Don't lean out like that," I say.

"Why not?"

"Because it scares me, that's why."

"Are you afraid of losing me?"

"I'm very afraid of losing you."

"You're going to, you know."

"Yes, I know that."

She looks at me and I see something written on her features. A strength and a calm that seem far superior to anything I can muster.

"I wasn't thinking of jumping, Lucy, if that's what you imagine. It didn't even cross my mind. I like the view from up here. Look, you can see where the deer have been crossing on the ice."

I force myself to look down, but all I can see is whiteness, the gorge of ice that has formed solid across the swimming hole, and the darker water emerging from the shelf of ice downriver.

"I can't see anything in this storm."

"Well, you could before it started snowing so hard."

"I'm sorry I lose it sometimes, like I did just now at breakfast. I don't think of you, of what you're going through."

She puts her arm around me. "Come sit close me."

"Joycelle, I hate this."

"What do you hate?"

"I'm afraid of heights."

"Just sit up slowly. There. You're not going anywhere. Just because you sit at the edge doesn't mean you're going over."

"I don't know."

"You know that broken mirror?"

"Broken mirror?"

"Yeah, leaning up against the wall in the barn."

"What about it?"

"I was looking in it the other day. Every once in a while when I see myself, I don't even know it's me anymore. And I was looking at this skinny woman and thinking how white she was, how pale, like a ghost, and how her hair was getting so thin. I always had great hair, you know. My eyes looked so big in my face. I looked at myself for a long time because it seemed like I was seeing a me I ought to get to know. You know what the funny thing was?"

"No. What?"

"The more I looked, the more I thought I liked this person better than I've ever liked her in my whole life. That's because of you. Because of us. And because it's my last chance."

"Have I told you how much I love you?"

"No. Never," she says.

"I do."

"That's good. That's all I need right now. I mean right at this moment."

"I wish—"

"Don't say it. You want to get down from here, don't you?"

"How can you tell?"

"I think it's the way you're shaking."

"Let's go down and build a fire."

Halfway down the cliff, the dogs come bounding up the steps to meet us, full of energy, barking and leaping before us. We bend down to greet them, petting their wet heads. When we stand up, Joycelle turns and embraces me. We stand there, holding each other for a long while, two figures, halfway down, or halfway up. And then, holding her hand, I let her lead the way down the path through the whiteness of the storm.

ABOUT THE AUTHOR

Judith Freeman is the author of *Family Attractions*, a collection of short stories, *The Chinchilla Farm*, and *Set for Life*. She reviews books regularly for the *Los Angeles Times*. *Set for Life* received the Western Heritage Award for Best Novel. She lives in Challis, Idaho, and Los Angeles with her husband, photographer Anthony Hernandez.